"O'Dwyer, you look different," Smith said, actually initiating a conversation with her.

"I left my helmet home."

"Jeez! Can't you ever be serious?"

"It's hard since I never leave home without my sarcastic wit. Besides, I never know what kind of mood you're going to be in."

"I just wanted to say I like what you've done with yourself."

She shrugged. He didn't have to know how hard she'd worked to get that way. "All I did was put on a dress and apply some makeup."

"Well, it looks nice. You look like a...a real...woman."

Like the excruciatingly shrill screech of chalk scratching a blackboard, he'd gone and pressed the wrong buttons, as usual, causing something to short-circuit in Marcie's head. Before she could stop herself, her eyes narrowed to slits and her nostrils flared with fury as she spewed, "I knew you'd say something sexist like that."

"Damn, O'Dwyer. That's not how I meant it," Smith replied angrily.

"Really?"

Visibly gritting his teeth, he replied, "Really!"

By this time, every eye at the table was watching, every ear listening, as though the two of them had forgotten where they were. Marcie ignored everyone and turned completely around in her chair to look him squarely in the eye. However she saw no defiance or anger. Instead she saw something she'd never seen in his eyes before. Had he actually been telling the truth? Could he be capable of giving a woman an honest compliment? She wasn't certain how to respond. For the sake of the others at the table, she chose to believe him and go from there.

"To tell the truth, Smith, I wasn't sure how you meant it. I mean, we're not on what you would call the best of terms."

"True. However we're at a wedding, O'Dwyer. Try to be civil."

"Civ—" The nerve of that man. She was about to blow again when Smith placed a finger on her lips. Lucky for him, she didn't try to bite it off.

"Truce, O'Dwyer?"

Praise for more Highland Press Books!

THE CRYSTAL HEART by Katherine Deauxville brims with ribald humor and authentic historical detail. Enjoy!
~ *Virginia Henley*

* * *

CAT O'NINE TALES by Deborah MacGillivray. Enchanting tales from the most wicked, award-winning author today. Spellbinding! A treat for all.
~ *Detra Fitch, The Huntress Reviews*

* * *

HIGHLAND WISHES by Leanne Burroughs. This reviewer found that this book was a wonderful story set in a time when tension was high between England and Scotland. She writes a well-crafted story, with multidimensional characters and exquisite backdrops of Scotland. The storyline is a fast-paced tale with much detail to specific areas of history. The reader can feel this author's love for Scotland and its many wonderful heroes.

This reviewer was easily captivated by the story and was enthralled by it until the end. The reader will laugh and cry as you read this wonderful story. The reader feels all the pain, torment and disillusionment felt by both main characters, but also the joy and love they felt. Ms. Burroughs has crafted a well-researched story that gives a glimpse into Scotland during a time when there was upheaval and war for independence. This reviewer is anxiously awaiting her next novel in this series and commends her for a wonderful job done.
~*Dawn Roberto, Love Romances*

* * *

THE SENSE OF HONOR by Ashley Kath-Bilsky has written an historical romance of the highest caliber. This reviewer was fesseled to the pages, fell in love with the hero and was cheering for the heroine all the way through. The plot is exciting and moves along at a good pace. The characters are multi-dimensional and the secondary characters bring life to the story. Sexual tension rages through this story and Ms. Kath-Bilsky gives her readers a breath-taking romance. The love scenes are sensual and very romantic. This reviewer was very pleased with how the author handled all the secrets. Sometimes it can be very frustrating for the reader when secrets keep tearing the main characters apart, but in this case, those secrets seem to bring them more together and both characters reacted very maturely when the secrets finally came to light. This reviewer is hoping that this very talented author will have another book out very soon.

~ *Valerie, Love Romances*

* * *

FAERY SPECIAL ROMANCES - Brilliantly magical! Ms. Rogers' special brand of humor and imagination will have you believing in faeries from page one. Absolutely enchanting!
- *Dawn Thompson, Author of The Ravencliff Bride*

* * *

IN SUNSHINE OR IN SHADOW by Cynthia Owens - If you adore the stormy heroes of 'Wuthering Heights' and 'Jane Eyre' (and who doesn't?) you'll be entranced by Owens' passionate story of Ireland after the Great Famine, and David Burke - a man from America with a hidden past and a secret name. Only one woman, the fiery, luscious Siobhan, can unlock the bonds that imprison him. Highly recommended for those who love classic romance and an action-packed story.

~ *Best Selling Author, Maggie Davis,*
AKA Katherine Deauxville

* * *

INTO THE WOODS by R.R. Smythe - This Young Adult Fantasy will send chills down your spine. I, as the reader, followed Callum and witnessed everything he and his friends went through as they attempted to decipher the messages. At the same time, I watched Callum's mother, Ellsbeth, as she walked through the Netherwood. Each time Callum deciphered one of the four messages, some villagers awakened. Through the eyes of Ellsbeth, I saw the other sleepers wander, make mistakes, and be released from the Netherwood, leaving Ellsbeth alone. There is one thread left dangling, but do not fret. This IS a stand alone book. But that thread gives me hope that another book about the Netherwoods may someday come to pass. Excellent reading for any age of fantasy fans!
~ *Detra Fitch, Huntress Reviews*

* * *

ALMOST TAKEN by Isabel Mere is a very passionate historical romance that takes the reader on an exciting adventure. The compelling characters of Deran Morissey, the Earl of Atherton, and Ava Fychon, a young woman from Wales, find themselves drawn together as they search for her missing siblings.

Readers will watch in interest as they fall in love and overcome obstacles. They will thrill in the passion and hope that they find happiness together. This is a very sensual romance that wins the heart of the readers.

This is a creative and fast moving storyline that will enthrall readers. The character's personalities will fascinate readers and win their concern. Ava, who is highly spirited and stubborn, will win the respect of the readers for her courage and determination. Deran, who is rumored in the beginning to be an ice king, not caring about anyone, will prove how wrong people's

perceptions can be. **Almost Taken** by Isabel Mere is an emotionally moving historical romance that I highly recommend to the readers.
~ Anita, The Romance Studio

* * *

Leanne Burroughs easily will captivate the reader with intricate details, a mystery that ensnares the reader and characters that will touch their hearts. By the end of the first chapter, this reviewer was enthralled with **HER HIGHLAND ROGUE** and was rooting for Duncan and Catherine to admit their love. Laughter, tears and love shine through this wonderful novel. This reviewer was amazed at Ms. Burroughs' depth and perception in this storyline. Her wonderful way with words plays itself through each page like a lyrical note and will captivate the reader till the very end. The only drawback was this reviewer wanted to know more of the secondary characters and the back story of other characters. All in all, read HER HIGHLAND ROGUE and be transported to a time that is full of mystery and promise of a future. This reviewer is highly recommending this book for those who enjoy an engrossing Scottish tale full of humor, love and laughter.
~Dawn, Love Romances

* * *

PRETEND I'M YOURS by Phyllis Campbell is an exceptional masterpiece. This lovely story is so rich in detail and personalities that it just leaps out and grabs hold of the reader. From the moment I started reading about Mercedes and Katherine, I was spellbound. Ms. Campbell carries the reader into a mirage of mystery with deceit, betrayal of the worst kind, and a passionate love revolving around the sisters, that makes this a whirlwind page-turner. Mercedes and William are astonishing characters that ignite the pages and allows the reader to experience all their deepening sensations. There were moments I could share in with their breathtaking romance, almost feeling the butterflies of

love they emitted. This extraordinary read had me mesmerized with its ambiance, its characters and its remarkable twists and turns, making it one recommended read in my book.
~ Linda L., Fallen Angel Reviews

* * *

REBEL HEART by Jannine Corti Petska - Ms. Petska does an excellent job of all aspects of sharing this book with us. Ms. Petska used a myriad of emotions to tell this story and the reader (me) quickly becomes entranced in the ways Courtney's stubborn attitude works to her advantage in surviving this disastrous beginning to her new life. Ms. Petska's writings demand attention; she draws the reader to quickly become involved in this passionate story. This is a wonderful rendition of a different type which is a welcome addition to the historical romance genre. I believe that you will enjoy this story; I know I did!
~ Brenda Talley, The Romance Studio

* * *

BLOOD ON THE TARTAN by Chris Holmes is the powerful tale of a little known ugly time in Scotland, where raw, fighting Scottish spirit gathers itself to challenge injustice. In Catherine Ross and Ian Macgregor the reader is treated to a rare romance and love triumphant as they fight for Scottish honor.
~Robert Middlemiss, A Common Glory

* * *

RECIPE FOR LOVE - I don't think the reader will find a better compilation of mouth watering short romantic love stories than in RECIPE FOR LOVE! This is a highly recommended volume – perfect for beaches, doctor's offices, or anywhere you've a few minutes to read.
~ Marilyn Rondeau, Reviewers International Organization

* * *

Christmas is a magical time and twelve talented authors answer the question of what happens when **CHRISTMAS WISHES** come true in this incredible anthology.

Christmas Wishes shows just how phenomenal a themed anthology can be. Each of these highly skilled authors brings a slightly different perspective to the Christmas theme to create a book that is sure to leave readers satisfied. What a joy to read such splendid stories! This reviewer looks forward to more anthologies by Highland Press as the quality is simply astonishing.
~ Debbie, CK2S Kwips and Kritiques

(*One story in this anthology was nominated for the Gayle Wilson Award of Excellence*)

* * *

HOLIDAY IN THE HEART - Twelve stories that would put even Scrooge into the Christmas spirit. It does not matter what *type* of romance genre you prefer. This book has a little bit of everything. The stories are set in the U.S.A. and Europe. Some take place in the past, some in the present, and one story takes place in both! I strongly suggest that you put on something comfortable, brew up something hot (tea, coffee or cocoa will do), light up a fire, settle down somewhere quiet and begin reading this anthology.
~ Detra Fitch, Huntress Reviews

* * *

BLUE MOON MAGIC is an enchanting collection of short stories. Each author wrote with the same theme in mind but each story has its own uniqueness. You should have no problem finding a tale to suit your mood. BLUE MOON MAGIC offers historicals, contemporaries, time travel, paranormal, and futuristic narratives to tempt your heart.

Legend says that if you wish with all your heart upon the rare blue moon, your wishes were sure to come true. Each of the heroines discovers this magical fact. True love is out there if you just believe in it. In some of the stories, love happens in the most unusual ways. Angels may help, ancient spells may be broken, anything can happen. Even vampires will find their perfect mate with the power of the blue moon. Not every heroine believes they are wishing for love, some are just looking for answers to their problems or nagging questions. Fate seems to think the solution is finding the one who makes their heart sing.

BLUE MOON MAGIC is a perfect read for late at night or even during your commute to work. The short yet sweet stories are a wonderful way to spend a few minutes. If you do not have the time to finish a full-length novel, but hate stopping in the middle of a loving tale, I highly recommend grabbing this book.
~ *Kim Swiderski, Writers Unlimited Reviewer*
* * *
Legend has it that a blue moon is enchanted. What happens when fifteen talented authors utilize this theme to create enthralling stories of love?

BLUE MOON ENCHANTMENT is a wonderful, themed anthology filled with phenomenal stories by fifteen extraordinarily talented authors. Readers will find a wide variety of time periods and styles showcased in this superb anthology. *BLUE MOON ENCHANTMENT* is sure to offer a little bit of something for everyone!
~ *Debbie, CK²S Kwips and Kritiques*
* * *
NO LAW AGAINST LOVE - If you have ever found yourself rolling your eyes at some of the more stupid laws, then you are going to adore this novel. Over twenty-five stories fill up this anthology, each one dealing with at least one stupid or outdated law. Let me give you an example: In Florida, USA, there is a law that

states "If an elephant is left tied to a parking meter, the parking fee has to be paid just as it would for a vehicle." In Great Britain, "A license is required to keep a lunatic." Yes, you read those correctly. No matter how many times you go back and reread them, the words will remain the same. Those two laws are still legal. The tales vary in time and place. Some take place in the present, in the past, in the USA, in England... in other words, there is something for everyone! Best yet, profits from the sales of this novel go to breast cancer prevention.

A stellar anthology that had me laughing, sighing in pleasure, believing in magic, and left me begging for more! Will there be a second anthology someday? I sure hope so! This is one novel that will go directly to my 'Keeper' shelf, to be read over and over again. Very highly recommended!
~ *Detra Fitch, Huntress Reviews*

***

LOVE UNDER THE MISTLETOE is a fun anthology that infuses the beauty of the season with fun characters and unforgettable situations. This is one of those books that you can read year round and still derive great pleasure from each of the charming stories. A Wonderful compilation of holiday stories. Perfect year round!
~ *Chrissy Dionne, Romance Junkies*

A Heated Romance

Candace Gold

Highland Press Publishing

High Springs, FL

A Heated Romance

Copyright ©2008 Highland Press Publishing
Cover copyright ©2008

Printed and bound in the United States of America. All rights reserved. No part of this book may be reproduced or transmitted in any form or by any means, electronic or mechanical, including photocopying, recording, or by an information storage and retrieval system-except by a reviewer who may quote brief passages in a review to be printed in a magazine, newspaper, or on the Web-without permission in writing from the publisher.

For information, please contact
Highland Press Publishing,
PO Box 2292, High Springs, FL 32655.
www.highlandpress.org

All characters in this book have no existence outside the imagination of the author and have no relation whatsoever to anyone bearing the same name or names, save actual historical figures. They are not even distantly inspired by any individual known or unknown to the author, and all incidents are pure invention.

ISBN: 978-0-9815573-0-4

HIGHLAND PRESS PUBLISHING

Circles of Gold

This book is dedicated to all
women who persevere
despite the odds.

Special thanks to
Patty Howell, Senior Editor

Chapter One

Monday morning after breakfast, Marcie O'Dwyer busily swept the kitchen floor. She looked up to see a dark-haired, handsome, incredibly built guy with broad shoulders walking toward her. His well-muscled body moved with easy grace.

Before she could say a thing, he said, "Hot damn! This is some sweet deal I got myself into."

"Can I help you?" she asked.

"*We'll* discuss *that* later. I can't believe they've hired a woman to clean for the house."

She looked at him as if he were crazy. "*Who* did you say you are?"

"I didn't. You're pretty damn nosy for a cleaning woman."

"*I'm not the cleaning woman!* I'm a *firefighter*, bud."

"You?" He chuckled. "You're putting me on, right?"

She shook her head, blood pounding in her ears. Leaning on the broom handle, she glared directly into his green eyes. "Damn serious!" she squeezed out between clenched teeth.

"A female doesn't belong in a *fire*house. She belongs in a house surrounded by a white picket fence with a bunch of kids to take care of." His reply knocked the heated banter squarely back into her court.

Marcie gripped the broom handle so tightly her knuckles turned white. She had a mind to whack the guy right over his thick skull with it.

"O'Dwyer, I see you and Smith have met." Assistant Chief Lenny Wiebolt walked into the kitchen. "He's the new transfer from downtown, replacing Logan."

Wiebolt was tall, with thinning sandy-blond hair. He

was a fair guy who treated everyone equally no matter their gender. This fact alone endeared him to Marcie.

"He's a real charmer," she spat, glowering at Smith before putting the broom away. "If you'll both excuse me, I have things to do." She suddenly felt the need for fresh air and walked outside.

A small, innocuous pebble lay on the concrete apron in front of the firehouse, and she gave it a swift kick. Mentally, she replayed the scene with Smith and fumed all over again. This guy was something else. To look at him, she saw every woman's hottest fantasy—a near perfect male specimen. However, all that was just icing. Too bad the cake beneath was rotten. She'd had her fill of male chauvinists. In her opinion, macho firemen were the worst. Even her dad had been one.

Marcie hated having to prove herself every time a new fireman joined the squad. Needless to say, as the only female firefighter in town—and a damn good firefighter at that—the onus fell on her. But she was fed up with being forced to go through the drill. If some ego-inflated Neanderthal couldn't deal with it, well that was *his* problem, not hers. This time she swore would be the last. She was damn tired of having to justify her worthiness.

More in control, Marcie walked back inside just as the fire alarm clanged. The dispatcher announced over the intercom that a car had wrapped around a telephone pole on the corner of Remsen and Oakland, six blocks away. The driver was still trapped inside.

One fire truck would be needed to deal with the situation. Marcie knew she and Jerry Dodd were definitely going out on the call. That was good. He was a good friend and they worked well together.

Her eyes scanned the other suited men looking for Smith. Yeah, sheer stupidity, but she couldn't stop herself. Their eyes locked. Did she detect a hint of merriment in his emerald eyes? Damn! She wasn't interested in him and didn't want him to think otherwise. She'd only looked out of curiosity to see if the Assistant Chief would send him out right away to get his feet wet. She forced her eyes away. Too bad his smile was still imprinted in her mind.

Everyone jumped onto the truck. She and Smith ended up standing on opposite sides in the back. As the fire engine sped down the street the houses and buildings flew by in a kaleidoscopic blur. She stayed focused on the surroundings to keep herself from looking at *him*. Her priority was the call. Nothing else. Then why was this obnoxious guy so damn distracting?

Five minutes may have passed, but it felt like thirty by the time they arrived at the scene of the accident. Policemen directed traffic and kept a small crowd of onlookers back. An ambulance pulled up from the other direction.

The squad jumped from the fire truck. The car, a Honda Civic, looked like it had been rammed by an eighteen wheeler. Assistant Chief Wiebolt ordered Marcie and Dodd to stabilize the vehicle in order to prevent it from igniting. DiMaggio, a squad veteran, used the butt of his axe to knock out the remaining glass from the driver's side so Smith could use the 'Jaws of Life,' a hydraulic tool, to remove the doors and roof, if necessary.

There was only one occupant, the driver, and he was wedged tightly between the dashboard and seat. The guy wore a suit and Marcie wondered if he was on his way to work or a meeting of some kind. He appeared middle-aged and probably had a family that had no idea where he was at the moment. She hated to think that if they didn't save him, some police officer would be paying the family a call later. She banished the negative thoughts from her mind. The man was still alive and they'd get him out somehow.

It took twenty grueling minutes to free the victim. Marcie's stomach rolled and the sour taste of bile filled her mouth as she saw the man's body lifted onto the stretcher—completely covered in blood. But, he was alive and that was what counted in her book. It was what the job was all about: to protect and serve.

No sooner had she calmed her stomach than

Wiebolt got a call on the truck's phone. He yelled, "Load up! We've caught a heavy fire at the apartment complex on Mercer Road."

A one-alarm blaze had escalated quickly and their squad had been ordered to join the other two engine crews already at the scene. When their fire truck got there, Marcie groaned at the sight of the roaring, yellow-orange flames shooting out of the top floor windows.

"This isn't going to be a picnic," she muttered under her breath as she jumped from the back of the truck.

The squad split into two groups and headed to the roof to hit the hot spots. Sweat trickled into her eyes from the intense heat. Marcie swiped it away with her glove and followed in Dodd's wake, mindful of where she stepped. One false move and she could fall through a soft spot or part of the roof weakened by the flames. With equally careful steps, DiMaggio moved closely behind her. Their task was to battle small flare-ups as they looked and listened for trapped civilians.

Without warning, she heard a loud, splintering crack behind her as DiMaggio cried out. She swung around and gasped as she helplessly watched him fall halfway through the roof.

Marcie lunged to grab onto him before he disappeared. "Hang on! I got you! Dodd! I need you!"

Dodd hadn't gone far and heard her call. He turned and started to make his way back as quickly as he could.

Sweat stung Marcie's eyes as she held onto DiMaggio. She felt the muscles in her arms pulling under his weight. "Hold on, guy." She tried to wedge her body, not knowing how long she could continue to hold him before her shoulders gave way. Just then she felt another set of hands grab DiMaggio's straps. Dodd came into view and together they pulled DiMaggio to safety. A few minutes later, Smith and Wiebolt reached the three panting firefighters sprawled on the roof.

"You okay?" the AC asked. "Wanna go downstairs?"

DiMaggio flexed his legs. "Nah! I'm okay, thanks to O'Dwyer." He flashed a thumbs up along with a grin of thanks in her direction before turning back to the commander. "Hand me my axe and let's get back to work."

Two hours later, with the blaze extinguished and the building deemed safe, the fire personnel began to depart. Marcie and her squad drove back to the firehouse, hopeful there'd be time for some dinner and rest before the next call.

Thoroughly exhausted, she removed her gear and groaned when she remembered she had kitchen detail, which included preparing dinner. Not a gourmet chef like a couple of the other guys, she usually selected something fast and easy. Before jumping into the shower to scrub all the grime and dirt off, she put a huge pot of water on the stove to boil. Spaghetti, leftover meat sauce, salad and Italian bread should do the trick to feed the guys. She chuckled to herself. Wouldn't that old crone who taught home economics and had the gall to flunk her be surprised to know she'd gotten this far in food preparation? Before she could give it another thought, Smith came strolling in to retrieve the bag he'd left in the kitchen when the fire alarm had gone off.

"You *do* seem to know your place, don't you?" Smith grinned, obviously pleased with himself.

Marcie's whole body tensed. She wanted to wipe that stupid smirk off his face. "Easy there, Mr. Testosterone, you can be replaced by a zucchini." Her voice dripped with unmistaken anger as she waved the one she'd just retrieved from the refrigerator inches from his handsome face.

Smith's green eyes lost their merriment and narrowed a moment before he stomped out of the room.

Yes! Marcie thought to herself. She'd won a round against the Neanderthal. Then why did she feel so depressed?

The rest of the evening remained thankfully quiet, and by eleven everyone was ready to catch some shuteye before the alarm sounded again. After the confrontation in the kitchen, Smith had stayed out of her space. She smiled, pleased that he must be finished provoking her.

As she prepared for bed, she soon discovered he'd only been warming up.

"Want me to come tuck you in and read you a bedtime story, O'Dwyer?" Smith cooed from the other side of the partition.

Snickers and muffled laughter came from the other guys.

"Not necessary,"—she wished he'd give it up—"I'm not afraid of the dark."

"Are you sure? I can come right over and—"

"I already have my Teddy bear. Didn't anyone ever tell you three's a crowd?"

Marcie's response clearly cracked the other guys up. But everyone was beat, and the laughter quickly died and was soon replaced by snoring.

Lying in the darkness, an unbidden, Technicolor image of Smith formed in her mind. No denying it—the man was handsome, a solid 10 on her man scale. She liked tall men and he was well over six feet. And his raven-black hair was thick—the kind she loved to run her fingers through. Nor could she forget those mesmerizing, emerald green eyes, fringed by long, black lashes any woman would give an arm for. She lowered her mind's eye to Smith's lean, muscular body, chiseled in all the right places. Yup, definitely buff. He'd be so perfect. A damn shame he was in dire need of a 'tude' adjustment.

In truth, Smith's attitude toward a female in the profession was no different from most people she encountered. Few *really* believed women should be firefighters. She'd decided to become one right after her father had been killed in a four-alarm house fire. Coming from a long line of firemen, she'd wanted to carry on the family tradition. Unfortunately, she received little support from family or friends.

When she'd told her girlfriend, Joanne, she'd signed up for the fireman's test, the girl had nearly freaked. At least she'd expected *her* to understand. They'd been resting on a bench at the mall sipping on iced frappucino grandes. Joanne had lowered her cup and looked at Marcie.

"Are you nuts?"

"Why?"

"Because you signed up to take a test for a job title that doesn't end with the word *woman*."

"I aim to change that." Marcie had punctuated her declaration with a hefty swallow and had promptly given herself a brain freeze.

"Since when did you become such a women's libber?"

"Look, why are you so shocked? You know how long I've wanted to become a firefighter."

"Yeah, but I thought it was like gas and would eventually work its way through your system."

"Well, it wasn't and it didn't and I'm damn serious about following in my dad's footsteps," Marcie had replied.

"Too bad both your feet together fill only one of his shoes."

The barb hit home, knowing Joanne meant that in stature and not shoe size. After all, Marcie did have big feet. "Where's your sense of achievement? Don't you realize women can do most any job as good as a man?"

"Yeah, but I do think your chosen profession is a definite turnoff to most guys in general, and will probably prevent you from getting married."

"How can you say that?" Marcie had slammed her drink down on the bench.

"Seeing you dressed in complete fire combat gear would intimidate any man."

"Oh! Well, you can put your fears to rest."

"Why, what do you intend to do?"

"When I go on a date I promise to leave the axe at home."

Starting off with a definite strike against her, Marcie had worked hard, perhaps twice as hard as most, because she constantly had to prove herself. At the end of her probationary period she'd been honored with a commendation for bravery. Yet, this meant nothing to new male recruits who joined the squad. They still wound up giving her the usual teasing about being the weaker sex.

Marcie had to laugh when she thought about it. Far from a *shrinking violet*, she stood 5'11" in her stocking feet and worked out at the gym at least four days a week on the weightlifting and cardio equipment. In fact, she could lift and drag a hose as easily as any man. And by using the right technique, she could carry an adult twice her size down a ladder.

Despite her resentment toward his treatment of her, visions of the hot new transfer swirled through her head before exhaustion finally shut down her overactive mind and she drifted off to sleep.

Chapter Two

O'Leary's was the hangout for the firehouse, serving as a place to get together and, no pun intended, shoot off steam. Basically, the watering hole was a dump. The bar, which had once been light oak, had darkened over the years from spilled drinks, sweat and tobacco stains. Food was on the menu, but a four-star gourmet restaurant it wasn't. You ate at your own risk. An ancient jukebox stood in the corner that sometimes worked, but always took your money. Several lighted beer advertisements decorated the walls.

No respectable critic would write a blurb on the place for any upscale decorator magazines. Marcie often wondered when Ralph, the establishment's owner, would eventually fix the Bud 'Lit' sign. The 'e' had been burned out since she first walked into the place over three years ago. Perhaps he was waiting for another letter to go out to make it worthwhile.

It had been a relatively calm day and most of the squad gathered at O'Leary's after work to celebrate the arrival of Jerry Dodd's first kid. He and his wife, Cheryl, had been trying for ages, and after two miscarriages they had a beautiful little girl. In Marcie's book, it couldn't have happened to a more deserving couple. She genuinely liked Dodd. He was one of the few guys who'd accepted her as an equal from day one. He was also a good friend.

Everyone had downed a beer or two and seemed mellow enough to feel little or no pain. Marcie sat at the bar talking to Dodd when Smith slid into the seat on her other side. Her body sensed he was there before she did.

"Another beer, Ralph," he called. She could feel his eyes fixed on her like green laser beams.

"So, O'Dwyer, tell me, does cold cream really help

keep your complexion soft after you remove all the soot from a hard-working day?"

She turned to face him. "Is that supposed to be funny?"

"Haven't you had enough thrills acting like a man? Aren't you ready to act like a *real* woman?"

A collective "Ooh," could be heard from the others in the room followed by complete silence. Everyone had stopped their conversations and tuned into theirs.

"I *am* a real woman, but you're obviously too blind or ate too much stupid for breakfast to see that."

"Whoa, I'm leaving before there's bloodshed." Dodd quickly vacated his stool.

"I wouldn't spill his blood, Dodd. We have no contamination containment facility here."

"You're a real funny lady, O'Dwyer. When you quit the squad, you can become a comedian."

Marcie glared at him through narrowed eyes, trying to control the myriad of nasty thoughts whirling around like darts inside her head. Unfortunately, he didn't drop it and added to the caustic remarks he'd already spewed.

"Just remember one thing, O'Dwyer. If my life is hanging by a thread, I want a *real* man to hold it, not you."

"I'll keep that in mind and let *you* dangle." She stared icily into his green eyes, fighting the desire to scratch them out.

Suddenly, Lenny Wiebolt materialized behind them. "Okay, you two, before you do something crazy, why don't you put all that steam you're spouting into some healthy competition?"

Marcie glared at Smith and he glowered back. Neither spoke.

"Come on, you both had a great deal to say a moment ago."

Silence in the bar. All eyes were on the three of them, waiting.

"Okay then. Here's the deal. Right after roll call tomorrow morning, instead of the planned drill, you two will gear up and haul hose to the top of the training building. That should put all this bull-slinging to rest. Agreed?"

He looked at Smith with one eyebrow cocked and his jaw set before repeating, "Agreed?"

Smith gave out something that sounded like a grunt. No surprise coming from a Neanderthal.

"And you, O'Dwyer?"

Marcie nodded—like she had any choice.

The Assistant Chief said, "Okay then," and walked off. Smith picked up his beer and stomped away.

Marcie watched his muscles ripple under his tight tee-shirt. She wasn't quite sure how she felt—angry or sad that he was such a male chauvinist. Whatever, she was angrier with herself for letting him get to her and allowing him to ruin her good time. She said goodbye to the rest of her squad and drove home to the studio apartment she rented on the other side of town.

Basically, it was a large room that had been divided into a bedroom and living room by a stationary wall of louvered doors bolted to the floor. A kitchenette and bathroom finished the place. The furniture consisted of a small, round glass table with two wrought iron chairs, a couch and a queen-size bed. Her bed took up most of the bedroom area. Eventually she hoped to move into a one-bedroom apartment, but for now this was all she could afford and have a place to call home. Though her mother had never asked her to move out—and on more than one occasion asked her to return home—Marcie valued her independence and sanity above all else.

She put together something to pass off as dinner that even a hospital wouldn't serve. No matter how hard she tried to improve her cooking, culinary arts would never be her thing. In school she had the honor of being the only student the home economics teacher begged the guidance counselor to transfer into a shop class, claiming Marcie proved too much for her nerves to handle. Surely the teacher had been overreacting. After all, she'd only made a few mistakes like getting her thumb caught under the presser foot of the sewing machine and having it impaled by the needle. And she'd only stitched the apron she was hemming to the skirt she was wearing once.

While she ate, Marcie kept reliving the confrontational scene with Smith. Why on earth did it bother her so? In the past whenever something like that happened with other guys she'd let it roll off her back like water on a rain slicker. But this time, doing that wasn't so easy. She found she couldn't stop thinking about Smith. And that annoyed her even more.

Marcie fixed a cup of soothing herbal tea and crawled into bed with a book. She hadn't read more than a few pages before she fell asleep. Sleep often scared her. It's the one place where a person had no control over their thoughts. As a kid, her colorful imagination had sparked more than her share of nightmares. On those occasions her dad would calm her fears and put her back to bed. Now she had to face her nighttime demons alone.

That night her demon was a muscular, green-eyed firefighter who kept chasing after her everywhere she went, demanding she return to the bedroom where she belonged. He wouldn't let her put out a fire because she was a female and forced her to watch as it burned to the ground.

She bolted upright, gasping for breath.

Recalling the dream, Marcie called out, "Damn you, Smith!" Now she was even more upset he'd invaded her dreams. She decided the best way to deal with someone like him was to avoid him. Perhaps with fewer confrontations she'd be able to keep him out of her dreams.

Too upset to fall back to sleep, she got out of bed and shuffled into the bathroom. She gazed at herself in the mirror. Her blue eyes had more dark rings than Saturn. She splashed cold water on her face after pushing her thick red hair away from it before padding back to bed. After punching and propping her pillows to get them right, she grabbed her stuffed Goofy and soon fell sound asleep.

This time Smith had the good sense to stay away.

Chapter Three

The following morning Marcie dragged herself out of bed and stumbled into the bathroom. A shower shocked some of the neurons in her brain into functioning, but it took an extra strong cup of coffee to finish the job. Although she no longer felt comatose, she hoped the people living in the city she served would be extra careful that day and try not to burn down their homes or businesses.

Driving to the station, a sudden coldness pervaded her body. It wasn't the wind-chill factor kicking in, thanks to the cold hello Canada was sending in the form of an Arctic blast. Nor was it the fact she'd shortly be competing with Smith to prove she was as good a firefighter as he, though neither could be discounted. The momentary freezing of the blood in her veins came from the recollection of having promised to have dinner at her mother's that evening. If her mother was still cooking on a schedule, Wednesday night meant spaghetti and meatballs. Marcie didn't have a problem with the meal—only the people who'd be there eating with her.

Recently she and her mother had agreed to a shaky peace pact concerning her job as a firefighter. According to the pact, her mother would refrain from sniping about Marcie's career choice, a skill her mother had honed to perfection, if Marcie refrained from bringing it up, especially at the dinner table. Not too long ago the two of them couldn't be in the same room fifteen minutes without an argument ensuing. Somehow her work always got dragged into any conversation. Her mother actually thought Marcie was undergoing some kind of identity crisis and begged her to see a psychologist. To her mother, there was no logical reason for a young woman desiring to ride around in big trucks, putting out fires.

"Why on earth are you doing this?" her mother constantly asked.

"I want to make a difference and help people."

"If you want to help people, be a nurse," was her mother's response.

"I don't want to be a nurse."

"I knew I shouldn't have let your father take you for rides on the fire truck. And your grandfather with his tales of glory..."

"Look, I really like my job, Mom, and would like your support."

Her mother adamantly shook her head. "Chasing fires isn't a good career for a woman, honey. Getting married and raising a family is. Where did I go wrong?"

Okay, just because her mother didn't verbally say something, it tacitly came across in her reproving eyes. Marcie doubted her mother would ever accept the fact Marcie hadn't chosen a more feminine career—like marriage and motherhood. Her mother ascribed to the same school of thought as Ray Smith, which absolved Marcie of all guilt when she referred to him as a throwback.

Her older sister, Eileen, who Marcie didn't adore on her kindest days, got married as soon as she graduated high school. As the whiney child, the one who'd make the most noise to get attention, she'd never ridden in the fire truck because she 'didn't want to get her dress dirty.'

Marcie's biggest thrill was when her white mouse escaped from his cage. Eileen fled screeching from the house, vowing not to return until he was caught. Marcie had really taken her time in rounding up the poor timid creature, which seemed to be more frightened of her sister than the other way around. All her high-pitched shrieking must have hurt his little pink ears. Thoroughly enjoying the moment and reveling with delight over Eileen's torment, Marcie had considered asking her father to buy her a snake for Christmas.

Now six years later, Eileen the Perfect had two kids, both girls, who seemed to have inherited her award-winning whining genes. Her husband, Larry, the real estate tycoon—Eileen's description not Marcie's—was myopic and possessed a one-track mind. It seemed his entire life revolved around the buying and selling of houses. If those beady, little black eyes of his happened to spy a 'For Sale' sign, he'd break every law of the road and gravity in order to speak to the owner of the property. Why anyone would ever trust an oily-looking guy like him was beyond her. In her book, the only thing he lacked was a long, curly mustache, black top hat and a whip.

Her mother would often tell her, "Go find someone like Larry and make a life for yourself." Marcie had often found herself wondering, what did her mother think she was now, comatose?

The *blessed* union of Eileen and Larry had produced only two children, which probably was a good thing. Sarah, a slight, dark-haired girl, was ten and the oldest. She was the whinier of the two only because she'd had longer to practice. Jessica, a smaller version of her sister, was only six and therefore still had time to perfect her whine. Being her only grandchildren, Marcie's mother doted on the girls and enthusiastically displayed their crude modernistic-looking drawings on the refrigerator. Had she ever stopped and taken a long, hard look at some of their pictures? Some of the people depicted in Sarah's drawings were missing hands and feet, a fact that chilled Marcie to the bone. She certainly hoped for all their sakes, as well as that of their neighbors, it was because the kid had lost her flesh-colored crayon.

Gramps was the only person out of the bunch whom Marcie actually looked forward to seeing. Like any elderly person, he had his good days and bad days. As a kid, she often sat on his lap and listened as he retold tales of the firemen he'd known and the fires they'd battled. She loved the way his eyes would shine and sparkle with life as he spoke. Now, as a safety precaution, Gramps was no longer encouraged to talk about the good ole days because he'd 'get too riled up.' When he fell into one of those spells, and an emergency vehicle happened to pass the house, its siren would 'call to him.' He'd grab his old fire hat and join the dogs already chasing it. The part about riding on the vehicle seemed to escape him. Nearly being hit by cars on numerous occasions had made her mother quite apprehensive, which was definitely understandable.

While Eileen got her genetic makeup mainly from her mother, Marcie inherited hers from her dad. Getting dirty never bothered her. She was a tomboy and had to be hog-tied to get her to wear a dress. As she drove, Marcie realized she really hadn't changed much.

She still loved the excitement of riding the shiny red trucks and being a firefighter. When she showed up at roll call, she never knew what kind of day would greet her because no two days were ever alike. Usually she couldn't wait to get there. Today was different, though. This morning she'd rather be heading to any other place on the planet but the firehouse.

As everyone waited for AC Wiebolt to start roll call, the tension in the room was so thick it'd need a chainsaw to cut through it. The entire squad was there early or on time for fear they'd miss any of the fireworks. Marcie felt the unmistakable signs of a headache developing and was in no mood to run up a ton of stairs toting a hose just to prove a stupid point to some jerk. Too bad she'd been pressured into competing with Smith. But she couldn't back out now.

Speak of the devil, she saw Smith leaning back in a chair with his arms folded across his chest wearing a self-satisfied look. By his actions, Marcie surmised he was assuming he'd already won because she was a woman. She bet he was just itching for the contest to begin.

When she sat next to Dodd, Smith spoke up, "Didn't think you'd actually show."

She assumed a tough-looking expression and tossed

the statement back at him. "You might say I thought the same about you."

Smith let out a long, hard chuckle. As others joined in on the laugh, Marcie felt the heat begin a slow boil in her body.

Dodd touched her shoulder. "Save your strength for the run."

On that note, the AC strode into the room and began the roll call. The buzz in the room ceased immediately.

Zoned out, worrying if she would get through the grilling exercise, she hadn't paid much attention to what Wiebolt had to say. It wasn't until the guys stood that she realized roll call had ended.

The entire shift, including the AC, made its way outside to an adjacent lot where a vacant, ten-story apartment building stood. It was their training facility, and where the competition would take place. She and Smith would put on bunker gear, the name given to the protective coat and pants firefighters wore, and run up the steps to the roof carrying coiled hose on their shoulders. Whoever finished in the least amount of time would be proclaimed the winner.

Wiebolt flipped a coin and Smith won the toss. He chose to go first. Marcie watched as he suited up. The man was solid muscle. How in the world could she ever hope to beat his time? She sighed. All she could do was give it her best shot. She'd love to walk away now, but that wasn't an option. The slight throb in her head had increased in intensity as Smith's chauvinistic rat-pack—Rory Mulvane, Sal DiMaggio and Jim Maguire—cheered him on.

Look on the brighter side, she told herself. At least they weren't doing the run wearing full gear. That would have been totally unbearable. Had they geared up for a real fire, they'd be wearing a special fire-resistant hood under their helmets to protect their neck and ears. And attached to the helmets would be the SCBA, the self-contained breathing apparatus equipment that prevented them from breathing in toxic smoke and succumbing to the heat. It consisted of a mask, air hose, regulator, air bottle and harness. The air bottle, strapped to the firefighter's back, provided fifteen minutes of oxygen, but wasn't the lightest thing to tote around on one's back. It was decided not to have the competitors carry an axe or pike pole to prevent them from using the equipment on each other.

The only thing they had to carry was the coiled hose and that sucker was heavy enough.

The AC accompanied Dodd, acting as the official timekeeper, to the roof. DiMaggio gave the signal and Smith charged up the stairs. The guys cheered him on. Everyone was caught up in the moment. Marcie felt her heart beat in sync with the seconds ticking away. Finally she heard Dodd shout: "Time: five minutes, twenty-three seconds." It was terrific time and was going to be hard to beat. Her personal best was six-and-a-half minutes.

Now it was her turn. She suited up. Lifting the coiled hose, which felt more like a pile of bricks on her shoulder, she anxiously waited for the signal. Nobody really expected her to beat Smith's time, and she knew it. All bets were based on how much she'd lose by.

"Go!" DiMaggio yelled and she took off, beginning her ascent at a decent clip. It would be a few more flights before she'd start to get winded. She hated that sensation when her lungs began to burn, feeling as if they were going to burst and each breath she sucked in felt like her last. Step after tortuous step she plodded on, telling herself it would be over soon. And she'd definitely proven herself to the last man. No more sucker bets. She intended to give *never again* new meaning.

The top flight was now in her blurry sight, her eyes stinging from the sweat running in rivulets from her brow. Her shoulder felt as if it were on fire and going to snap off. With each flight, she swore the hose had magically gotten heavier. The burn in her lungs hurt like hell and she feared each gasping breath was her last. It was a good thing she didn't have far to go, because she couldn't take much more.

"Come on, O'Dwyer! You're almost there!" Dodd shouted. Her ears rang so loudly he sounded as if he were under water. As she reached the last step, she collapsed at his feet, hitting the floor of the roof with a loud thud. He grinned at her. "You done real good, lady."

"Am...I...dead, yet?" she asked between gasps.

The Assistant Chief gave her two thumbs up. It looked like four with her double vision.

Trying to catch her breath and talk at the same time, she rasped, "Ho...how long?"

"Five and-a-half minutes!" he shouted for everyone to hear.

Smith had only beaten her by seven seconds. Okay, she may have lost the competition, but she'd certainly proven herself to him and everybody else—and surprised herself, as well. Too bad she was half dead and good for nothing, as a result.

"Let's head down." Dodd gave Marcie a hand, tugging her to her feet. "Here, give me the hose."

She gladly handed him the hose and together they made it down the steps where the others waited. She'd have given him anything to carry her down in place of the hose, though. At the bottom, Smith leaned against the wall calmly waiting for her, acting as cool as a cucumber with that stupid narcissistic, superior look she detested plastered across his face.

"You surprised me, O'Dwyer. That was quite a show you put on."

"You weren't so bad yourself," she replied, trying to get a better grip on her breathing.

"Though, in your case, luck played a great—"

"Luck!" she screeched with the last bit of breath that remained in her body, leaving her light-headed from oxygen deprivation.

"Yeah, luck. Women aren't—"

"Don't start that again," she said through clenched teeth. Lucky for him she didn't have the strength to scratch his eyes out.

"Whoa, you two. The competition was supposed to

settle this." Wiebolt stepped in between them to avoid bloodshed.

"He's too pigheaded—"

"Me?"

"Enough! Both of you!" Wiebolt shouted. "Go shower and cool off. As far as I'm concerned you both did damn good and deserve a round at O'Leary's. Time to put this baby to rest. Save your energy for fighting fires."

She and Smith stood glaring at each other like two alley cats eying the same cornered rat.

Dodd forced them to shake and call a truce. Knowing Smith, Marcie guessed he had his fingers crossed behind his back. Too tired to give it another thought, she dragged her body straight to the locker room. Her head throbbed and she could smell herself. She needed a shower in the worst way, though a stiff drink would probably do more good.

Hope for a quiet day literally went up in smoke when the first alarm sounded. A car had caught fire as the result of a fender-bender on the north side of the interstate. The two occupants of the car, a man and his teenaged daughter, were able to get out of the car before it went up in flames. Luckily for the squad, the fire was quickly contained and the gas tank didn't explode.

No sooner had they returned to the station than they were dispatched to a house fire on Maple Avenue. Unfortunately, these civilians hadn't been as lucky. The elderly couple died of smoke inhalation. Neighbors reported they'd heard a loud bang and then saw flames shoot out of the victims' basement. It sounded like a gas leak, but they wouldn't know for certain until after the fire inspectors issued their report.

The rest of the day proved less eventful—unless a kitten stuck in a tree was considered earth-shattering. Marcie was certain its owner had a different take on the situation, though. Regardless, the kitten was returned to the woman who owned it unscathed. And it was almost time for dinner with the *Addams Family*.

Chapter Four

A black pickup truck was parked in front of her mother's house. Unless Larry had loosened up and traded in his BMW, she had no idea who it belonged to. Then, as she began to open the door of her Jeep, it occurred to her that her mother might be trying to match her up with one of her friends' sons again. Every so often, fearing her youngest daughter was never going to marry, she'd get nervous and arrange one of her *perfect* dates. Then it was the same old, tired conversation—again. The last one was still fresh in Marcie's mind. It had taken place in the kitchen following dinner after her sister had taken her brood home. Marcie was helping her mother dry the dishes.

"Mom, I'm not going on this date," she replied, trying to restrain herself from conking her mother on the head with the frying pan she was drying.

"Of course, you are, dear."

"*No*, Mom, I'm not."

"Don't be silly."

"I told you this the last time you tried to set me up."

"I can't remember."

"Conveniently. I'm serious this time, Mother." She struggled in the worst way to control her temper and not commit murder. "I'm not going."

After reflecting a moment and allowing reality to set in, her mother replied, "Why not?"

"Because, I *hate* blind dates."

"This one's different."

"They're all *different*, that's the problem."

"No, I'm serious. He's really quite a catch."

"Charlie the Tuna is a catch."

"Go ahead. Make a joke, Miss Smarty Pants. All I want to do is dance at your wedding before I join your father."

"Stop being so melodramatic. You're not going any place for a long time."

"You've got a crystal ball?"

"No. Somebody has to take care of Grandpa."

"Look, Marcie, just go this once and I promise never to set you up on any more blind dates."

"Uh-huh. I think I've heard that before."

"I mean it this time," her mother had placed a hand on Marcie's shoulder.

"Do you honestly promise this time will be the last?"

Then her mother nodded and gave Marcie her most earnest smile. Marcie figured she probably had her fingers crossed behind her back. She'd begun to believe everyone lied when it suited them.

Despite the warning advice coming from the tiny voice in the back of her head to go home while she still had the chance, she got out of her car. She ignored it, reasoning she was already here. Besides, she was starving and her mother was a damn good cook, a trait Marcie so sorely lacked. She might be able to hook up a hose to a pump in seconds flat, but flat was the way her cakes always came out of the oven, looking more like a pancake.

"Here she is now," Marcie heard Gramps say as she opened the front door and stepped inside.

Her grandfather often sat by the front window watching for emergency vehicles to pass. She looked to see who he was talking to and nearly freaked. That small voice in her head now shrieked, "I told you so!!!"

"What's *he* doing here?" she demanded, not believing what her eyes were seeing. Smith was in the process of snaring a cocktail frank with a plastic toothpick. Her mother, fearing splinters, always bought plastic ones. In a fraction of a second, she took the entire scene in as Smith continued to stuff little cocktail wieners into his mouth like a squirrel gathering nuts. If her mother had broken out the hors d'oeuvres, she obviously thought Smith was potential husband material. She suddenly got the sick sensation of vertigo as if she were falling through a time warp, hurdling toward some parallel universe where everything was totally out of whack.

Her mother chided her, "That's not a very nice way to greet a guest of your grandfather."

Grandfather? Now, she *was* positive he was suffering from dementia. However, she had no intention of helping him entertain his *guest*.

"Um, seeing how the table's going to be really crowded, I'll just take off—"

"Stop right there, Marcie O'Dwyer!" her mother commanded. "No one is leaving before their belly is full. In my house there's always enough room and food."

She wasn't certain about the room part, but as for the food, they probably could feed some poor third-world country. But with her mother standing there, waving a knife that could possibly pass for a small machete, she took off her leather bomber jacket and threw it over a chair.

"Hey, O'Dwyer, I'd like to have a word with you in private." Smith had ceased stuffing his mouth in order to speak and had the unexpected decency to swallow first.

She couldn't help noticing how hot he looked tonight in his jeans and tee-shirt. He could be the center photo on her wall calendar anytime. She tugged at her straying thoughts and brought them back to the business at hand.

"Come on, we can talk in here." She led him into the den and closed the louvered doors behind them. "You can start off by explaining what the hell you're doing here."

"First off, let's get something straight. If I'd had any idea you were Charlie O's granddaughter, I'd never have set foot in this house and we wouldn't be having this conversation. That man's considered a saint in my house having saved my grandfather's life."

"Well, don't get too attached to Gramps."

"You don't have to worry. I don't intend to return. Stupidity doesn't run in *my* family."

Her mother discreetly knocked on the door and shooed them into the dining room. Of course she seated Smith and Marcie together at the table. The air that separated them could have cooled a freezer. While they were in the den talking, her sister and her family had finally showed up. Sarah was in rare form whining about something. It didn't take long for Eileen to notice Smith and the implications of his presence.

Giving Smith a huge, toothy smile, she said, "Say, Marcie, how about introducing me to your new *boyfriend*."

"Smith and I are only co-workers, Eileen. That's all!"

"So you're a fireman, too," Larry said.

"Yeah," Smith replied. "Me and your gramps, there," pointing to Marcie's grandfather.

Right then and there, Marcie started plotting his demise.

"How do you feel about working with a woman?" Larry proceeded to ask, having completely missed the insult the jerk had already delivered to her.

Marcie choked on the sip of water she'd just taken, having swallowed and taken a breath at the same time. Coughing and sputtering in an attempt to speak before Smith answered, she interjected in a tight, high-pitched voice, "Larry, you know my mother hates talking about the fire department at the dinner table." What she had actually wanted to say was, *shut that stupid piehole of yours before I stuff my size-ten-and-a-half foot into it.*

Smith looked at her and smirked. She knew exactly what he was thinking as she busied herself sculpting a mountain out of her mashed potatoes. Somehow potato sculpting seemed a lot more fun when she was a kid.

"By the way, Marcie, when are you going to fix that damn bumper on your Jeep?" Larry asked.

"Haven't had the time. Why?"

"Because it's a damn nuisance. I nearly ripped my slacks on it tonight."

"Well, if you're in such a damn hurry, you can get it fixed for me," she replied, ending the conversation.

That was about the moment Grandpa became completely lucid and started talking. "It began as a quiet night at the station." Every eye at the table turned to him.

Marcie's mother covered her face with her hands and shook her head, obviously not a happy camper.

Grandpa continued. "It had been a quiet evening. Joe Smith, Louis Savage, Bill Murtha and I were playing poker. I had two pair, finally pulling my first decent hand all night, when suddenly the alarm went off, killing the game and my lucky hand. It turned out to be a mother of a fire." Seeming as sharp as a tack, he proceeded to retell the entire story of how he saved Smith's grandfather without leaving out a detail. I knew because I'd heard the story so many times when I was little. Listening to this man, you'd never believe his brain was being attacked by senility.

They were all lost in the spell of the story he wove—except her mother, of course—when an ambulance rushed by. Instinctively, Grandpa stood and was about to flee.

Breaking out of the trance, Marcie realized what he intended to do and yelled to Smith, "Help me stop him! Block the door and for God's sake, don't let him out!"

Moments later, with Smith on one side and Marcie on the other, Gramps was guided safely back to the table.

"What was *that* all about?" Smith inquired.

"If we hadn't stopped him, he'd be half-way down the block by now, chasing the ambulance."

Smith found humor in what she'd said and chuckled. She couldn't help but notice how adorable he looked when he laughed, but shook that annoying thought off like fleas on a hound dog, which was closer to how Smith usually acted.

Since Eileen's kids had been relatively quiet up until this point, Marcie thought maybe they'd been sedated, which in their case was a good thing. At least Sarah had stopped behaving like a dog. Less than two months ago, whenever she came here for dinner, a bowl was placed on the floor for her to eat from. Eileen allowed this crazy behavior for fear she'd stifle her child's creative juices. She even had her name printed on the bowl. Come to think of it, Dr. Frankenstein had been creative, too, and look at what he'd produced.

Marcie had just washed down some pot roast—not meatballs in honor of Smith—with a sip of water when she got this strange look from the man-of-the-hour, which had started out as one of surprise and then transformed into a smirk.

"What?" she asked, not knowing what was going on.

"I knew you had the hots for me," he whispered.

"Are you crazy?" She'd said it loud enough to attract everyone's attention.

When everyone went back to minding their own plates, Smith whispered again, "Wait until later."

"For what?"

"Don't be coy."

"You're one-hundred percent certifiable. Can't you see I'm trying to eat?"

"Ooh, how did you do that?"

"Do what?" Marcie put down her fork and looked at him.

"That."

"I didn't do anything."

"You didn't?"

"No. I didn't." Both my hands were on the table.

At that point, she and Smith looked underneath the table and saw her niece, Jessica, crawling quickly back to her chair.

"Never mind," he grunted.

After she figured out what had happened, she exploded into a wide grin. And then all hell broke loose.

"Where's Sarah?" Eileen asked Larry, who was busy seeing how much food he could stuff in his mouth at one time. He must have come from a 'first come, take all' kind of family.

"HowshooIno," he replied, spraying food as he spoke, reaffirming why one shouldn't talk with a mouth full of food.

"She's your daughter, too," Eileen whined.

Some things never changed as Marcie prepared for one of their arguments. Why couldn't they just save it until they got home? But no! For some bizarre reason audiences never seemed to bother them. Marcie just thought it rude to fight at her mother's all the time.

"She's in the house somewhere." Mom attempted to calm Eileen who was beginning to lose it. "We'll find her."

Gramps and Larry continued to eat as if nothing had happened. She knew her grandfather's excuse. Nothing could excuse Larry.

Smith wiped his mouth and rose from his chair, taking command. "Let's go look for her. We'll each take a room."

Marcie headed upstairs. She looked in all the bedrooms and the bathroom. If Sarah was hiding any place up there, she'd become invisible. Feeling confident she wasn't upstairs, she headed downstairs. She entered the kitchen just in time to see Smith open the cabinet under the sink and find her niece, lying there in a fetal position sucking her thumb.

"I used to hide from my brother under our sink," Smith said.

"Well, thanks for finding her," Marcie said.

He gave her a no sweat grin and she called to Eileen, "Crisis over! She's in here!"

Gramps never got up from the table. He was waiting for dessert. Larry it seems had gone to the bathroom. She was prepared to put the 'Condemned' sign up after he vacated. 'Use at Your Own Risk' was also acceptable.

Smith left shortly after the apple strudel and coffee. He thanked her mother and patted her grandfather on the back. She got a nod from him as she made one of her trips out of the kitchen to gather stuff off the table. Since it was a civil nod, she figured things would settle down between them for now and she wouldn't have to worry about her back.

Eileen and her brood left soon after Smith and the house grew quiet again. She finished helping her mother clean up before going home and straight to bed. She'd had quite a day and fell sound asleep the minute her head hit the pillow and she didn't move a muscle until the constant ringing of the phone woke her. And she nearly slept through that.

Chapter Five

"Marcie! Marcie, are you there? Wake up! Marcie, wake up!"

Through the veil of leftover sleep, which clung to her like a mummy's wrap, Marcie could hear her mother's voice, only it sounded hundreds of miles away in her head. She fought her way to the surface of consciousness and gave out a yawn which sounded more like a grunt. Despite being in good shape, every muscle in her body ached from the strenuous workout she'd given it the day before.

"Marcie! Get up!"

"Where are you, Mom? Did you take a trip? You sound so far away..." she replied as the tentacles of sleep began to reel her back in and she gave out a huge yawn.

"Marcie! Get out of bed and go wash your face."

"I did last night. It's clean. How can you see through the phone?"

Her mother groaned. "Wake up, Marcie."

Marcie tried to obey, but yawned again as tears trickled from the corners of her eyes. She tried to blink them away. "Couldn't this call have waited, Mom? It's my day off and I'm exhausted."

"Would I have called if it weren't important?"

No, never. "What's wrong?"

"I took Grandpa to the hospital early this morning."

"Is he all right?" Marcie came wide awake as fear fluttered within the pit of her stomach.

"They're doing tests on him right now trying to rule out a stroke and heart attack."

"Did you call Eileen?"

"Yeah, but she's got a headache and is resting in bed."

Poor Eileen needs her rest. What am I, a stepchild?

I'm the one who should be in bed.

She gave out a huge sigh and attempted to stretch. "Ouch!"

"Marcie? What happened?"

"Nothing, Mom. I'll be there as soon as I can." She hung up and sat on the edge of the bed.

She didn't have to ask which hospital they'd taken him to because she knew old Gramps had his favorite. According to him, Central General had the prettiest nurses on their staff.

"I can die in any hospital, mind you. So when it's time for me to cash in my chips, the last thing I want to see on this earth is a pretty face. Make sure you take me to Central General," he'd always said.

She pushed herself up off the bed before she had a chance to fall back to sleep. She took a long hot shower, shrugged into her jeans and slipped on a sweater. After she brushed her unruly mop of russet hair into a ponytail, she had a quick breakfast before heading out to the hospital.

By the time she arrived at Central General, Grandpa was being admitted. He'd had a bad case of heartburn, which the doctors thought was GERD at first. GERD, which is Greek to most people and stands for gastro-esophageal reflux disease, was not the reason for his getting admitted. The tests revealed Grandpa's heart was a ticking time bomb. His arteries were so clogged it was a miracle any blood reached his heart at all. They were going to operate later in the day.

Marcie had known all along she had to get to the hospital and rescue her mother. Even though Mom put on a brave face, she didn't do too well in hospitals and hated them. Yet in a way, she was like the perennial designated driver, always there when someone in the family died. When her father, a milkman took his last breath, she'd been holding his hand. He'd died after being shot by some derelict who'd robbed him before he'd started his deliveries. Then there had been her younger brother, Tommy, who caught influenza when he was three. He'd lingered for a day in the hospital before he died. Her mother was rushed to the hospital complaining of chest pains and died four hours later clutching her daughter's hand. No wonder her mother had a fear of hospitals.

The worst hospital visit she'd experienced, though, was reserved for her husband, Marcie's father. Over seventy-five percent of his body had been burned fighting a fire. Swathed in oozing bandages from head to foot, he died from complications six hours later with her sitting at his bedside.

Marcie was certain there were others, but at the moment thinking only made her head hurt more.

Gramps had fallen asleep, or so they'd thought until he opened one watery-blue eye and focused it on them. "What are you two fools goin' to do, watch me sleep all day? Go on, scat until they cut me up later," he barked.

"Are you sure, Grandpa?"

"Don't add deafness to your list of deficiencies, girl." Marcie looked at her mother, who tilted her head in the direction of the door. You could never argue with Gramps when he was in his feisty, argumentative mode. Since he was scheduled for surgery at 4:00 o'clock, Marcie went home with her mother to keep her company. Had she known beforehand what the topic of discussion would be, she'd have reconsidered.

First her mother distracted her by making sandwiches to die for from last night's leftovers.

She must have taken two bites before she heard, "Smith's quite a guy."

"I'm glad you like him. I'll give him your number."

"Stop talking like an idiot. I meant for you."

"Not interested."

"Why not?" she asked.

"Because, he's not my type."

Her mother stared at her for a few seconds as she mulled over what Marcie had said, acting as if it were the answer to the riddle of life. A beat later, her eyes widened suddenly with that *I should have known look plastered all over her face*. Then she paled, letting out a sound like a half-moan, half-groan. "Oh, no..."

"Mom, what's wrong?" Marcie nearly jumped from her chair over to her mother. She feared she'd be rushing her back to the hospital.

"I...didn't know. Why am I always the last to know?"

"Know what? What the devil are you talking about?"

"It's a good thing your father's dead."

"What?"

"That you're gay. Your father must be turning over in his grave."

She had no idea which was more ridiculous. Her father doing acrobatics in his coffin or the fact her mother thought she was gay. "I'm not gay."

"No?"

"No."

"Not even just a little...what do you call that?"

"Bisexual? Not in the least. I prefer men, Mom."

"Oh, thank goodness!" She expelled a huge breath of air. Then added, "So what's wrong with Smith?"

"Are we back to that?"

"We never left the subject."

"Look, Mom, he's just not my type."

"You don't like tall, handsome men? Are you into dwarfs with pointy ears this week?"

Marcie rolled her eyes. "He may be handsome, but he's a Neanderthal. He doesn't approve of women in the Company."

"Well, neither do I. I like him even more now."

"Told you he was more your type," Marcie answered, feeling quite smug with herself.

"I think you two would make a nice pair," her mother replied.

"Too bad you're the only one who thinks that way. And don't let this shock you too much. He likes me *even less* than I like him."

"I didn't get that impression."

"You have selective vision. You see only what you want to see. Besides, I'll never give up my profession for a man."

"If you remain so stubborn, you'll never get married," her mother replied, stirring more sugar into her coffee.

"Marriage isn't everything, you know."

"Oh, ending up alone like me is?"

"How do you know Smith is the marrying kind?"

"All men are when they meet the right woman," her mother declared.

"Well, thank goodness that leaves me out." She took another bite of her hoagie.

"That's what you say now," she said under her breath, but loud enough for Marcie to hear.

The conversation changed direction and went to her other favorite topic, Eileen and her family. Every now and then Marcie felt guilty that she didn't love her two nieces. She did try to relate to them, but Eileen must have been snatched by aliens and impregnated on their starship. That was the only way to explain their bizarre behavior.

Finally she'd had enough and went to take a nap. She gave her mother explicit instructions to only wake her if the Assistant Chief called her into work, the President needed advice, Grandpa took a turn for the worse, or the world was coming to an end, but she scratched the last reason.

Gramps' surgery went well. The attending nurse knew he was coming around in the recovery room when he reached out and pinched her behind with his free, unattached hand. Thank God for her sake, and probably his by the look on her face, his other hand was attached to an IV tube.

She related this to Marcie and her mother with a straight face after Gramps was brought back to his room.

They stayed and visited with him for forty minutes more before wishing the nurses good luck and going home.

That old man is something else, Marcie thought as a huge wave of relief replaced her earlier apprehension. Gramps was the personification of a dirty old man.

Chapter Six

Following the competition between Marcie and Smith and their being thrown together at dinner at her mother's, an obvious cessation of hostilities seemed to be in place. Their truce, if it could be called that, could be better translated into 'You stay out of my way, and I'll do likewise.'

Marcie told herself she was honestly okay with that. Never in a million years would she dream of hanging out with some guy whose principles were rooted in the Stone Age.

It was actually ironic in a way. As a fireman, Marcie thought having to cook and clean for the entire shift from time-to-time should help broaden his horizons. However, Smith was truly a hard case and she doubted anything short of shock therapy or a frontal lobotomy would help.

The squad had just finished dinner when the fire alarm clanged. Dropping everything, they dashed to the poles and into their gear. Marcie rode in the lead truck with Dodd and Assistant Chief Wiebolt. Bob McLaughlin drove. Sal DiMaggio was on the back of the truck. In the other truck was the rest of the team, Smith, Frank McGuiness, John Calderone, Rory Mulvane and Jim Maguire. Ed Clark drove the EMS SUV.

According to the dispatcher, a tanker had overturned on the 257, a major highway. The squad prepared for the worst since an overturned tanker was always a potential disaster. Just how bad, they'd have to wait and see.

The AC tried to lighten the mood by cracking one-liners. He got on the truck's horn, or mobile phone, which also served as an intercom between the trucks, and asked if anybody remembered the marshmallows. A reply came back, "No. But we got lots of wieners." Of course that drew laughter.

As the scene came into view, they didn't see the dreaded fire or even a whiff of smoke. Instead, it looked more like a scene from a vintage Three Stooges' movie.

The tanker had collided with a large open-bed truck transporting cages of live chickens. The squawking livestock flapped their wings wildly as they fled from wooden cages that had fallen off the truck and had broken open on the road. Between flying feathers and general pandemonium, men from both trucks chased the crazed escaping chickens. It would have been less comical, had the tanker not ruptured in the collision and begun to leak.

"Is that oil from the tanker they're slipping around in, Assistant Chief?" McLaughlin asked.

"I hope to hell it isn't oil, man." He jumped from the cab of the fire truck to find out. "All it needs is a spark. Wait on my order."

The squad watched as Wiebolt approached one of the several cops trying to maintain what little order they could. Marcie saw the AC shake his head as his hands flew up to the sides of his helmet. Her heart's pace ratcheted up a notch. New beads of sweat formed under her helmet and armpits.

"It must be real bad," McLaughlin said.

The squad prepared for the worst as Wiebolt trudged back toward the trucks. Before they could ask any questions, he got on the horn and called in for a dump truck of sand and a payloader. Knowing the implications of such a request, Marcie now feared the worst. Finally, their supervisor turned to face them. Not a soul moved. All eyes were on him. Tense silence blanketed the group.

"There's good news and bad news." Wiebolt stated flatly, showing no emotion.

"What are we facing," Dodd asked.

"Well, it ain't no oil slick."

"Then that's good," McGuiness said.

"Yeah, but we may have worse problems."

"What is it then?" Marcie asked, thinking toxic waste.

"Molasses."

"Molasses?" they all said in unison, looking at one another.

"Too bad we have no flapjacks," McGuiness quipped.

Marcie gathered that had been the good news. There wouldn't be any fire to battle. The AC had used the word 'worse.' There had to be more. And she was right. The bad news was they had to help catch the escapees and supervise the clean up. What a God-awful mess! Traffic throughout the area would be snarled for hours and then some.

Trying to catch frightened chickens covered in molasses might sound funny to the average civilian, but it was far from that or easy. It turned out to be one of the biggest challenges Marcie had ever faced. For starters, staying on her feet without taking a header into the mess was her first priority and also the most difficult. She also quickly discovered it was just as impossible. They were slipping and sliding into one another as if they were on an ice rink without skates. More than once she butted heads with Smith, only this time physically and not mentally. She also banged into Mulvane and Dodd. She felt as if she were at the amusement park on the bumper car ride. The squad also had to hunt down and chase the chickens that had managed to avoid getting stuck in the slippery goop and found their way into the backyards of nearby private homes.

By dusk, with the light waning, they were forced to pack it in. Luckily, most of the chickens had been rounded up. Now the squad would have the tedious chore of cleaning molasses off their equipment and themselves. What an experience!

She declared to Dodd, "If I never have molasses on my pancakes again, it will be too soon."

Later that night, they caught a call to put out a blaze

at the Stevens Department Store, located in the older part of town. The department store had been there long before Marcie was born. Rumors circulated from time to time that some rich entrepreneur had bought the place and it soon would become a restaurant or office building, but nothing seemed to come of them. She guessed the store hadn't been doing well lately. Between the malls and the factory outlets, those old established businesses often had a tough time competing.

The squad slid down the poles and put on their gear. Marcie rode in the truck next to the AC. She often thought about him, wondering if she could do his job. Lenny Wiebolt must have had nerves of steel. Even though the Chief ran the department, it was the Assistant Chief who made the split-second, crucial decisions at each fire as to who would do what and when. If he was wrong, it could cost their lives as well as those civilians they came to help—not to mention the loss of property.

She remembered the first time she'd ridden with him to a fire. She'd been a rookie. He clowned around, referring to the fire as a barbecue and even asked if she'd remembered to bring the marshmallows. At the time, she thought he was a little out of line or perhaps had been in one too many fires and was out of his mind. That was before she got to know him. All that humor was merely a cover up. The man was just as nervous and scared as the rest of the crew. Aware of the gravity of his position, he was able to compartmentalize his fears and apprehensions, never allowing them to get to him. He had a clear head and was able to make life and death decisions on the spot. In her opinion, the man was simply amazing.

Like most of the men in the company, he had a great deal at stake. His wife was pregnant with his fourth kid. And she was due soon. The chance of leaving her a widow had to enter his mind every time he went out on a call. When running into a burning building, he had to think about the possibility of not coming out.

As they approached an intersection, Wiebolt

grabbed the siren wire and tugged on it a few times to warn the public of their approach. Out of nowhere, an idiot driving a van pulled away from the curb directly into the fire truck's path.

Bob McLaughlin swerved out of the way and nearly hit an oncoming car on the opposite side of the street. The Assistant Chief slid sharply into Marcie, banging her shoulder against the door.

Great! We'll all be killed before we even get to the fire.

"Asshole!" McLaughlin screamed and flipped the idiot the bird.

"He probably has no clue about what just happened," Wiebolt yelled.

It was hard enough keeping the truck steady in normal conditions, let alone trying to make hairpin corrections. Thank God, McLaughlin was a good driver. Then, in the middle of all these dire musings, a humorous thought popped into Marcie's head. If Smith had been driving, he probably would have stopped the truck, gotten out and beat the crap out of the other guy. Now *that* would have been quite a scene.

Even though they had made good time, when they arrived at the scene, they found the entire building engulfed in flames. At that point, all they could do was contain the fire and prevent it from spreading. They had to fight it from the outside. Minutes later, the entire roof caved in. Luckily no one was in the building. It had been a fast blaze, spreading quickly. Usually a fire like this was indicative of accelerants and perhaps arson, but there was no way to know that for certain now. Once it was completely out, the fire inspector would sift through the rubble and submit his report.

Two other companies had responded and together hosed the building down without a mishap. It took over three hours to make certain the fire was out. No one wanted any flare-ups.

"Good job, guys," Wiebolt said as the squad hauled their tired bodies back into the fire truck and headed home.

Marcie hoped they wouldn't have to respond to any other fires before they got some sleep. Unfortunately, fires didn't take time off or schedule vacations.

As tired as she was, Marcie couldn't sleep. Her body was restless and her brain wouldn't shut down. To remedy the situation, she went to the kitchen to warm some milk. Allergic to most dairy products, she was the only one in the house who drank soy.

When the milk was warm, she poured it into a cup and sat at the table to read.

"You couldn't sleep, either?" Dodd walked into the room. He opened the refrigerator and poured himself a glass of orange juice before joining her. "I notice things have quieted down between you and Smith."

She looked up from her reading, "Yeah, I showed him who the boss was."

Dodd chuckled. "Yeah, thanks for whipping him into shape for us. We're eternally grateful."

Marcie pursed her lips as she replaced the bookmark and closed the pages. Things had definitely cooled down between her and Smith. In fact, it seemed he was going out of his way to avoid her. Now she wasn't certain if she was happy with that.

"He's not so bad when he keeps his mouth shut," she said.

Dodd shrugged. "I guess some guys feel a woman should be safe at home."

"He doesn't have to proselytize."

"I don't think you have to worry about what he says, O'Dwyer. The rest of us know and respect what you do."

"Thanks. I need to hear that every so often. So what's keeping you up?"

Dodd stared at the half-empty glass he was holding. It seemed he was about to say something. However, when he looked up all he said was, "Nothing...really. Guess I'll go back and try to get some sleep."

A few minutes after Dodd left, Marcie decided to attempt sleep herself. The milk had done its job.

Smith lay awake on his back, looking up at the ceiling, his hands clasped behind his head. His mind was filled with thoughts he'd rather not have. O'Dwyer had become a problem. She was definitely a good firefighter and dedicated. Contrary to what he'd told her, he wanted someone like her to be watching his back. But, she was a woman and that upset and infuriated him—and now scared him as well.

Why weren't women content just to marry and have children? Okay, if they wanted a career, why couldn't they choose a safe one? Why couldn't they be content to leave the perilous jobs to men?

He turned on his side and scrunched the pillow under his head. Still sleep wouldn't come. He knew exactly what upset him the most about O'Dwyer. She reminded him of Robin—from her red hair and tight body with those endless legs, to her feisty wit. At least he could *now* think about Robin without ripping off the scab covering the hole in his heart.

High school sweethearts, he and Robin had made plans to marry as soon as he made sufficient money to support them. Robin had wanted to help out and had gotten a job also—as a cop. The harder he'd tried to dissuade her from joining the police force, the more insistent she'd become. She'd been riding some self-felt zealous high to help fight crime, convinced that what she was doing was right and could make a difference.

Almost a year from the date she'd joined, Robin was fatally shot by some hopped up junkie. Though being a firefighter was dangerous in many ways, getting up close and personal with bullets was deadly. Her death had been a waste and had devastated him. She'd been his one true love and he'd vowed there would be no other.

Until now...

Smith *did not* want to go through all that again. Then he finally admitted to himself he was falling for O'Dwyer. Not if he could help it, he mused. He still had time to apply the brakes. There was no way he'd willingly get involved with a woman firefighter. What was it his grandmother would say: "Jumping from the frying pan into the fire?" Thinking of the play on words, the cliché described the situation to a tee.

He was definitely not going to make the same mistake twice. He had to avoid her. That was the only way he would be able to protect himself—and his heart.

Chapter Seven

Marcie's next shift was fairly quiet compared to the last one. The squad had a practice drill in the morning and did some well-needed house and truck cleaning. She power cleaned all the trucks. Afterward, she stood back to admire how they gleamed as the sun's rays bounced off the red paint and chrome. Even as a child, she'd loved to see the shiny red trucks after they'd been washed.

In the afternoon the house got a call from airport officials requesting the Hazmat truck to check out a suspicious smell emanating from the baggage area. Bioterrorism was the new fear weighing heavily on everyone's mind. The squad donned their 'space suits' and headed for the small private airport a few miles away.

Much to everyone's relief, and to the chagrin of the airport officials, it turned out to be a raccoon that had somehow wandered inside and got stuck in the equipment and died.

Phew! Marcie thought. If that smell could somehow be put into a guided missile and shot into a nest of terrorists, they might look for other work.

Some of the guys started up a poker game that night. Marcie hadn't been too crazy about poker ever since she'd lost big-time in a coed strip poker game when she'd been fourteen. Around the table sat Mulvane, McGuiness, Smith, Calderone and Dodd. She wasn't sure where McLaughlin and Clark were. She ambled into the kitchen, made a cup of hot chocolate, and sat down to read. Since the guys were in the next room, she could hear the conversation—when they weren't yelling at one another to hurry up and bet or deal.

One topic that came up was the price of gas. That led to a political discussion on how the US should become less dependent on foreign oil. She blanked them out and got back into the book again. Politics didn't thrill her any more than poker did.

It wasn't until McGinnis asked Rory if his wife was expecting that her attention shifted back to the guys again.

"No. Why do you ask?" she heard Rory reply.

"I happened to pass your place the other day and it looked like you were putting on an extension," McGuiness answered.

"It's for Angie. She wants her own gym so she can work out in the comfort of home without having to drive ten miles."

Marcie thought about Angie and the way she pampered herself. She never appeared in public with a hair out of place and always had her nails freshly manicured. She wore only designer clothes and expensive jewelry. How nice—and costly—it must be to be treated like a princess.

Marcie accepted her own fate, knowing that maxing out her plastic wasn't in the cards for her.

She heard Dodd yell, "I call!" and the subject of Angie was dropped.

Unable to get back into the book, she decided to give her mother a call to see how Gramps was doing.

Marcie often worried about what would happen when her grandfather finally passed on to that big firehouse in the sky. Her mother's place wasn't large—only three small bedrooms—but being alone without even a bowl of goldfish for company no matter how cozy the house, wasn't a hot idea in her book. Though worried, she wasn't traumatized to the point of thinking about moving back in. Insanity only ran through certain members of her family.

Besides, if she did return home it would make things worse since she and her mother got along like oil and water. She loved her mother, but there was no way she could live with her. They existed in different worlds.

From time to time, she'd bring up the subject, but usually got her mother's stock reply, "Don't worry, Marcie, I'll be just fine."

Her mother was dead serious about being able to take care of herself. Her reply acted as a Band-aid and mollified Marcie for a while, until the scab worked its way off. And like the seasons, this conversation was cyclical.

When her grandfather had his scary bout with GERD and his subsequent bypass, the worries rose to the surface like pond scum. Marcie couldn't get beyond them and knew she'd have to speak to her mother and deal with them.

Before she had the chance to do so, the Almighty intervened and played one of His colossal jokes.

Heading toward her mother's place for dinner, the price of the phone call—the one she'd made when she couldn't get back into her book—she felt the usual trepidation forming in the pit of her stomach as the tiny voice in her head began to stir. The feeling grew stronger the closer she got to the house. She'd already wrestled with the urge to call and tell her mother she couldn't make it for one reason or another, but her mother usually found just the right words to push Marcie's guilt buttons. And if that didn't work, she'd revert to her unfailing last resort and whine, "This may be the last time I'll get both my girls together before I die." This further reinforced the idea that Eileen whined in her mother's footsteps.

When she pulled up in front of the house, she noticed her sister's van parked in the driveway. Chauvinist Larry never allowed Eileen to drive him anywhere and he wouldn't be caught driving anything less than his BMW, so Marcie wondered what was up.

Dozens of scenarios quickly popped into her head as she parked and got out of the Jeep. In Technicolor, she pictured Larry running to the door of some prospective homebuyer's abode and tripping over a garden hose, breaking his leg in multiple places. Or even better, meeting the business end of some angry dog's mouth.

She found her mother and Eileen in the kitchen having coffee. Everything looked and smelled normal. Several pots on the stove bubbled, filling the air with delicious odors. The two little she-monsters were watching TV in the den, no doubt a horror movie.

When Eileen noticed Marcie, she dabbed at her eyes with a tissue and whined, "My life is over; Larry's left me."

This was even better than she'd imagined.

Honestly, her first instinct was to break out in laughter. She quelled the urge, realizing the situation called for a little more sensitivity, and instead replied, "Umm...gee...sorry, Eileen." It might not have been much, but at least it wasn't a more truthful, "I told you so." Also trying to squash a giggle bubbling in her throat was truly difficult and above and beyond her sensitivity.

In what could only be termed an Olympic feat, Eileen was able to condense her sad melodrama into a ten-minute diatribe. The essence of which was that her smug, self-centered, obnoxious cretin of a husband had left her for a twenty-four-year-old bimbo. She nearly left out the most important fact that the bimbo had just inherited her parents' two-and-a-half-million-dollar estate on the Florida Gulf Coast. It was probably the best thing to happen to her sister and the kids, but Marcie had the distinct feeling she was the only person who thought that way at the moment.

Larry had already put the house up for sale and Eileen and the kids were preparing to move in with her mother. Marcie groaned inwardly when she heard this. Why was there always a drawback to everything? Yet again, she was in the minority looking at the situation from that point of view, for her mother actually seemed happy. She guessed when her mother had become a grandparent she'd left her common sense in the hospital nursery.

"Marcie, call your grandfather to the table," her mother instructed. Eileen punctuated the command with the honk of her nose as she blew it into an already well-used tissue.

Grandpa was entertaining his giggling great-granddaughters by making his hand speak to them. His lipstick-outlined imaginary mouth had teeth—his—which he'd removed from his mouth.

"Okay, Grandpa, pop your teeth back in. It's time to eat." Marcie turned to the girls. "Go wash up."

Instantly her eldest niece whined, "I'm not dirty."

"That's okay. Humor me and take your sister into the bathroom and wash anyway."

Sarah rolled her eyes, but took Jessica by the hand and led her to the bathroom. Marcie returned to the kitchen to see if her mother needed help.

Eileen was moaning quietly. "No warning. All he left me was a note. Said he found someone he loved more."

"I think it's her family estate he loves more," Marcie said.

Mom threw her a look.

"Come on, Mom, you know the guy; you know I'm right."

"He took all his clothes...and his shoes," Eileen added.

She had added his shoes to the statement as an afterthought as if it were a unique item to take along with one's clothes when leaving. Then Marcie reminded herself it was Eileen who was speaking, so didn't give it another thought.

Her mother herded everyone into the dining room to start eating. As Marcie reached for the potatoes, she thought about how Eileen's moving in with her mother would affect her. The idea wasn't doing much for her appetite.

Without warning, things went from bad to worse. Her sister calmly turned to her and declared, "This is all your fault."

Marcie nearly choked on her dinner roll. "What did you say?"

"You heard me!" Then Eileen repeated it word for word.

"Are you crazy?" The words exploded from Marcie's

mouth along with crumbs from the dinner roll.

"It's true, you know."

"How is it *my* fault? I'm not the other woman. I'd need a frontal lobotomy for that."

"If Daddy hadn't loved you more, I wouldn't have gotten married."

"You got married because you were knocked up!" Marcie informed her sister, who'd evidently forgotten the real reason for her rushed marriage.

"Marcie! There are kids at the table," her mother cautioned.

"I didn't start this, Mom."

"Let's just drop it and eat in peace," Mrs. O'Dwyer said firmly.

"Nah! Keep yapping. There's more for me," Grandpa interjected.

Marcie fought the desire to grin at the old man. "That's fine with me."

Eileen looked like she was about to say something else, but clearly changed her mind.

Nothing further was said about the subject. The tenuous truce held, and Marcie left after helping her mother clean up. She didn't go home, though.

Following that wonderful and insightful meal, which had merited a spot in the all-time top ten winners, Marcie needed to unwind. She was so tense she feared snapping like some overstretched rubberband.

She headed directly to O'Leary's for some liquid medication.

As she drove, it occurred to her that she no longer had to worry about her mother being alone, now that Eileen and her two girls would be there indefinitely. Expanding her thoughts along that path, maybe her mother wouldn't notice if she didn't show up for dinner every so often. Then, again, maybe she should be more careful about what she wished for next time.

Marcie walked into O'Leary's and found the place half-filled with firefighters, but none from her house. She didn't mind. All she needed was beer, not company or small talk. She spied an empty seat at the bar.

As soon as she sat, Ralph came over. "Beer?"

Marcie nodded.

"You look like you've had a mighty long day." He poured the cold amber liquid into a thick mug for her. Her taste buds were already doing a Mexican hat dance.

"Thanks." She savored the first foamy sip. Acting somewhat ladylike, she wiped the foam mustache from her face with a napkin.

"Your buddy's here. Went to the john."

She nodded. Probably Dodd. Good. He was the only guy she could possibly tolerate now. A great listener, he also gave honest advice. However, it wasn't Dodd who slid onto the stool next to her.

Smith signaled Ralph for another beer. He turned to her. "You moonlighting or something?"

"What's it to you?"

"You look like hell."

"Well, thank you."

"Don't take what I said wrong and get bent out of shape."

"Really! How *should* I take it?" She was too strung out to verbally spar, even with him.

"I was only stating a fact and meant nothing by it."

Marcie didn't quite see the subtle difference, if there was one, but at the moment she didn't really care.

"I just had dinner at my mother's. It wasn't fun. Any other questions?"

"No."

Not another word was spoken between them until he finished his beer. He laid enough money on the bar to pay for hers, too. "See you at the house." Then he walked out.

She stayed for another beer and thought about Smith. Unfortunately, she'd found herself doing a great deal of that lately. Not that she truly wanted to. She'd be thinking about something else entirely unrelated, then out of nowhere, bam! Suddenly, Smith was in the picture. Often she'd daydream about running her fingers through his thick black hair. Sometimes she'd imagine lots of other things—like being held in his strong arms, or how he'd taste—before she managed to change the mental channel.

But she'd noticed something was going on with him. He wasn't as forceful as he'd previously been. Like tonight, there was really no bite to his behavior. And lately when she wanted him around—and she had to admit there were now occasions when she did—she had the distinct impression he was avoiding her.

Yes, something was definitely going on, and she wished she knew what.

Chapter Eight

The weather was changing and the days were getting colder. The brief warm spell had ended. Marcie expected any new precipitation would come down in the form of sleet or snow, depending upon how far the temperature dipped. Firefighters were always conscious of climatic conditions. Wind especially, because it always played havoc with a blaze.

If it hadn't rained in a while and things were dry, fire could spread rapidly. A carelessly thrown cigarette in a heavily wooded area had the potential of becoming a devastating inferno. Add strong wind gusts and disaster could develop instantaneously. These scenarios occurred all the time in western states. On a windy day a residential fire could spread quickly, jumping from one house to another, often consuming an entire block.

Icy conditions always caused problems. At best, they slowed an emergency vehicle's response time and made it difficult to hose down a building. These adverse conditions caused accidents and navigating around them with a fire truck was never easy. Not to mention how the wet and cold elements could affect a firefighter's exposed skin.

On that note, arthritic firefighters were practically nonexistent. They'd never survive upstate weather. Thinking about all this and the impending snow, she made a mental note to have the tread on her Jeep's tires checked and rotated.

At the firehouse, after the chance meeting with Smith at the bar, things between them were back to normal—they hardly spoke. Marcie figured this was probably for the best, for every time she and Smith actually talked, he somehow managed to set her off. Was it because he pressed the wrong buttons or was she overly sensitive? The entire situation with that man was getting to her.

Why should she even care? He wasn't her type. Her ideal man would have already evolved from the cave dwelling mentality.

Thankfully, the day had started off quietly. Nothing pressing was discussed at roll call except that Mrs. Avery, a fifth-grade teacher at the Elk Street Elementary School had requested two firemen to come and speak to her class.

"Anyone willing to go speak to a bunch of kids, come see me later," Assistant Chief Wiebolt had said.

Visiting some school and talking to a bunch of kids wasn't considered fun by most of the guys. Instead, they considered it an intrusion into their time. Marcie had a different take. If the kids listened, they might learn how to protect themselves better. Not counting her two weird nieces, she really liked kids. However, that didn't mean she was going to rush and have any—even if she did get married. She'd tell Wiebolt she was interested and to sign her up.

Some of the guys started a poker game in the common room. Marcie found a quiet place to read. As a kid she read all sorts of books, but as she got older, suspense novels grabbed and held her attention. She liked the kind of book that kept the reader on the edge of their seat, its plot twisting and turning as it kept one guessing. Romances just didn't do it for her. It was a fairytale to believe all relationships turned out with a happy ending. Hardly any of the marriages she knew of had been made in heaven. And judging from the relationships in her family, she was far better off reading thrillers.

Her mother talked as though her father was a saint. No way would she have described him that way before his death. In all honesty, her father had been a very difficult man to live with. As far as male chauvinism went, he would've made Smith look like an amateur. Her father believed her mother belonged at home caring for his children and castle. She had to be faithful and keep the torches burning for him. He, on the other hand, believed in the double-standard that men were different and didn't have to adhere to the same rules set forth for their women.

He'd often come home plastered to the gills, long after O'Leary's had closed. When Marcie was old enough to understand, she'd heard her parents arguing over the smell of perfume on his clothes or the errant lipstick stain on his collar. He'd also used his fists on more than one occasion, when his words weren't sufficient enough to end the argument. Her mother had tried using makeup to hide the bruises from Marcie and her sister, but she never could cover them all. Yet, despite his faults, he loved her mother in his own way. He had a romantic side and never forgot her birthday or Mother's Day.

Marcie had come to believe if that was what romance was all about, she didn't want anything to do with it, Hallmark Cards and all. What she wanted was a man who'd love her alone. To her that meant one-hundred percent loyalty and giving her *all* of his business.

The fire bell clanged, interrupting her thoughts. She dropped the book. In less than five minutes the squad was rushing to a residential neighborhood. The call had come in from a man who said the house across the street from him was on fire. Aside from an address and the person's name that made the call, the squad usually had no idea what they were up against until they arrived at the scene.

The dispatcher often had to interpret what the frantic person on the other end of the line had said. Sometimes even getting an address was difficult. Panic and fear affected people differently.

When they pulled onto a short block of cookie-cutter houses, they saw a woman with black, frizzed hair sticking out from her head in coils like the spiral decorations of a May Pole. She wore a bulky-knit sweater and wielded a garden house like David fighting an angry Goliath of a fire that had already decimated her garage and was now in the process of devouring her house.

Wiebolt moved the woman, probably in her late twenties or early thirties, to safety as Marcie attached the fire hose to the nearby pump as quickly as she could. Dodd started hosing down the fire. Afraid the fire would leap over the driveway to the next house, the Assistant Chief directed the guys from the other truck to hose down the surrounding houses. There wasn't much they could do. The woman's home had nearly been destroyed by the time they got there. Half the roof had already collapsed and the other half seemed held up by a prayer. One good gust of wind would probably knock it down. Hopefully she had insurance and a place to stay in the meantime.

When asked how the fire started, she gave quite a story. Her name was Annie Block. She was divorced and lived alone, supporting herself as a waitress at a local restaurant. Today had been her one day of the week off.

"So how did the fire start, Mrs. Block?" the AC asked.

"Call me Annie. I ain't no missus anymore, thank you very much."

"Okay, Annie, what happened?"

"I had this spider problem, you see..."

"Where? In the house, garage?"

"Oh, in the garage, of course."

"So, what did you do?" Wiebolt asked, trying to keep his face expressionless.

As Marcie and the others listened to the conversation, she already suspected the woman wasn't the brightest crayon in the box.

"Well, I went to get my can of Raid, only it was empty. I hate bugs. They're nasty and—"

"Mrs. Bl—I mean Annie," he said, trying to keep her on track, "what did you do next?"

"I had to kill them, so I grabbed my can of hairspray. It was a large, economy size. Now that I'm on my own I try to save money..."

She stopped talking when she saw the Assistant

Chief's expression change to one of annoyance, despite his attempts to keep it neutral.

"Sorry. Spraying them with the hairspray only stunned them, which pissed me off. That's when I decided to set them on fire. So I took out my lighter from my pocket like this—"

Wiebolt grabbed the lighter from her before she could open it. The woman looked confused, but he prodded her to continue.

"When I tried to burn them, everything around me went up in flames. I rushed to get my garden hose to put out the fire and then you came." She pursed her lips and shrugged.

"Eh, thank you, Annie," he said.

As the Assistant Chief walked away, she called after him, "Can I have my lighter back?"

This had to be one for the books and was going to be discussed at O'Leary's for a very long time. Obviously the people in this jurisdiction needed more exposure to fire safety. It was another good reason for going to the elementary school to talk to the kids. But hey, hadn't her mother ever warned her about playing with matches—or lighters?

Chapter Nine

"Hey, O'Dwyer, the AC wants to see ya—now," Calderone said.

Marcie tried to read the expression on his dark-skinned face. She wondered if she'd screwed up somehow on the last call out. However, there was no message to be read from his dark eyes. Okay, she'd find out when she spoke to Wiebolt. With a dose of apprehension she made her way to the Assistant Chief's office.

She knocked on the closed door.

"Enter!"

Opening the door she came face to face with Smith. Her heart plummeted. She hadn't expected him to be there. Now what? Her trepidation mushroomed.

"You wanted to see me?" She hardly recognized her own voice.

"Yup. Now that you're both here, sit down."

Marcie couldn't fathom what this might be about. Had Smith complained about her?

"It turns out you two are the only ones willing to visit the school. Is that going to be a problem—with your history and all?"

Marcie felt her heartbeat slow down. She took a deep breath. She'd forgotten about speaking at the school.

Smith shook his head and she cleared her throat and said, "No."

"Good. You'll need to collaborate on the presentation. The teacher wants you there next Thursday." Wiebolt's attention returned to papers on the desk. He looked up. "Well, what are you two still sitting here for? You've got work to do." He dismissed them.

Smith held the door for her. "I have some stuff left from another school visit I made at Central," he said as they walked out.

Stunned at this revelation, Marcie slowed her steps and gazed up at him. "Hey, that's great. When do you want to discuss this?"

He shrugged. "Now's as good a time as any."

"Okay."

"Let's go outside and I'll tell you what I've got."

They walked together in the yard, which had a little garden thanks to a few of the firefighters' wives. Perennials kept the area behind the firehouse in color during the spring and summer. The early frost had virtually killed them off, but a hint of color remained. The sweet smell of the flowers had been replaced by the acrid smell of gasoline, rubber and motor oil.

The person walking beside Marcie was a stranger. The man speaking wasn't the same guy she knew and verbally jousted with much of the time. No, this definitely wasn't the same individual. This had to be the *good* twin. She liked the way his green eyes gleamed with excitement as he told her about the presentation he'd made to a sixth-grade class at Central. Marcie realized Smith had most of the entire pitch put together already. He'd kept the old diagrams and pictures. All they needed was to fine tune what they'd say to the class. Along with the diagrams, they'd bring various pieces of equipment to demonstrate. And copies of the safety and prevention rules to hand out.

"Sounds great. I'd like to see some of the stuff."

"I'll bring in what I've got tomorrow to show you."

Then he turned toward her and actually smiled—a warm engaging expression that seemed in stark contrast to the frosty vapor that usually emerged from his mouth when he spoke. She noted how much she liked his smile.

"Good idea," she replied. "So, we'll go with three major topics: How a fire is caused; how to prevent fires; and what to do if a fire occurs."

He nodded. "Yeah. That's exactly what we'll do."

"And when we've got all the info together, we'll talk about what each of us will say."

"Sounds like a plan," Smith said lightheartedly.

As they returned to the firehouse, a thought hit her. They'd been talking civilly for the very first time since that morning he'd walked into the kitchen.

Over the next few days, she and Smith devoted whatever time they could squeeze in to the project. Still underneath an umbrella of cooperation, they headed to the elementary school to give their presentation to Mrs. Avery's class. They entered the classroom wearing full firefighter's gear. With their protective masks on, some of the kids thought they were astronauts. When Marcie took off her helmet to explain what Smith and she were wearing, a tall boy with neatly combed, sandy-blond hair raised his hand.
"What do you do?" he asked her.
"I'm a firefighter; I fight fires."
"But you're...a girl."
"And you're very observant."
Mrs. Avery and a handful of kids laughed.
Ignoring the laughter, the boy didn't seem satisfied. "Girls can't be firemen."
"They're not. They're firefighters. And we do the same job."
"If you say so..." The kid sat, but as a budding chauvinist, he didn't quite believe her.
Marcie just knew Smith had been laughing behind the mask. After telling the class, "Women can be anything they put their minds to today," she moved on with the presentation.
The primary goal was to teach the children about fires, how to prevent them and what to do if one occurred. Through the use of equipment, pictures, and face-to-face talking, it was their job to make the kids more proactive in fire prevention. The statistics showed that children caused way too many fires. Perhaps by teaching these eager students some of the basics, none sitting in this classroom would play with matches or grow up and burn their homes down due to carelessness or ignorance. She didn't want to meet any more people like Annie Block who used hairspray to kill bugs.

The kids were very enthusiastic during the entire delivery. When finished, Mrs. Avery and the entire class thanked them.

Exiting the building, Marcie felt good. It wasn't just about reaching the kids, which both she and Smith believed had been accomplished.

No, she felt something else—a feeling she couldn't readily identify at first. It didn't take her long to figure out what it was.

Smith had been more than civil toward her. He'd been friendly. They'd bonded over this project. She wasn't certain if this would blossom into real friendship, but she found herself liking him as a person and enjoying his company. A totally different side of the man—a tender one—one she'd never have expected had emerged. He liked kids and they liked him.

Marcie was beginning to view Smith in a new light. This one softened her tough stance and she more than hoped their relationship had taken a new direction. She was willing and ready to let bygones be bygones. What happened next depended on him.

When she thought about Smith from this new perspective, she was finally able to admit that even though he annoyed the hell out of her at times and brought out the worst side of her, he tended to invade her subconscious and dreams. However, she was just as certain he didn't expend one moment of his precious time thinking about her, except of course, to devise different ways to exasperate her.

Despite this, she constantly caught herself dwelling on *him*. To make matters worse, embarrassing even, some of these thoughts were X-rated. On the bright side, at least no one, especially Smith, could read her mind. Consequently, so long as she kept this problem under wraps, no one would be the wiser. That, of course, depended entirely on Smith.

Smith said nothing during the short ride back to the firehouse. He was too lost in thought. Apprehension began to replace the euphoria he'd been experiencing in the classroom. It wasn't just being with the kids, but being with *her*—being with O'Dwyer.

She'd gotten under his skin from the beginning and he'd tried to deal with it. Since Robin, he'd protected his heart. Don't put it on the line, it won't be broken. The problem was, he liked her and enjoyed hanging out with her. Her honesty was refreshing. She was definitely not like the women he'd met recently who played head games. Today, the temptation had dangerously increased and he'd nearly suggested dinner.

That would have been a colossal disaster. He had to keep his feelings covered up. It was the only way he'd survive having his heart broken again. Time to go back to the way it had been, which meant keeping her at a distance.

Chapter Ten

In every fire company there was always one guy who was one of the nicest people to know. The one person who could be trusted with the deepest, darkest secrets. The one who would merit the first halo, if they were ever given out. He never cussed or said a mean thing about anyone. It was doubtful he'd ever had a bad thought his entire life. Sometimes you wondered if he was too good to be true, like an angel who fell off the heavenly wagon and broke his wings.

In Marcie's squad, Ed Clark was that man. She thought he would've made a terrific minister had he desired to become one. Instead he'd chosen the career of paramedic/firefighter. In addition to being mild-mannered and able to hold his tongue, unlike some of the hotheads around, he was an eternal optimist. He always saw the best in everything, no matter how bad. His cup was always half full—never half empty.

Tall, thin and lanky, Ed could wield a fire hose as if it were a garden hose, often surprising those who didn't know him. He could be a ringer in an arm wrestling competition. His straight sandy-brown hair never stayed in place. A lock or two always hung down his forehead giving him the look of a big kid. But he was no kid, for he possessed the collective wisdom of someone well beyond his thirty-odd years.

Marcie often wondered about him. She'd never seen him with a woman on a date or at special functions like confirmations and weddings. Since he was a minister's son, she had the impression he was naïve or just chose to walk the straight and narrow alone. Now that she thought about it, she couldn't recall ever seeing him at O'Leary's. It was probably way too sordid a place for him. That was why she could have been blown over by a gentle summer's breeze when she received the wedding invitation.

He was marrying a woman named Laura Most. Marcie had never heard him mention her and wondered who she was. She made a mental note to ask Sal DiMaggio, the resident gossip. Sal and his wife, Josephine, seemed to know the backstory to everything.

Marcie pushed hangers around in her closet. Just as she suspected, she had absolutely nothing to wear. Grabbing the phone, she immediately called Joanne to set up a date to go shopping.

"I'm glad you called, Marcie. I could use a good mall run. Barry has already seen me in three of my outfits."

"Do you really think he cares about you wearing something more than once? Besides, how long does the outfit actually remain on?"

"You do have a valid point. However, would you open the same book twice?" she countered.

"You're unbelievable, Joanne."

"I know. That's what keeps them coming back for more."

"Oooh, that hurt!" Marcie winced.

Joanne had been her best friend for longer than Marcie could remember. When it came to attracting the opposite sex, well, she was unbelievable. She oozed sex appeal. Her pheromones were so strong they could be sensed a good block away. Men tended to flock to her like cats to catnip. To top it off, though one might expect her to be conceited and way too self-centered to think about others, just the opposite was true. She worked in an assisted-living complex for seniors as an activities coordinator and helped keep the elderly men's hearts pumping. Beautiful, dark-haired Joanne had just as much, if not more, fun as blondes and didn't need to brag.

"You're getting a new dress to impress Smith, aren't you?" Joanne asked out of the blue.

Whenever they spoke, not too unlike her mother, she seemed to manage to bring Smith into the conversation. Just because she'd met the guy of her dreams—for that week anyway—Joanne thought Marcie had to pursue all available hot leads, which meant Smith.

"No. I-I don't even know if he's going."

"Uh-huh. Tell me another—"

"I just want to look nice."

"For whom?"

"Me. Can't I look nice for myself?"

"Of course." Joanne's voice dripped in sarcastic skepticism. Obviously, she hadn't believed a word Marcie said.

They checked calendars, settled on a mutual day off, and made plans to meet at the mall. Marcie gave a great deal of thought to what Joanne had said. The woman often knew Marcie better than she knew herself. Was it possible she subconsciously wanted to look nice because Smith might be there? Nah! The Neanderthal probably wouldn't even notice.

Marcie met Joanne in front of the Macy's East entrance at the Oxford Mall. Since it was mid-week and a school night, fewer kids hung out cruising the stores. They hugged hello and then, as if Joanne suddenly remembered why they were there, a look of determination covered her face. She asked, "Ready?"

"As ready as ever." They walked into Macy's.

After two hours of intensive search and try-on procedures, the final decision was made and Marcie had purchased the perfect dress and shoes. This had followed the only minor mishap when Marcie got her head caught in the sleeve of a tight dress. At that point they realized they were famished and stopped at the food court for a quick snack.

Joanne brought the subject of Smith up again. Until this point, Marcie had been on a high. She'd just purchased a great dress that looked as if it had been designed for her and a pair of heels that complemented the dress. So, she couldn't understand why Joanne was sticking a pin into her bubble of contentment and blowing everything.

"Smith's eyes will pop when he sees you in that outfit."

Marcie practically choked on the chicken sandwich that stuck in her throat as if she'd swallowed a bone. She grabbed her drink and sucked heartily to dislodge it.

"Have I mentioned to you he's not my type and I don't care what he thinks?" she snarled through tightly clenched teeth after regaining her composure.

"Well, maybe you should." Joanne totally ignored her anger.

"Why should I? He's not the only guy in the world."

"In yours, he is."

"That's a stupid thing to say," Marcie snapped, dropping her sandwich onto the plate, letting her annoyance with the entire conversation show.

Joanne dabbed her mouth with a napkin. "Not really. When was the last time you had a relationship with any guy—or even went on a date?"

Marcie opened her mouth to answer, but didn't get beyond, "I-I...went..." before finally admitting she couldn't remember and shut up.

"Neither do I, and that's my point. You've got to get over Jack and get on with your life."

Folding her arms across her chest, Marcie was indignant. "I *am* over Jack, thank you."

"Sure you are," her friend replied, obviously not believing a word of it.

"Yeah, really," she repeated defiantly. "He's ancient history."

"Really?" Joanne challenged, the pretty woman's nose only an inch or two away from her own.

"Definitely."

"Then stop tarring all men with the same brush."

"FYI, I have given Smith his own personal brush and bucket of tar."

Joanne rolled her eyes. "What am I going to do with you?"

Marcie gave her one of her smug looks, which elicited a chuckle.

"I love you, but you know that. I just don't want to

see you end up a cat lady all alone."

"You have nothing to worry about Jo; that will never happen."

"How can you be so sure?" she asked.

"I hate cats."

Joanne waved both hands at her. "I give up!"

She giggled. "I love you, too, Jo. Now let's get me an evening bag to go with my knockout ensemble."

When Marcie first opened the invitation to Ed's wedding, she wasn't really sure whether she'd attend or not. Not having a date to take, she hated the prospect of sitting alone at the table while everyone else got up and danced. Anybody walking into the room from outside would automatically think she'd forgotten to put on deodorant. However, after learning about the woman he was marrying, she decided she wouldn't miss the wedding for the world.

Laura Most had been a victim of spousal abuse. Ed met her at an outreach program run by his dad's church. A volunteer, he spent many of his days off at the church trying to help the victims of abuse free themselves of the vicious psychological chains that kept them tethered in place, preventing them from moving on with their lives.

Ed told her it took many months for him to gain Laura's trust and get her to open up to him. Just when he thought he'd reached her and she was going to leave her husband, John, the worst possible thing happened.

John unexpectedly came home early the very night Laura intended to leave him. Laura smelled the liquor on his breath as he entered their bedroom. He caught her in the act of packing. Seeing the half-packed suitcase drove him over the line and he grabbed his gun out of his nightstand and shot her. Thinking she was dead, he then turned the gun on himself. Luckily, their little girl was safe with Laura's parents when all this took place.

Laura had survived, a miracle in itself, and she and Ed grew close as she healed. If ever two people should be together, it was those two.

Because of that, Marcie made it a priority to attend their wedding and celebrate their happiness. That was another reason why she took the pursuit for the Holy Grail of dresses so seriously. With Joanne at her side, she knew the mission, however impossible, would be successfully completed in the end. Jo was a *do or die* kind of woman when it came to shopping.

Chapter Eleven

Marcie felt great when she pulled open the heavy, ornate wooden doors and stepped inside the church. Not just because she was wearing a stylish, black silk dress that fit her like a glove and showed off every curve, but because God didn't strike her dead for not having visited one of His houses sooner. In fact, as she looked up at the beautiful stained glass windows depicting Jesus' life and those of His Apostles, she couldn't remember the last time she'd been to a mass with her mother, who religiously attended St. Andrews every Sunday, rain or shine. A devout Catholic, she couldn't understand her daughter's secular ways and worried she'd end up hurdling down the rocky road to Hell if she didn't mend them.

However, nothing—not even the dreaded flames of Hell—could dampen Marcie's spirits on this particular day.

She looked terrific, and she knew it. Her thick, red mane was down, gently brushing the tops of her shoulders, and she felt like a clown's apprentice with all the makeup she'd applied. But, by the time she'd finished dressing, she hardly recognized the attractive person staring back at her in the mirror.

"Eat your heart out, loser," she mouthed silently to Smith. She had no intention of playing any more of his games. He needed to get a life—or better still, a psychiatrist. That man's head was definitely on wrong. And they talk about women having mood swings.

The church buzzed with a cacophony of conversations. She walked down the main aisle, and joined her fellow firefighters sitting on the left. She couldn't miss Angie, Rory Mulvane's wife. Her bright red dress stood out in a sea of muted black, grey, beige and blue. Her diamond earrings and necklace played havoc with the fluorescent lighting.

When she saw the Dodds, she slipped into an empty seat near Cheryl. There was no disguising her pregnancy, so Marcie congratulated her. They chatted a bit before Marcie's attention waned. She was distracted and found it hard to stay focused on Cheryl.

Marcie's eyes strayed to the front door. She didn't have to be a rocket scientist to figure out why.

Smith, the obvious target of her door-watching, walked in only a few moments before the organist, a white-haired woman who looked every bit as old as the church, began to play *Here Comes the Bride*. Marcie turned away to face front, but not before she saw him take a seat way in the back on the groom's side.

Laura made her entrance on her father's arm looking as radiant as the first day of summer as she joined Ed at the altar. Her wedding dress was beautiful, but it paled in the glow of her smile. Happiness was certainly contagious. The entire place was grinning, or crying from happiness. It was a simple service performed by Ed's dad. The bride and the groom then read their pledges to one another. That drew another round of audible sobs and a few sighs from the guests.

After the new bride and groom kissed for the first time as man and wife, the guests followed them outside and pelted them with birdseed. They ran to a white limo that whisked them away to the reception at the Knights of Columbus Hall a few miles away.

"We'll meet you at the place," Cheryl Dodd said as they bid goodbye at the church.

"Save me a seat," Marcie said jokingly.

"No problem, I already can fit in two," Cheryl replied.

With a wave of her hand, Marcie said, "No way."

Cheryl smiled and said goodbye as a smiling Jerry Dodd lovingly took her hand and led her away.

Walking into the hall, decorated with flowers on the tables and wedding bells and cupids on the walls,

Marcie got her first shock. It was a sit-down dinner and the guests had assigned seating. For some reason she'd expected a buffet. According to her place card, she was sitting at table five. Quickly she scanned the other cards on the table to see who would be with her. She sighed in relief when she saw one for Mr. and Mrs. J. Dodd. She looked for Smith's name, but he must have picked up his seating assignment before her. Hopefully he'd be at another table. Certainly Ed would want peace at his wedding and have the common sense to separate Smith from her. She couldn't believe how things had deteriorated between them so quickly, especially after they'd worked so well together organizing and giving the presentation to Mrs. Avery's fifth-grade class.

Wrong again! By the time she got to the table after a quick pit stop in the ladies' room, there was only one open seat at the table and it was next to—of all people—Smith. This had to be some kind of sick joke. Looking at him from afar was okay. However, to be stuck for three or four hours next to him was going to be torment. As she thought about her dilemma, she figured she had two choices. Either sit down and make the best of a terrible situation...or try to find a chair at another table.

A quick look around the room showed most of the tables were filled. One thing about firefighters, they were a punctual bunch who loved to party. The latter part was understandable. A dangerous job required letting off some steam. There was no way she'd be able to sit at another table without causing a fuss and drawing attention to herself.

She sighed and sat next to Smith, who took in all of her as she slid her legs in. He had to be the handsomest guy in the entire place. His navy-blue pinstripe suit fit him so well it looked like it had been ironed on. She never realized how broad his shoulders were. With his face cleanly shaven and his hair neatly trimmed and combed, he looked like a guy right off the cover of *GQ*. He could grace any month with those opaline green eyes and full kissable lips. A girl could... Then she realized she was obsessing about him and stopped.

She said hello to everybody collectively and settled in. The waiter came around and took drink orders. Knowing she'd be needing lots of fortification to get through the afternoon, she was raring to go. Since she believed in trying to maintain her health, she ordered a screwdriver, basically vodka and orange juice. She might end up sloshed, but at least she'd be getting her daily requirement of vitamin C.

"O'Dwyer, you look different," Smith said, actually initiating a conversation with her.

"I left my helmet home."

"Jeez! Can't you ever be serious?"

"It's hard since I never leave home without my sarcastic wit. Besides, I never know what kind of mood you're going to be in."

"I just wanted to say I like what you've done with yourself."

She shrugged. He didn't have to know how hard she'd worked to get that way. "All I did was put on a dress and apply some makeup."

"Well, it looks nice. You look like a...a real...woman."

Like the excruciatingly shrill screech of chalk scratching a blackboard, he'd gone and pressed the wrong buttons, as usual, causing something to short-circuit in Marcie's head. Before she could stop herself, her eyes narrowed to slits and her nostrils flared with fury as she spewed, "I knew you'd say something sexist like that."

"Damn, O'Dwyer. That's not how I meant it," Smith replied angrily.

"Really?"

Visibly gritting his teeth, he replied, "Really!"

By this time, every eye at the table was watching, every ear listening, as though the two of them had forgotten where they were. Marcie ignored everyone and turned completely around in her chair to look him squarely in the eye. However she saw no defiance or anger. Instead she saw something she'd never seen in his eyes before. Had he actually been telling the truth? Could he be capable of giving a woman an honest compliment? She wasn't certain how to respond. For the sake of the others at the table, she chose to believe him and go from there.

"To tell the truth, Smith, I wasn't sure how you meant it. I mean, we're not on what you would call the best of terms."

"True. However we're at a wedding, O'Dwyer. Try to be civil."

"Civ—" The nerve of that man. She was about to blow again when Smith placed a finger on her lips. Lucky for him, she didn't try to bite it off.

"Truce, O'Dwyer?"

She pursed her lips together and took a breath before she nodded. He then removed his finger from her mouth, demonstrating he also hadn't trusted her not to bite him. Wanting to have the last say, she whispered, "Don't you *ever* dare do that again."

Grinning, he whispered back, "Why, you gonna bite my finger off?"

"Yeah."

"Thought so."

The waiter returned with the drinks and she nearly gulped hers down. It didn't take long before she signaled him for another. She'd forgotten she was drinking on an empty stomach and the alcohol went straight to her head, quickly blurring all the sharp edges and angles around her. Their salads came and she ate it, not tasting a morsel, along with another drink. The alcohol warmed her blood and lightened her head, clearly a nice sensation. However, her common sense floated off along with her inhibitions.

The DJ began to play slow songs. Everyone got up from the table leaving just Smith and her. Marcie played with the stirrer in her glass. She felt his eyes upon her.

"Hey…O'Dwyer."

When she turned to face him, he wore a goofy, sheepish-looking smile. Perhaps he was feeling just as uncomfortable with everyone gone. She was feeling no pain and actually returned the smile. Perhaps that gave him the courage to extend his hand and say, "Let's dance, O'Dwyer."

The alcohol had truly messed with her judgment, big-time, for seconds later she was on her feet. She glided into his open arms and he drew her close—real close—and they began to dance. Marcie liked the way he smelled and put her head on his shoulder. It was simply nice being in his big, strong arms. She chalked it up to being quite heady from the volatile combination of liquor on an empty stomach, Smith's aftershave, and the fact she hadn't been in the arms of another man since her ex, Jack.

The music continued and so did they. Marcie actually enjoyed dancing with him. If anyone was watching, they were probably truly shocked. But she wasn't checking around to find out and quite frankly, she didn't care. She merely wanted the dance to go on and on. She felt light on her feet, as if her heels had sprouted wings.

Smith seemed to be enjoying himself just as much. She thought she noticed a smile on his face when she furtively glanced up at him once or twice. After the fourth—or was it the fifth dance, she knew he was. His nuzzling her neck gave it away. Damn! He'd hit that spot right under her ear that always made her squirm with delight.

She began to feel that sensual burning deep inside when she got turned on. Right now it was only at the simmering point. Two hours later when Smith hoarsely whispered in her ear, "Let's get the hell out of here," it had become a five-alarm blaze. Whoever said 'a thin line separated love from hate' must have known what they were talking about.

They fled outside to his pickup. No sooner had they gotten inside than Smith crushed her to him, taking her mouth with a savage intensity that sent a tingling all the way down to her toes. And it wasn't from tight shoes. Whatever reservations she'd had about Smith were long gone. The kiss had sent a shock wave straight through her and she returned it with the same intensity.

They necked like that for a few more minutes before

the temperature inside the cab of his truck began to steam up the windows. Smith pulled his lips away from hers and started the engine. He gunned it out of the lot and headed for his place, which turned out to be a trailer.

From the outside it looked like a giant tin bullet set on wheels. However, on the inside it possessed every creature comfort imaginable, though the only thing she cared about at that moment was climbing into a bed. She was so worked up that even a bunk bed would have sufficed. With Smith's lips glued to hers and his hands running up and down the length of her body, they made their way past the bright stainless steel kitchen, the elaborate oak wet bar and the large-flat-screened TV on the wall opposite the sumptuous blue, crushed velvet couch in the living room and found themselves in the bedroom.

The bedroom was a regular love nest done up in red. Marcie suspected he got his decorating tips from a pro. The bed itself was round and comfortable. Underneath the fur-like comforter were sensual silk sheets.

Smith didn't ask what she thought of his interior decorating. Instead, she hardly had her coat off before she was in his strong arms, her mouth his captive again. Kissing and petting as they slow-danced their way toward the bed, they dropped bits of clothing with each turn. His lips had found the soft spot of her neck again, driving her wild as his hands located the zipper on her dress and slid it down. She stepped out of it as his hands fumbled for her bra clasp. She ran her hands through his hair, twisting and grabbing it with abandon, before running them up and down his well-muscled back as he buried his face in her chest. Oh, it felt sooo good.

They fell back onto the bed and their lips met again, their tongues entwined. He rolled over her and his hardness pressed into her thigh. Marcie had never wanted a man as much as she wanted Smith. She'd stopped listening to the little voices of reason in her head by the third drink. She reached down and freed his member from his slacks and positioned herself so he could slide inside her.

Finding their rhythm, they rocked the bed and probably the trailer, as well. Between the grunts and the noise of their breathing that probably sounded to any passerby like two steam engines on the fritz, they climaxed within seconds of each other.

Smith smiled down and kissed her nose.

"That was good for a warmup, O'Dwyer." He got off the bed and removed the few articles of clothing he still had on. She felt the same way. They'd just tasted the icing and were now going back for the rest of the cake. He had one terrific body and she had the overwhelming desire to touch every part of it.

He climbed back onto the bed and they began to make love again, only nice and slow this time. Now that the urgency had passed, they explored each other's bodies and delighted in one another—all night.

Some time later, Marcie opened her eyes and discovered the body in bed next to her wasn't Goofy. She lay there a few moments before falling back to sleep, thinking about Smith. In a way, what happened might have been inevitable. They were bound to get it together, if they didn't kill one another first. There were a number of factors involved, of course. They worked together in the same firehouse and saw each other for twenty-four hours at a time. They'd been thrown together constantly, first that crazy dinner at her mother's, the school presentation, and finally the wedding. The alcohol at the reception served as the catalyst. On the other hand, if they hadn't been seated together, they would have probably killed one another instead.

The following morning, when Marcie opened her eyes she hadn't remembered her nocturnal thoughts. Instead, when she realized she wasn't at her apartment and looked under the top sheet and saw she was naked, she nearly freaked. Slowly the events of the night before began to dance through her head, which felt heavier than a lead sinker at the moment. With a great deal of effort she turned her head and saw Smith lying next to her. At that moment only one word came to mind. *Oops*!

She suddenly wondered if she'd done the right thing. Obviously, it would have been better to have had such thoughts last night. Before she could pursue this line of thinking any further, Smith opened his eyes. And gave her a 100-watt smile. The heat of that smile melted all those negative thoughts away.

"Hi," he said.

"Hi, yourself," she replied, feeling more alive.

Smith reached over and swept the stray strands of hair from her eyes. His touch reawakened the sweet sensations she'd felt the night before, chasing away whatever remnants of sleep remained. As he pulled himself on top of her and covered her mouth with his, she knew she was a goner. Firemen were real good at *starting* fires, too.

Chapter Twelve

Living in a close-knit community had disadvantages. The biggest one was everybody knew everyone else's business. Gossip was a sport like football or baseball. To put it more bluntly, in such a community, when a woman discovered she was pregnant, the entire neighborhood knew before her significant other.

Some people enjoyed living in such a place. Marcie didn't. She didn't relish greeting a neighbor who knew her business. Take this notion, compress it into a smaller venue, and that was what living in the firehouse was like. Residing with guys twenty-four hours at a clip, it was hard not to feel like living under a microscope.

That was exactly what happened when Smith and Marcie started dating. They didn't have to say a thing to anyone. Whoever saw them dancing at the wedding knew it all and what they didn't know they made up as they went along. Marcie and Smith couldn't have done a better job had they placed an ad in the newspaper. She was amazed to overhear that she and Smith had made it in the cloakroom of the Knights of Columbus Hall. God, they were good!

They tried to keep things on a professional level at work. Sometimes it proved challenging, like when she had to restrain herself from jumping his solidly gorgeous bones. One benefit of having the same time schedule at work was it gave them the same time off. They had ample time to be together, and that turned out to be good and bad. Marcie was crazy about Smith, but there was a drawback to being together too much.

She'd wanted to take things with Smith nice and slow. She realized it would be difficult closing the barn door after all the animals had escaped. But, jumping into bed with Smith before they'd even gone on an

A Heated Romance

official date wasn't the way to start a relationship. After all, where did you go from there?

She was honestly scared. For one thing, what if they crashed and burned before they had the chance to really get to know one another? But, that wasn't what really frightened her. She'd never felt about another guy—not even Jack—the way she did about Smith. It was so...intense. Nearly every waking moment was filled with fantasies that centered on him. All she cared about was making him happy. Luckily, he had the power to bring out the wantonness in her and she had enough tricks in her bag of charms to keep him satisfied. She found herself wanting to do things to him she'd never done with any other man. This part of her, that she hardly knew existed, terrified her. It was as if she'd turned into another person.

She'd become a woman in love. And that was the most frightening thing of all.

Because of Jack she'd kept her heart in a cocoon and not allowed herself to become serious about any guy. For the longest time she couldn't bear to even say or hear his name without feeling sick. The pain was too severe and she feared getting hurt again. If she wasn't vulnerable, history couldn't repeat itself, she reasoned. And now she'd fallen head over heels in love with Smith. Could lightning strike twice? she worried.

She and Jack first met at her senior prom in high school. He'd been Mary Evans' date. Mary was a tall, lovely blonde and together they made an attractive couple. Marcie had gone to the prom with Tommy Jenks, the guy she was dating at the time. Her grandfather, who was considerably less fond of Tommy than she, referred to him as Tommy Jerk. They'd been out a few times, nothing special. Joanne's guy of the month was Chuck Ryder, a tall basketball center and the heartthrob of many of the other girls.

They'd all sat at the same table with another couple who'd turned out to be friends of Mary Evans. Afterward, Joanne and Chuck, and she and Tommy had gone to a club on Jackson Avenue. Fifteen minutes later, the other two couples arrived at the club and sat with them. They all spent the rest of the night together.

From the first moment she saw Jack, she thought him handsome. She found herself copping sneak peeks at him from the corner of her eye. She found herself listening intently to whatever he had to say. At twenty, he acted years older and way more mature than Tommy Jenks. He had an air of confidence, and seemed very sure of himself, especially around women. One look at him and she came away with the feeling he knew who he was and where he was going. And somehow she wanted to be on his train bound for success.

A few weeks after the prom, Marcie bumped into Jack at the supermarket. Surprisingly, he remembered her and they talked a few minutes. She'd been in a hurry and began to walk away. That was when he grabbed her arm. "Wait, please don't go."

She turned to face him, clutching on to the butter, milk and bread she was purchasing for her mother.

"At least...not before you give me your telephone number."

She nearly replied, *for what*? Flattered, astonished, whatever, she gave it to him. Even more unexpected, he called that very night, and they made a date for the following Saturday. By that time, she'd heard from the grapevine that he and Mary Evans had broken up, making him a free agent.

One Saturday date led to another. Marcie found him to be a really sweet guy when there was no one around to impress. Besides, he really knew how to treat a girl. He sent flowers and never forgot important days. Three months later, they were going together. She fell in love with him and actually thought he felt the same way about her. She hadn't known they had different views on what constituted a relationship. She believed in being faithful, and to a great extent, so did he. Only, there was a hitch. They ran into a snag over interpretation. She meant with each other and he interpreted it to mean with several women.

To make a long story short, she'd discovered Jack in bed with another woman. It hurt, but somehow she found a way to forgive him. After all, didn't true love conquer everything? Everyone makes mistakes and Jack had promised never to cheat again with another woman. She naïvely believed he'd give her all his business from that moment on and they continued as a couple—until months later when she found him in bed again. This time with a man.

There's that interpretation problem again.

Marcie could compete with another woman. She didn't know how to compete with a man. That was it. She did what any other jilted, red-blooded woman would do. She threw his key at him and told him to stuff it where the sun *don't* shine, that is, if there were any room.

He ran after her, but stopped at the front door when he realized he was naked. Marcie left his apartment an emotional mess. Seeing him with another man opened up a nasty can of unanswered questions. Aside from the usual pain one experienced when a normal relationship went down the toilet, she now had the added implications of wondering if Jack had been AC/DC all along or if this was a casual aberration. Either way, it freaked her out.

Jack tried to win her back, but she somehow found the strength to solidify the mass of sobbing jelly she'd become and ignored all of his overtures. She couldn't bear to share him with another person—woman or man. And she wasn't *that* forgiving. In her book, she didn't wait around for strike three to toss a person out. Her favorite new song was *Hit the Road Jack,* by Ray Charles. It said it all.

Post-Jack, Marcie had been protective of her heart, never wanting to put herself in harm's way again. It took way too long to mend and she'd erected a strong barrier. And then along came Smith.

She was apprehensive about her relationship with him. It wasn't that she didn't trust his feelings toward her, for she doubted his kisses lied or the way he touched her was deceiving. It was something else.

She hardly knew him.

He was as open as could be about his present life. However, his lips were sealed as tight as a zip-lock-bag when it came to his past, especially his childhood. It was as if it had never existed. Well into their relationship she did discover there was a history of mental illness in his family, despite his cavalier protest at her mother's house. Marcie suspected he feared he carried the bad genes. Perhaps he felt if he didn't speak or think about it, it would never happen. If it hadn't been for something her grandfather had mentioned and recalling some talk at a barbecue between several of the firemen's wives about some crazy lady who burned her house down, she might not have put the facts together.

Smith had mentioned he'd been raised by an aunt after his dad died. His mother was already dead. He never told her how she died. The truth was she'd been suspected of killing four of her children in a fire. Luckily, Smith was out of the house when all this took place. She'd set the fire in the middle of the afternoon and then went down to the basement, where she hanged herself. This was what the authorities had pieced together, according to an old news article she'd found in the library archives. Taken alone, this would be hard for a guy like Smith to handle. However, adding the fact his maternal grandmother had committed suicide as well, was downright scary. She couldn't fault him for being somewhat *apprehensive* about it.

Because of this, Marcie never invited Smith to accompany her for dinner at her mother's place during the time Eileen and her children lived there. Fearing it might dredge up bad memories about his past or in the least make him uncomfortable, she thought it best not to expose him to any of the kids' weirdness. Marcie doubted Smith knew she'd found out about his mom or grandmother. Of course, she never brought the subject up for fear of his reaction, and he never spoke about it. It wasn't until Eileen moved out to live with a biker that

Marcie began to invite Smith to her mother's. They went practically every week. He and Gramps talked about the old days, despite the less than happy look on her mother's face when they did.

Regardless of all the unwanted reminiscing, she knew her mother liked Smith. She looked at him as a *live* one—a future son-in-law. It wasn't long before Marcie figured out that anyone who drew breath without the use of a ventilator was suitable material. It was her mother's mission in life to get Marcie married. Though she spoke of Eileen's divorce as a temporary setback, she didn't want her other daughter to miss any opportunities. So when Smith became a regular at her table, she broke out Eileen's old wedding list and began to update it. It never occurred to her that Smith might be showing up just for her free home-cooked meals.

After shopping for a new bedroom lamp, she and Smith went back to his place. Their pillow fight the night before had proved deadly for the one which had been on his night table.

Smith plugged it in. "You're right O'Dwyer, this one is nicer than the old lamp."

"Wanna redecorate?" Marcie asked, reaching for a pillow.

"No, not now!" he yelled as he tackled her.

Pinned down and unable to move, she chided, "This is how the other one got broken."

He smiled down at her. "I know."

Their lips locked and things soon became heated. Smith knew her weakness and went right for that spot on her neck. A few minutes of nuzzling and Marcie was a goner. Clothes flew across the room as they hurriedly removed them. It might have been a great deal easier if they'd disengaged their lips first.

"Oh, yes," Marcie said as Smith slipped inside her.

The phone rang.

"Ignore it."

Moving his mouth to her ivory breast, he muttered, "The machine will pick it up."

"Oooh, Smith, do that again."

"Marcie, I know you're there. This is important. Pick up."

All movement on the bed stopped as they looked into each other's eyes.

Following one of the nights Smith had come for dinner, her mother had called her sounding excited.

"There's a sale on evening dresses at Macy's."

"And you're telling me this because...?" Marcie asked.

"I was wondering if I should buy a dress for...you know..."

"If I knew, would I be wondering if you took the wrong meds this morning, Mom?"

"Oh, you know all right, Marcie. Why are you playing silly games with me?" Exasperation sounded in her voice.

Sometimes her mother acted stranger than usual. This was definitely one of those times. It was like talking to a person who kept using only pronouns and constantly changed subjects. One never knew what the devil they were talking about.

"Okay, Mom. What would you need the dress for?"

"A wedding."

"Who's getting married?" Marcie asked.

"You. When were you going to tell me?"

"*Me*?" It finally dawned on her what was happening. "I'm not getting married."

"Why not?"

"Well, for one thing, Smith hasn't asked me. It's usually the man who asks the woman. Unless of course she pulls an Eileen. Is that what you're hinting?"

"No. No, of course not," her mother replied quickly.

That soured the conversation and ended it prematurely without the outcome her mother had been hoping for. She half expected her mother to tell her to snare him exactly like her sister had snared Larry.

A lot of good it had done Eileen in the long run.

Chapter Thirteen

The West Burg Fire Department had thirty-six personnel to cover twenty-four hour response to its citizens. The department's primary mission: to prevent loss of life, to care for the sick and injured, to prevent fires and to protect the property of the community. Marcie, like the other firemen at the firehouse, had taken courses in CPR and emergency procedures, but there were four trained EMTs: Ed Clark, Jay Gould, Harry Johnson and Tom Haber.

Marcie was aware most people thought firefighters were superheroes, going around putting out the evil flames of fires. Actually, firefighters were mere mortals who risked their own safety to save and protect the community. And like ordinary people, they sometimes cracked and fell apart when the stress of the job or home life got to them. This factor necessitated a psychologist on staff who counseled personnel. Witnessing death and destruction on an almost daily basis, often messed with a person's mind, no matter how strong that person was. Jay Singh was there whenever anybody needed his help. In some cases, after a major crisis, personnel were ordered to see him.

That morning was a quiet one for the West Burg firehouse. Beautiful and on the warm side for late winter, it made everyone hopeful for an early spring. When the remaining birds shivered in the leafless tree branches, it signaled time for a change. Marcie was beyond tired of being able to write messages in the cold mist she left every time she opened her mouth to speak.

With nothing pressing, she and Smith puttered with a motorcycle he was refurbishing. They'd already bought matching helmets to wear in anticipation.

"As soon as I get this baby going, I'm gonna take

Grandpa out for a ride," Smith said. "Hand me that screwdriver."

"My mother will have a stroke."

"Yeah, but it will be worth it. The old man will have himself a blast."

"It'll certainly beat chasing fire trucks," she replied.

The fire alarm clanged. There had been a three car pile up on 17. Both Smith and Marcie wiped the grease off their hands and rushed to their gear. She was assigned to the ambulance with Ed Clark and Tom Haber, while Smith rode the hook and ladder to the scene along with McLaughlin, Wiebolt, and DiMaggio. Their biggest fear was that one of the cars would go up. And if there were people trapped inside...

Traffic had already backed up and they were forced to ride along the side of the road. Most of the problem was caused by rubberneckers. Police had set up flares and were attempting to control traffic. Other officers at the scene were in the process of removing the last of the people from the cars.

To assess the situation, Wiebolt jumped out and spoke to the officer in charge. He returned and barked his orders before getting on the horn and calling for two more ambulances.

The first car, a compact, was so compressed it looked like half a car. The back seat had been pushed entirely into the front. Miraculously, the driver and passenger were alive, but both suffered multiple fractures to their legs and bruises to their torsos. Airbags had deployed and tempered the impact, saving their lives. They lay under blankets on the side of the road awaiting transport to a hospital.

The car in the middle looked like an accordion. Marcie could hardly believe it had been a small SUV. When she and Smith reached it, a cop was trying to calm a hysterical woman. He thought she was screaming from the pain of her trauma. She was wedged between the door and the dashboard, sitting next to her husband who had a shard of glass protruding from his lifeless right eye. Apparently he'd been killed on impact.

Listening more carefully, Marcie picked up on the word children.

"Smith, she had kids in the car."

The back of the car was a mess of debris.

"We've got to get this door open," Smith replied. "Hey, give me a hand."

Together they maneuvered the demolished door off its broken hinges. He reached inside and began to toss twisted metal and plastic out of the car. Dobbs and McGuiness were attempting to extract the mother from the front of the car.

"I see a little girl!" Smith yelled. Marcie allowed herself a sigh of relief as Smith disentangled the child from the seat and handed her to Ed Clark.

Then something the woman said nagged at Marcie... "Didn't she say children, Smith?"

"There's no other kid. Maybe she's delirious and the child wasn't in the car?"

Marcie's gut instinct disagreed. "No. I think a mother would know, no matter what. We gotta take another look."

Something she'd never seen was being registered loud and clear in Smith's opaline eyes. Fear.

Maniacally she began to throw the mangled pieces of the car out behind her. Smith, in the line of fire, went to the other side and tried to pry open the door. When he got it open, he removed debris from his side.

"O'Dwyer, there's no other kid."

"There's gotta be—keep looking!" Then she saw a shoelace dangling under the demolished seat. "I found her! Help me get this off of her."

"Jesus!" Smith grabbed his side of the twisted metal around the seat as Marcie tugged at hers. Slowly it began to give and as he held up the broken seat, Marcie carefully extracted the little girl.

Tom Haber performed CPR on her before gingerly carrying her to the ambulance.

Despite attempts to save her, they later learned she'd died from internal bleeding. Stuff like this chips away at a person's emotions. In the blink of an eye, an entire family had been destroyed.

The last vehicle involved in the mishap was a pickup truck. No airbags had been installed in its dash and both passengers were killed on impact, one civilian had been ejected through the windshield.

When Marcie first started as a firefighter, all the gore and bloody dismembered body parts played havoc with her stomach contents. More often than not, she'd upchuck. Though she never truly got used to seeing such horror, she could now control herself better. However, this was one horrific scene and she couldn't wait to leave.

Soon the accident inspectors appeared at the scene to take depositions from eyewitnesses and snap hundreds of pictures before they allowed the road to be cleaned and traffic to resume.

Around one in the morning the fire bell clanged. The dispatcher barked out the details he'd been given. A fire had broken out in a store on Main Street near Higby's Tools. Weather conditions were favorable, clear skies, little wind, but by the time the trucks got there, the store had been gutted and the ravenous blaze had moved on to the next business.

They hooked up the hoses and watered down the surrounding buildings as a team went inside the second building to douse the flames. Marcie was part of that team; her task, punch ventilation holes with her pike. Though the night air was around 30 degrees, the blaze made it feel like a super-hot sauna. Sweat continually dripped into her eyes, stinging them and blurring her vision, not that it was easy to see through the smoke.

Marcie's adrenaline pumped as she gave her shoulder muscles a workout. The fire in the second building, having been caught early, was contained and put out quickly. They were able to return to the station before dawn.

Chapter Fourteen

By the time Marcie was able to keep her eyes open for at least thirty-minutes, it was two in the afternoon. The last twenty-four hours had drained her. Along with normal exhaustion, her hip felt tender to the touch. She removed her nightshirt and found a bruise the color and size of an eggplant. Definitely a not-so-nice side effect of being a firefighter. Hardly a day passed without finding a bruise of one kind or another somewhere on her body. This one was a beaut. No doubt she'd banged into something. Luckily, it was in a spot where no one would see. Then, remembering she was seeing Smith later, she chuckled at the conjured image of him kissing her *boo-boo* and making it feel much, much better.

After feeding her growling stomach which had been on empty, Marcie straightened up the apartment. Neatness wasn't one of her top-ten behavioral qualities. The apartment usually had to undergo a major overhaul whenever she expected company, which before Smith, was hardly ever. Beginning in earnest, she started at one end and worked toward the other. She considered cleaning her place like being on a treasure hunt, for she often found missing items and other things she'd forgotten she owned. Actually, she cleaned because it was necessary to ensure the safety of her guests. How would it look if the tabloids got hold of 'unsuspecting guest sits on deadly fork' or 'guest trips over pantyhose and splits skull open on bathroom floor'?

By the time Smith rang the doorbell, the place was passable. Of course the apartment would never be listed in Home Beautiful, but it was capable of passing a health inspection. She opened the door. He stood there holding an open box of aromatic Chinese take-out. The smell alone made love to her taste buds. And she was famished. She'd been so busy cleaning she'd barely eaten anything all day.

"Mmm!" Marcie pecked his lips and yanked him inside.

"Hungry, O'Dwyer?"

"Starving." She pawed through the containers. "There's so much here. What did you do, get something from every column of the menu?"

"Just about. Had no idea what you liked."

His thoughtfulness touched her heart, but did nothing for her stomach. Only food could help at this point, so she filled her plate. Clearly, this didn't surprise Smith. They'd already shared many meals together. More than once he'd mentioned how much he liked her healthy appetite. What was it about men and women's appetites? It seemed most men admired a woman who could pack food away. Perhaps it had something to do with the old saying, *the way to a man's heart is through his stomach.* Or some such nonsense.

Sitting across the table from him and sharing small talk about their job, Marcie felt like a married woman having dinner with her husband. The role wasn't exactly a perfect fit at that moment, but she'd gladly work at it.

"I've got a confession to make, O'Dwyer."

Confession? I'm all ears.

She quickly put a look of concern on her face, thinking it would be the right touch for a moment of truth.

"You're something else."

That's it? Hey, I expected something juicy. All wasn't lost she realized, as he reached across the table and took her hand in his.

"You're tough and can haul rope like any man...and yet...you're soft like a woman should be."

Was that it? I guess for Smith it was quite a mouthful. She smiled.

Then he brought her hand, reeking from the barbecued spareribs she'd just demolished, up to his mouth and kissed it. However, all thoughts of smelly food were quickly forgotten and replaced as her brain detected ripples of anticipated pleasure that stirred within her. She nearly gave in to the urge to sweep everything from the table and pull him on top of her. But the distant memory of spending an entire day cleaning was still way too strong to allow her to carry out such an impulsive act.

Thus began the part when actions spoke louder than words. Smith, not one for spouting pretty words, took Marcie into his arms and kissed her, greasy lips and all. She'd decided awhile back not to complain about his lack of romantic words. That was after she'd discovered one kiss from him had her heart beating in triple time. Every nerve ending tingled and she couldn't wait for his hands to start calming her quivering body.

She led him into the bedroom. Even though the floor was empty of stray clothing items she noticed his eyes dropped down towards his feet, playing it safe. No one ever wants to get tripped up by a stray bra strap or shoe.

They romantically fell onto the bed and Smith let out a very audible, "Ouch! O'Dwyer, what the hell?"

She watched in dread as he reached behind and held up her stuffed Goofy by his black nose for examination. "Goofy, O'Dwyer?"

"Some people don't like to sleep alone," she murmured in defense.

"Three's a crowd if I remember correctly." He tossed poor Goofy across the room. "Now where were we?"

A fraction of a second later all was well in Marcie's world. Smith's lips crushed hers as his hand sought lower ground. Though his hands were calloused, Smith had a gentle way about him that teased her, a touch that drove her crazy. As he kissed his way down her body, she squirmed in delight and would have worked herself off the bed had she not been under him.

Her moans filled the room. Smith had been kissing the soft flesh of her inner thigh. The man was pressing all the right buttons and she was about to detonate. A sudden urge to kiss him in the worst way possessed her, and she pulled him up. On the way, he slipped inside her, so it was a win-win situation for them both. This was where Goofy definitely couldn't cut it.

The following afternoon, after Smith had left, Marcie tossed her garbage into the dumpster when her next door neighbor, Mrs. Brass, came outside to throw hers away. She'd just pitched a huge black, plastic bag onto the trash pile. Her neighbor's plastic bag must have come from a bathroom wastebasket.

Mrs. Brass had a tiny little smirk-like smile on her bright red lips. A short woman, her height matching her width, she reminded Marcie of a Jack-in-the-box always popping up when you least expected her. Whenever she saw her, the woman was dressed in a bright tent-like dress that came down to her ankles. Small fuzzy slippers could be seen sticking out from the hem. Marcie's mother told her the dress was called a muumuu. She said women used to wear them as housedresses. She pictured Mrs. Brass' closet filled with these things, each with a different color or pattern. Probably got them half-price at a tent sale, Marcie thought, chuckling to herself.

She tended to avoid Mrs. Brass, for she'd learned the snoopy woman was the biggest gossip in the entire apartment complex. Nothing ever seemed to escape her beady little bird-like eyes behind those round thick, Coke-bottle glasses she wore. She must have kept her ear permanently glued to the adjoining wall of Marcie's apartment or had it bugged. How else would she know when Marcie was going out?

Clearly she was fishing for something. Why else traipse outside with only that tiny bag of garbage to throw away? Marcie realized anything she said would be turned around and used for Mrs. Brass' advantage. She had a reputation to keep up. Marcie guessed being the number one gossip of a development came with its own pressures. She also figured the less she said, the safer she'd be.

Mrs. Brass flashed her dazzling, *I got you* smile. "Hello, Marcie, my dear."

"Hello, Mrs. Brass. Nice muumuu."

"Well, thank you," she replied before throwing her a curve ball. "He's a nice one."

"Who?" Marcie queried, making an exaggerated effort of looking around.

"No, no, deary. Not anyone out here. I'm talkin' 'bout that handsome fella who stayed the night. You know, if he doesn't work out, I have a terrific grandson."

"That's okay, Mrs. Brass."

"My grandson, he's one of a kind."

Marcie pictured a guy her neighbor's height and width in drag.

Mrs. Brass threw out another teaser. "He makes oodles of money, you know."

"What does he do?"

"He's in real estate."

Definitely the wrong answer. Game over. "Oh, wow, gotta run. I hear my phone ringing," Marcie said.

"I don't hear anything," she said.

"There, you missed it again," Marcie said as she ran into her apartment and locked the door. She leaned back against it as she gasped for breath.

A moment later she peeked out the peephole to see if the gossip had gone back into her place. Marcie nearly jumped out of her sneakers.

The woman peered right back at her with one of her beady eyes.

Sheesh!

Chapter Fifteen

The weather was changing. The temperature slowly made an upward climb, subtly adding a few degrees as it tossed out a teaser, hinting at springtime. The dormant buds were ready to burst into blossom as Marcie's relationship with Smith had. He'd been alone for so long, she wondered if he was ready to complicate things by getting married. Of course, she didn't want to be the one to bring the subject up. Just because it was on her mind—nearly every waking hour— didn't mean Smith had been thinking about it.

On the other hand, if actions spoke louder than words, she should feel secure. When he kissed her, she felt loved. And when she gazed into those gorgeous green eyes, she saw a future filled with love and happiness—and possibly a few kids. She smiled whenever she thought about that—especially because of something Joanne had once said. "No man would ever marry a woman who's a firefighter."

Well, she'd found Smith, the exception to the rule.

No one could say their relationship was a fluke or a fly-by-night kind of affair.

They came to care for one another the hard way. It had been a steep upward climb—more akin to battle— before love hit them squarely between the eyes. She figured it had been an arrow from a near-sighted cherub.

Now it seemed they belonged together like bread and butter. They liked the same things—hell they did the same things, during and after work. Sure they still had disagreements. Every couple had them from time to time. But making up was always sweet. The bottom line was that she was happy and Smith seemed just as content. He'd accepted her, warts and all. Of course, she meant that figuratively, not having been kissed by any frogs lately. All her business went to Smith only. Could she see herself spending the rest of her life with him? In a heartbeat. Her tomorrows seemed destined to be filled with nothing but happiness...

It was Smith's birthday. She'd originally wanted to take him out to dinner to celebrate, but he'd mentioned he was tired and didn't feel like doing much that night. Define *much*. Was it like not staying up all night watching TV, but viewing only a couple of programs? Or on one's sex barometer, was it necking and/or petting, as opposed to sleeping together? These questions took center stage in Marcie's mind.

After a great deal of thought, she figured she'd surprise him with a cake. Not the kind one danced out of, but one that could be danced around—if so inclined. It didn't take much energy to chew. Besides, everybody loves cake. So she stopped at Benny's Bakery and picked up the gooiest cake she could find and had it decorated with *Happy Birthday Baby*.

Intent on surprising Smith, she parked her Jeep nearly a block away.

She was turning the row of hedges surrounding his bullet-shaped domicile when the door flew open and out stepped Smith. In the bright light over the door she could see he wasn't alone. On his arm was a dark-haired, well-dressed, beautiful woman. Her heart fell to her knees as she watched them embrace.

"I love you," the woman said loud enough for Marcie to hear.

"I love you, too, baby," Smith replied, each word stabbing Marcie's heart like a dagger.

Tired? I'll give him tired, she fumed. No wonder he's tired.

The woman got into her car and Smith stood in the drive, waving as she drove off. While Marcie watched, rockets went off in her head like photo flashes. Pop! Pop! Pop! How could he? History was repeating itself! How could she have been so stupid and blind? What the hell was wrong with her? She felt like a fool.

He turned to go back inside. This snapped Marcie out of her verbal self-flagellation mode. She took the cake out of the box and rushed up behind him. Lobbing the cake at him with all her strength, she hit the back of his head.

"What the...!" he roared.

"Happy Birthday, you two-timing snake!" she screamed at the top of her lungs before she ran back to her car.

"O'Dwyer! Wait! You got this all wrong!"

Yeah, real wrong. Wrong for getting involved with the likes of you, she thought, as the tears streamed down her face.

"Dammit! Dammit! Dammit!" Marcie pounded the steering wheel. Furious at him and herself, she started the engine and roared off. How she made it home in one piece was nothing short of a small miracle.

By the time she walked into her apartment, her eyes were red and raw. She threw herself on the bed, boots and all, ignoring Smith's voice on her answering machine.

"O'Dwyer, pick up. I know you're there..."

How could he do this to me? She hurt and seethed at the same time. He knew all about Jack. She'd told him one night during a heart-to-heart talk. The scene materialized in her frazzled mind as if it had happened moments before...

After they'd finished making love, she lay snuggled against Smith in the afterglow. He'd asked why she was so down on men.

"You mean it shows?"

"Like a beacon, lady, bright and sharp. Some are trustworthy, you know."

"You know any?" she'd inquired.

"You...you..." He'd tickled her into laughter.

The tickling and squirming had led to kissing before finally ending with sincere eye contact. "I'm serious, O'Dwyer. Some guys are capable of caring about only one woman."

"I've only met the male sluts of the species. Or those already taken."

"Well then, let me introduce myself." His lips covered hers.

After making love a second time, Marcie had told him about Jack and his infidelities. In no uncertain terms, she'd let Smith know she wouldn't go through it again. She couldn't.

So, with that in mind, how does one explain what happened tonight? Was Smith lying to her that night? She tried to remember where both his hands were. Maybe he'd had his fingers crossed.

The phone rang. Thinking it was Smith again, she picked the phone up and disconnected the line before leaving the phone off the hook. Knowing there was a chance he might come over, she grabbed her purse and keys and jumped back into the Jeep, heading for the first motel she found with a vacancy. She couldn't face Smith tonight—or any night. She just wanted to be alone and cry. Wallow in self-pity and get it out of her system. Then move on and not look back.

Chapter Sixteen

When Marcie opened her eyes she felt disoriented. Then it all rushed back to her like a wave crashing against a bulkhead. Her head throbbed, punctuating the pain in her heart. She got out of bed and struggled to get to her purse. She downed two aspirin with water, then padded into the bathroom.

She stared at her swollen eyes in the mirror and cringed. She'd let down her guard and allowed a man to hurt her. *Again.* What was wrong with her? Was she a magnet for the misbegotten? Or were all men bastards?

Realizing she'd be seeing Smith tomorrow made her stomach turn. She had to steel herself—she would not cry! She refused to show weakness. It would be best to go back to square one with him, as if nothing had ever happened.

She snorted ruefully. How could she even think that? The man had already gotten under her skin and was as much a part of her as breathing. She forced herself to stop right there. No more of that *type* of thinking. She'd been able to see herself through this kind of hurt before and would find the strength to do it again.

A tiny voice in the back of her head screamed, "But you love Smith more than you ever did Jack!"

"Shut up! Shut up! Shut up!" Marcie cried, burying her face in her hands.

When her pity party was over, she washed her face and renewed her vow to be strong. Smith would become history along with Jack. And that would be that. What she needed was a good shopping marathon. That usually cured most ills—except poverty, of course. She called Joanne.

"What are you doing?" she asked after her friend

answered her cell phone on the second ring giving Marcie hope.

"I was about to brush my teeth," Joanne replied.

"Does that mean you're off today?"

"Yup. Did you have something in mind?"

"I need some shopping therapy."

"What's wrong?"

"Nothing's wrong. Smith's a two-timing snake—just like Jack—"

"Stop yelling in my ear. I'll meet you at our usual spot by Macy's in a half-hour. You can tell me everything then."

Marcie hadn't realized she'd been shouting into the phone. She had to pull herself together. If she fell apart talking to Joanne, how would she act when Smith confronted her with his bullshit?

Over coffee, toasted bagels and tears, Marcie poured her heart out to Joanne. It felt like a sick rerun of the morning she'd told her about finding Jack in bed with another woman. Joanne was a good listener. Marcie had once thought it was because she'd rather eat her food while it was hot.

"And you haven't heard his side of the story?" Joanne inquired.

"What for?"

"Well...for starters...to know what really happened, Marcie—"

"I just *told* you what happened!" she said through clenched teeth, cutting Joanne short.

"No you didn't. You *only* told me *your* side of it—what you perceived happened."

Marcie's eyes narrowed. She didn't like the way the conversation was going. She came for Joanne's support. Getting beaten up was not on the day's fare.

"You know what you're doing, don't you?"

Marcie put the bagel she was holding down and looked at her. What little appetite she'd had was gone. She remained silent. She already had an inkling of what Joanne was going to say.

"You're condemning the man without a fair trial."
"You're just saying that because you like Smith."
Joanne rolled her eyes.
"I know what I saw."
"And what if there's an explanation?"
"I already know the explanation."

Joanne gritted her teeth. "No you don't. You're jumping to conclusions and tarring all men again with the same brush."

"With ample reason, I might add."

Joanne took a deep breath. "Marcie, here's my advice. You don't have to take it."

Marcie picked up the fork and stabbed at the uneaten bagel on her plate. Slowly she raised her eyes to look at Joanne. "What?"

"Give Smith a chance. Hear him out before you write him off."

"I need a new pair of boots." Marcie deflected the counsel in a vain attempt not to think about what Joanne had just said.

Joanne emitted a huge sigh and shook her head. "I can't do anything with you."

Smith tried to speak to Marcie before roll call the next day. She walked away and to avoid making a scene, he backed off. She had absolutely no desire to talk to him, even if he looked like he hadn't had a decent night's sleep in days. Could be an act, she cautioned herself. Jack had done practically everything to look contrite. No, she wouldn't fall for that again.

Did men think all women were stupid?

The Chief spoke briefly before the Assistant Chief went through the calendar of upcoming events. Marcie hardly heard a word the Chief or Wiebolt said, her mind busy wandering in all directions. When she caught herself thinking about Smith, she forced her attention back to the Assistant Chief.

She had maintenance duty and went straight to the garage. From the corner of her eye, she saw Smith follow her. She whirled around and said sharply, "I *don't* want to talk to you."

"At least give me a chance to explain."

She shook her head.

"She's my sister."

"Sister," she chuckled. "Now, there's a *good* one."

"It's the *truth*, O'Dwyer."

"Sure and next you'll be selling me a bridge."

Smith grabbed her arm. "O'Dwyer—"

"Take your hands off me. You don't want to make a scene," she snarled.

He released his grip and let her go, but not before telling her, "You're making a mistake."

Fifteen minutes later, the fire alarm went off and they geared up.

It was a two-family house. Visible flames ripped through the side of the house. The cops, who'd arrived only minutes before the firefighters, busily directed traffic and corralled a small group of people standing in the street. As soon as McLaughlin and Calderone stopped the trucks, everyone jumped out. Dodd and Mulvane hooked up the hoses while the Assistant Chief walked up to the people standing in front of an officer.

"Anybody know who lives here?" Wiebolt asked.

An elderly man spoke up. "The Jeffers. Father and mother live below. Son and daughter-in-law, with their three little kids, on the second floor."

McGuiness and Marcie rushed inside, while DiMaggio and Smith set up a ladder to enter through an upstairs window. Smoke hung in the air like a dense acrid fog. Marcie, who led the way, found the elderly couple in the kitchen slumped over the table unconscious, but alive. She hauled out the woman, McGuiness hefted the old man out to the ambulance where the EMTs waited.

She and McGuiness climbed the ladder and joined the others on the second floor.

The heat on the second story was intense. Marcie couldn't see a thing through the black, dense smoke. Flames blocked the way out of the room into the hall.

They'd have to back out and enter through a different room.

Marcie remembered seeing a ledge and motioned McGuiness to follow. She went back out the window and hugged the side of the building, slowly putting one foot in front of the other, inching slowly along the narrow edge toward another window. With her axe she smashed the window and quickly removed the hanging shards before they slipped through.

They found the others as they dropped the second of the children down to the waiting firemen holding a net. The father and two of the children had been rescued. The woman and a small child hadn't been found yet.

Suddenly Marcie's walkie-talkie came alive. It was Wiebolt. "Get out of there! The ceiling's gonna go."

Immediately following the Assistant Chief's warning, she heard a muffled cry. "Help!"

It came from another room. She motioned to McGuiness she was going to find the woman. He shook his head at her. He'd heard the AC's message loud and clear. Marcie didn't hesitate as she told the others to go. If she couldn't find and get the civilians out in a few minutes, she'd leave.

She heard the woman call again. Moving in the direction of the voice, a flaming ceiling beam fell, just missing Marcie. Cautiously she crept through the smoke filled hall. She heard a noise behind her and turned. Dodd dodged some falling burning debris. Marcie pointed to the door. He nodded he understood.

He stepped to the side as Marcie slowly reached for the door knob. She pulled back her hand quickly. Even through her glove she felt the heat. She carefully stayed to the side of the door as she broke it down with her axe. Then they both dropped to their knees as fire roared out from the room above their heads. They slowly crawled inside, searching for the woman. The woman saw them first and cried out. They followed the sound. Only a few feet away they saw her cowering in the corner. She clutched a child in her arms.

There was a swooshing noise and the entire ceiling

behind them came down in flames, blocking their way. The window was the only way out. Marcie moved quickly and smashed the panes as Dodd shielded the mother and child from flying glass. She climbed out the window and stood on the roof of the first floor as Dodd helped the frightened woman out. Then he handed Marcie the child and got out himself. The guys below were ready with the rescue net.

Marcie motioned for the woman to jump. She shook her head. Marcie had no time to plead with her. The entire place was going to go at any moment, so she gave the child back to Dodd and grabbed the frightened woman. With her arms clasped around the woman, Marcie jumped. Dodd held the little boy and followed Marcie and her civilian down. A moment later, the entire roof collapsed.

Wiebolt's face was full of fury as he screamed at Dodd and Marcie. "I distinctly gave you both an order to clear out. You disobeyed. I should fine you both. You could have been killed."

They took his wrath knowing, despite what he said, Wiebolt was proud of them. Fighting fire was like a crapshoot—unpredictable and risky. And like craps, sometimes you won and sometimes you lost. But like Lotto, if you didn't play, you couldn't win and oftentimes the chance was worth the prize.

Chapter Seventeen

Marcie, being her stubborn, myopic self, refused to talk to Smith and continued to avoid him. The truth was, she honestly didn't trust herself and avoidance made things easier for her. She feared she'd break down if too close to him.

Because of her unbelievably rotten attitude, Smith had clearly given up trying to penetrate the wall of ice she'd encased herself in. There were moments of weakness when she wished he'd turn up his blow torch and try a little harder, but they quickly passed following a foray at the mall. If nothing else, her wardrobe was growing by leaps and bounds. Too bad more clothes didn't equal more happiness.

The truth be told, she missed him. She'd never admit it to anyone else, though, so it remained her secret. And the subterfuge was killing her by degrees.

A month or so after she and Smith split up, everyone was at O'Leary's celebrating with the Assistant Chief the birth of his third boy.

In the back corner of O'Leary's stood an old pool table. The guys often challenged each other to a game. Sometimes, Marcie even played a game or two.

When Smith had first arrived, he'd ordered a beer, and taken it back to the pool table where he'd joined in a game with a couple of the guys from the 109th. Marcie watched him from the mirrored wall behind the bar, recalling how much he liked playing pool. He'd told her when he was little his grandfather used to take him to a pool hall downtown. Smith had taken her there several times and she'd been impressed when he'd taken out his custom cue stick from a case.

Marcie and Dodd sat at the bar joking with Wiebolt

about how he could forget about sleep for the next few weeks when she noticed in the mirror, two young girls walk toward the pool table.

Probably friends, they reminded her of two blonde bookends. They were dressed in similar short miniskirts and halter tops that swooped down on their left shoulders. She watched one of them saunter over to Smith and whisper something into his ear. The next thing she saw was Smith grinning as he placed his arms around her, apparently instructing her how to hold the cue stick.

The nerve of that little slut! A moment ago the bimbo hardly knew him. Now he's got his hands all over her body. A feeling of *déjà vu* passed over Marcie as she continued to watch them in the mirror. She imagined Smith's strong hands on her, nuzzling her neck.

"O'Dwyer, are you listening to a word I've said?" Dodd asked, bringing her back to reality.

"Yeah, sure," she replied quickly.

"So, do you agree with me or not?"

"About what?"

Wiebolt nudged Dodd and jutted his chin to the mirror.

Dodd realized what she'd been looking at. "You're impossible. Despite what you've said, you're still not over that guy."

Marcie pursed her lips and didn't answer.

"Funny thing is, I don't think he's over her, either," Wiebolt added to Dodd's comment.

She turned to face him. "From what I see, he's well over me."

"She means nothing to him. Any fool can plainly see that," Dodd said.

A moment later Wiebolt's cell phone chirped. He looked at the caller ID. "Gotta take this, excuse me." He walked off toward the restrooms.

Marcie used the interruption as an excuse to make a hurried exit. She had no desire to talk about Smith. She was far from a charitable mood and clearly Dodd felt she'd wronged the guy by not giving him a chance to tell his side of the story. As she strode to the Jeep, she was annoyed at herself for having a moment of weakness while around the guys.

The last thing she wanted was for Dodd to mention to Smith that she still cared for him. But she couldn't erase from her mind what Wiebolt had said about Smith still caring for her. And Dodd had said to her on several occasions 'what will be, will be' or that they were 'meant to be together.' Was it wishful thinking on Dodd's part or did he actually believe such silliness? Or did he see something she was too blind to notice?

Had Smith not cheated on her, they'd still be together and his hands would have been around her tonight at the pool table instead of that underage blonde slut. Yeah, she still loved him. They had something you just didn't find everyday. And she wasn't just referring to the dynamite sex. They enjoyed the same things—from rodeos and country music to moonlight strolls.

Every time Marcie thought about it her eyes filled with tears, and tonight was no exception. At times like this, she felt herself softening. Joanne chided her often for her stubbornness. Marcie didn't feel that was a fair interpretation. Hadn't she given Jack more than one chance? And look what happened.

According to Joanne, it didn't matter. No two people were the same and she should extend the courtesy to Smith as well. Unfortunately, she couldn't. She felt way too strongly that if he cheated once, he'd most likely do it again. The hardest part was always the first time.

That night, clutching Goofy, she cried herself to sleep.

Chapter Eighteen

Marcie lived in a decent-sized city in southwestern New York, not far from the Canadian border to the north and the Pennsylvanian border to the south. Like most of the area, West Burg was originally settled by farmers before succumbing to the industrial era. At that time, the entire area entered into a bustling manufacturing stage. But decades later, like most of the United States, it saw massive closings after American companies found it cheaper to set up factories overseas or just import the finished product from foreign markets.

Now a land of pencil-pushers, the U.S. manufactures little to boast about. Even so-called American-made cars are often built in Canadian factories.

As a result of factory closures and a significant rise in unemployment, urban blight hit parts of West Burg. From time-to-time, the West Burg firehouse was called to put out a fire in some abandoned factory. City consensus was that the derelict buildings should be torn down, but there was little money in the town coffers for urban renewal. So the structures stayed, becoming prey to the elements or arsonist. The factories that remained online lost revenue with each passing year despite the valiant campaigns of their owners to continue running. Now only a few remained until the capital dried up and the owners were forced to close their doors.

The call came in. A printing company was ablaze. Chemicals, paper and other flammable material were on the premises. It would be a virtual tinder box and very dangerous.

Although they responded quickly and arrived in record time, they found the six-story building engulfed in flames when the two hook-and-ladder trucks pulled up to the scene. Despite all efforts to contain the fire, the entire building was gutted in no time.

Normally, when a building went up so quickly, eyebrows were raised. However, with all the flammable stuff in the building, no one viewed it as unusual. The fire marshal would send in an inspector, but no one expected anything suspicious would be found.

A few days later, another large structure went up in flames—an office building on the other side of Route 17. Fires in buildings with central elevators tended to be tricky, especially when the fire could conceal itself in the walls. Playing hide and seek with a fire was a scary game.

When Marcie and her crew arrived, a car sat parked next to the fireplug. McLaughlin cursed aloud. Marcie looked at the Assistant Chief and asked what he wanted her to do as Dodd jumped off the truck to grab the hose.

"Smash the asshole's windows. I doubt if he'll ever park by a pump again."

She smashed the windows on both sides of the car. Dodd ran the hose straight through the parked car and began to spray the tongues of fire that lashed at them from the building.

"We've got to hunt this baby down," Wiebolt told them.

He split the firefighters in two groups to search out the site of the fire. Smith went with DiMaggio, McGuiness and Maguire; Marcie remained with the Assistant Chief, Calderone and McLaughlin. Group two got into the elevator while group one headed up the steps. The doors closed and Marcie hit the second floor button. They all held their breaths as the doors opened.

Nothing. Silence greeted them.

"Hit 3, O'Dwyer," Wiebolt commanded.

The bell dinged and the doors slid open. Again, nothing.

"I don't like this, man," McLaughlin said.

Marcie looked to Wiebolt, who creased his lips. Beads of sweat formed around the exposed skin not covered by his gear.

"Hit the next floor," Wiebolt said.

She felt as if they were playing Russian roulette. Would this be the floor? As the doors slid open, Marcie already knew the answer. The smell of acrid smoke hit them immediately; though the fire was out of sight, it was on this floor somewhere.

They exited the elevator. The walls felt hot, but the fire had retreated into one of the rooms. A thin trail of gray smoke snaked along the ceiling. By following the smoke trail and touching door knobs, they hoped to find the right one.

The Assistant Chief hurried over to a window and alerted Dodd who climbed up the extension ladder with the hose. He had to be in position when the door was opened. In many cases the fire would flash and engulf a firefighter. This was the scariest part—and very dangerous.

Marcie waited for Dodd to appear. Her mouth was dry and she was sweating like a pig, despite the fact the building was chilly. She wiped the beads of sweat that had formed on her forehead and swallowed hard for the umpteenth time.

The door was broken down. No flash. Probably because of the high ceiling. She let out the breath she'd been holding. Dodd sprayed down the wall, but the fire had already moved on. They were on the hunt. At the next door they saw a hint of smoke traveling across the ceiling, teasing them.

"Careful, man," the Assistant Chief cautioned. "It might flash."

"It might not." Calderone pointed at the high ceiling.

They'd been lucky once. Would their luck hold? It felt like a high-stakes poker game.

"Okay, let's deal with it," Wiebolt replied. Dodd held the hose, ready to contain the fire by hosing it down. Calderone slowly reached for the doorknob. He opened the door and suddenly the fire was sucked back inside.

Marcie screamed, "It's in the walls!"

"It's gonna get away!" Calderone shouted.

Just as he said that, there was a loud whoosh as the

fire came roaring across the floor, blowing out the windows.

"Here it comes!" Marcie yelled at the top of her lungs.

To their horror, Calderone was engulfed by the flames. He screamed and fell to the ground as Dodd quickly sprayed him down. A beam fell from the ceiling, knocking Dodd down. The hose fell from his hands and like a snake whipped from side to side, spraying everything around it. Marcie dove for the wayward hose, grabbed hold of it and finished putting out the flames on Calderone. Wiebolt had already called for medical assistance. Calderone moaned loudly in pain.

Dodd had only been stunned momentarily by the beam, and was all right. His shoulder and back would be sore later, but that appeared to be the extent of his injuries. Wiebolt helped him to his feet. They both joined Marcie, kneeling at Calderone's side.

"You're gonna be okay." She could hardly see through the tears in her eyes. The toughest part of being a firefighter was when one of their own went down.

"We've got to move him before the entire ceiling goes," Wiebolt said.

Together, they maneuvered the badly injured man into the hall as Ed Clark and Bloom, a trainee, rushed out of the elevator with a gurney and medical supplies.

They left Calderone in the care of the EMTs and went back to battle the blaze. Two more companies had been called in to assist. Finally they contained and put out the fire without any further mishaps.

Before the trucks headed back to the station, everyone stopped off at the hospital to check on Calderone, who was in intensive care with second and third-degree burns on most of his body. The poor guy. Marcie prayed he'd pull through. Usually touch and go with burns, infection was the biggest enemy.

Back at the station, dawn broke. Marcie, too tired and emotionally spent to appreciate the glory of the rising sun, crashed. The moment her head hit the pillow she was out for the count.

Chapter Nineteen

The company was on its way to the second high-rise fire in a week. Marcie hated this type of fire the most and thought about John Calderone who'd fallen victim to the last one.

Calderone was still in the hospital recovering from third and second degree burns. His condition was still guarded and could go either way with the doctors trying to keep his lungs clear. Marcie felt sorry for him and his family. She liked Calderone from the moment they'd first met. He was short with mocha-colored skin that reminded her of a chocolate latte. He wore a bushy mustache and always had a mischievous twinkle in his eyes.

Originally from Venezuela, his parents had come to the States looking for a better life. They worked hard to give their three kids everything they'd lacked while growing up in the slums of their native country. They were especially proud of John, their eldest, who had turned out to be a wonderful example for their younger children. He'd succeeded at everything he tried, being a good fireman and a devoted husband and father. Married to his high school sweetheart, Mary, they had three small kids.

Nearing the blaze, it crossed Marcie's mind that they'd responded to an unusually high number of fires lately. Was it simply coincidence? Or, she wondered, was there a pyromaniac out there setting fires because he liked to watch things burn?

Grandpa once told her a story about an arsonist. The story had enthralled her, but she'd only been eight, not old enough to understand how serious and scary the implications were. At the time, it had been like listening to a ghost story around a campfire. Now understanding what was at stake, especially with the potential loss of life, she shuddered as her grandfather's words came back to her...

"The guy was sneaky, all right. He'd set the fire and watch the flames engulf the place as he stepped back into the crowd that had gathered, enjoying himself as he watched us firemen come to put it out. At first it was one fire a week. But that didn't satisfy his need to see those flames dance. Soon it was two fires a week and then three. We realized we had some crazy on our hands, but who knew who he was? Or where he'd strike again? All we could do was continue to put those fires out as fast as we could."

"Was he ever caught?" she'd asked with a child's curiosity.

"Yes. But only because we caught a lucky break. The guy used gasoline to start the fires and accidentally spilled some on himself. As a result, he got burned real bad. When he went to the hospital emergency room, the doctor reported him to the police. If he hadn't screwed up, he may have never been caught."

In her little girl's mind she'd pictured the entire town having been burned to the ground.

Was this what they were now facing? Did the town have an arsonist in their midst?

They reached the fire and joined Company 109, already at the scene. From what Marcie could tell, most of the fire had been isolated to one area. Wiebolt gave orders and they rushed to join the other firefighters.

Marcie, Dodd and Wiebolt went to check on isolated flames in another wing of the building. Suddenly, a burning ceiling beam crashed down, falling so close it knocked the flashlight out of Marcie's hand. She jumped backward, ripping the tubing out of her air tank on an exposed pipe. She had no choice but to return to the truck and replace her broken equipment. She motioned to Wiebolt she'd be right back. Shaken from the close call, the fresh air would do her some good.

Marcie went outside and removed her oxygen mask and tank. The air stank of soot, but it was a great deal fresher than the air inside. It was also much cooler. She grabbed a new flashlight, checked the batteries and slipped on a new oxygen tank before going back inside.

As she reentered the basement, she saw another firefighter from her company standing several yards away.

What was he doing—he had no reason to be here?

This was where the fire had started, but the area had been put out long ago. Something about his behavior struck her as peculiar. She stopped, quickly stepped behind a large supporting beam, and watched. He sifted through the debris on the ground with his booted toe, apparently looking for something.

At first she figured he'd dropped something, but when he looked up every so often to see if anyone was coming, she got the feeling that wasn't the case. Marcie, her curiosity piqued, wondered what he was searching for. He turned to look behind him again, then stooped and examined the rubble. A moment later, he pulled a charred piece of plastic from the ruins and stood. He held it, studying it as if it were a treasure before shoving it into the pocket of his protective coat. Then he rushed up the steps.

Wondering who he might be, Marcie hustled to catch up with him in order to get a glimpse of the name on the back of his coat. Unfortunately, by the time she got upstairs, there were several men there. She had no idea which guy she'd chased.

What she'd just witnessed deeply upset her. At the same time, she found it downright scary. His furtive action provided evidence that her fears about an arsonist setting fires around town might hold water. If that charred object he'd pulled from the rubble was the remains of a trip box, then the fire they were battling had been set. His knowing the box was there probably meant he'd started the fire and had returned to retrieve it before the fire inspector came. Most of the time, the intense heat from the fire completely destroyed the trip boxes, leaving no evidence behind. But occasionally some trace was left and she thought this might be what he'd looked for.

Omigod! Marcie gasped as she realized that one of her fellow firemen could be an arsonist! She'd heard stories about this happening and now wished she hadn't witnessed that scene in the basement. She tried to refute what she'd seen, but what other explanation could there be? What else could he have been searching for in the rubble? What else could have been so important? Marcie couldn't think of a thing.

She rejoined the others and fought the few isolated blazes that still smoldered. By the time she got out of there, she was drenched and cold. Usually a long, hot shower stoked her inner heat and a large steamy cup of hot chocolate would finish the job. However, she doubted if anything could possibly warm the chill that had settled inside of her. To think that someone she knew and worked with, serving to protect the community from fire, could be the cause of the fires chilled her to the bone.

All the way back to the firehouse she tried to think of why a fireman might become an arsonist. She'd read somewhere how there was a thin line between sanity and craziness. Could the man have cracked and just crossed the line, setting fires during his down time? Or could he be doing it for money? Did everyone have his price, as the adage went? She doubted anyone could buy her. No amount of money could entice her to start a fire. Besides believing in the oath to serve and protect, she was unable to take a vow of abstinence, so she chose one of poverty instead. Unfortunately, not even her own bad humor could raise her spirits. This was serious shit and hardly a laughing matter.

Chapter Twenty

Marcie stood under the pulsating shower spray thinking and rethinking every second of what she'd seen at the blaze. Like several of the other recent fires, the buildings had burned quickly, suggesting the possibility of arson. But the other fires had been investigated and no accelerants or trip boxes had been found to link it to the work of an arsonist. And this one would probably have gone the same route had she not seen that guy pick up what could have been the remains of a trip box.

What bothered her was he could be just about anybody, including Smith. Her mind bent around the idea. Could he be involved in something shady in order to live above his means? The inside of his trailer did have some nifty toys that had cost big bucks.

The thought she was concerned that it could have been Smith troubled her. Why should she even care? The fact she already knew the answer irked her. She didn't want to think about him and yet she did. Why couldn't you turn love on and off like a water faucet? The next best thing would be to hope the well ran dry.

Marcie forced herself to focus on the main problem. What was she going to do about what she'd seen? Was she absolutely certain? At this point, she'd gone back over it hundreds of times in her mind. She ran her memory tape back and forth in an endless loop of slow motion stills, trying to remember every detail. She had to be one-hundred percent certain of what had gone down before she told the Chief—*if* she told him at all. That decision hadn't been made, yet—with good reason.

She was painfully aware of the serious consequences that would result from her accusations. Like tossing a rock into the middle of a pond, it would cause many ripples. Every firefighter on her shift that day would find himself under a microscope. At the least, it would destroy the harmony of the firehouse. And when it was discovered she was the one who leaked the information, she'd become a pariah. It would destroy everything she'd worked so hard for these past three years.

Then it occurred to her she had no idea if the guy had seen her. He'd looked in her general direction, but may not have seen her watching from behind the beam. However, if he had, he didn't know her identity any more than she knew his. In retrospect, she was the only witness and had she not gone out for new equipment and returned through the basement, she wouldn't have seen him. If she didn't tell the Chief, or anyone else for that matter, she could retain the status quo. But...was that really an option? Could she do that?

What if he continued to set fires? Would she be able to live with herself, knowing she possibly could have prevented them by notifying the authorities? Marcie had taken an oath to protect and serve the people living in her community. And what about Calderone lying in a hospital bed, seventy-five percent of his body burned in the last fire, which might have been caused by this bastard? How many more firefighters would be hurt fighting suspicious blazes set by him?

What motive could cause somebody to do such a terrible thing? He'd taken the same oath.

Was he deranged? Or did he do it for money? Money was always a strong motivator. Everyone needed money, but how many people would risk life and limb to attain it in such a perverse way? Or even gamble with the possibility of destroying one's career and family if caught?

Okay, one could argue whoever had done this wasn't out to hurt anyone intentionally because he struck at night when the building was empty. The only thing lost was property. However, he obviously didn't factor in the fact that accidents can happen. Calderone was a prime example. Thinking along those lines, if Marcie were to assume this wasn't the only fire set by this man, then the price had just ramped up and he'd become a murderer.

One of the buildings recently *torched* had hired a new night watchman following a series of attempted break-ins. This poor guy died in the fast-moving blaze, most likely never having had a chance.

Could she merely ignore what she'd seen as if nothing had happened? How could she knowingly continue to put out future fires started by this person? What would her father think of her if he knew? Marcie couldn't bring such disgrace to his memory.

Speaking of her father, Marcie wondered what he'd do in such a situation. Having known the type of man he was, the answer was simple. If he'd possessed such information, he wouldn't have hesitated a moment to go to the authorities. But then again, in all fairness, he never had to prove himself the way she had.

The very thought of him possibly watching her from above freaked her out. It also helped make her decision. She had to do something about what she'd seen. No way could she pretend it never happened. She turned the water off, stepped out of the shower and dressed quickly. Then she headed straight for Chief Mulvane's office—before she chickened out.

Chief Martin Mulvane had worked his way up through the ranks, picking up several citations for valor in the field along the way. Well-liked and considered fair-handed when dealing with issues concerning those under his command, everyone in the department sought his advice on personal matters as well as those related to work. Handsome and rugged, with a shock of auburn hair worn short and bearing a hint of gray at the sides of his temples, he was considered a man's man.

Firemen were a close-knit bunch, more like a tribe in many respects with their dances, barbecues, picnics and a hundred other reasons a year to get together. Growing up Marcie had seen a great deal of Martin Mulvane and his family. He hadn't been the Chief then. The man in charge had been an old, white-haired, bearded guy resembling Santa Claus, complete with a beer belly. Actually, he was more like Satan's helper. He might be smiling at you, but his calculating, beady dark-gray eyes told quite a different story. When Marcie got older and wiser she realized he was more than just a dirty old man. And unlike most dirty old coots, this one acted out his fantasies, which explained why her dad always held her hand tightly whenever they were in his presence. He'd died suddenly, opening up the position for Martin Mulvane. The official version was that he had a coronary. The truth was quite a different story. The teenage girl he was having sex with had given him the ride of his life.

Chief Mulvane's office was a shrine to his dead son, Jimmy. Both of his sons had joined the company, but it was Jimmy who was the rising star looking at a promising career. Rory, his other son, never quite lived up to his brother and father's legacies. He always seemed to be the last to offer help or volunteer.

Marcie's father had thought him a coward and a slacker. Years ago she'd overheard him and a few of the guys discussing Rory at a Sunday poker game at her parents' house. Her mom had sent her into the room, carrying a fresh bowl of chips.

"Night and day those two boys are," Dennis Sharkey had said.

"Yeah, makes you think that one was sired by the milkman," Joe Finney had added, laughing at his own humor.

"Which one?" Dad had quipped, trying to keep the joke going, but it was more a rhetorical comment.

"I'd rather have Jimmy watching my back, that's for sure," Joe Ciccone, Joanne's dad had replied.

"Rory would be too worried about his own hide," her dad had agreed.

Marcie had never forgotten that conversation. Nor could she forget the terrible blaze that took the lives of both Jimmy Mulvane and her dad. Jimmy had only been twenty-four. Rory had been their backup. She couldn't help but wonder had someone else besides

Rory been there, might they have survived?

Whenever she thought of Jimmy and Rory, she thought of Eileen and herself and how different they were, as well. But she wasn't thinking about any of this when she knocked on the Chief's door. All she kept thinking was if she'd seen correctly, one of her fellow firemen was rotten. And how many fires had he started?

Marcie heard Chief Mulvane bark, "Enter!" Then, "O'Dwyer. Nice work today."

"Thank you, sir."

"Something on your mind?"

"Yes, sir," she responded nervously. "It's about the blaze, Chief."

"What about it?" he asked, raising a thick, unruly eyebrow.

"Well, I ripped my breathing tube and needed to replace it. Going back into the building through the basement, I saw someone bend down and pick up something from the rubble and put it into his jacket."

"Did you see what it was?"

"From where I stood, it looked like partially burned plastic."

"Are you certain?"

Marcie sighed. "Pretty much."

"Did you see who it was?"

"No, sir. Couldn't read the back of his slicker from where I stood."

"This thing that he supposedly picked up, are you sure it came from the fire? It could have fallen out of his pocket and he bent down to retrieve it."

"That part I'm quite sure of. I watched him sorting through the debris too long to think it was something he'd merely dropped. I'm worried that it might have been a trip box, sir."

The Chief's eyes hardened and he sucked in his bottom lip. "You realize what you're suggesting, don't you?"

"Yes, sir, I do. I've thought about it a lot."

The Chief expelled a huge sigh and ran a hand through his thick head of hair. "Okay, run through what you saw exactly, O'Dwyer." His eyes had softened, but were now filled with pain.

Marcie slowly walked Chief Mulvane back over everything, trying not to leave anything out. After she finished, he sat silently rubbing his forehead with two fingers. She felt more and more uncomfortable as she watched him, guessing he was mulling the situation over in his mind.

"You're *absolutely* certain of this?" he said finally.

She nodded. "Yes, sir. He was *definitely* looking for something."

"And you're a hundred percent sure it wasn't something he might have dropped?" the Chief asked.

"When he found it, he held it up and inspected it a moment before putting it away. From where I stood, it didn't look like something a firefighter would carry in his pocket."

"You said it looked like plastic."

"Yes."

"And it wasn't a melted-down flashlight or something similar?"

"Why would anyone waste time sifting through smoking rubble for a flashlight when he could get another more quickly from the truck?" she asked. "It had to be something more important."

"And you think it was some kind of trip box."

"Yes, I do."

"You're certain?"

Marcie nodded, getting a little annoyed over the Chief's repetitive questions. She'd already told him all this. Why was he going over and over the same material? He knew she'd taken a forensics class and learned about fire-starting devices. After all, he'd signed off on the permission form.

"But, you have no idea who this firefighter was?"

"No." She tried to keep the rising frustration out of her voice.

"Did he notice you watching him?"

"I'm not certain. He could have."

"This isn't good. Not good at all." The Chief's entire

demeanor seemed to sag from the weight of what she'd just told him.

"I wish I were wrong, sir."

"Me too, O'Dwyer."

Marcie turned to go and he stopped her. "You'll probably have to make a formal statement concerning this matter."

She nodded. It wasn't something she didn't know.

Then he looked her squarely in the eyes. "For now, I think it best to keep what you saw to yourself and I'll take it from here."

She understood what he was inferring. "Fine with me, Chief. I just wonder..."

"What?"

"How many other recent fires might have been set?"

He didn't answer, but from the harried expression on his face, she knew he was thinking the same thing. At least she'd gotten it off her chest. Marcie left and closed the door behind her. She turned and walked smack into Smith who'd been standing off to the side.

"O'Dwyer! In to see the Chief?" he said quickly as if she'd surprised him.

"No, the plumber. Of course the Chief," she replied, wondering what he was doing there. "You need to see him, too?"

"Nah, I was looking for you."

"How did you know I was here?"

"One of the guys told me."

"Well, what do you want?"

"You know, I can't recall. It'll come to me later." He gave her a stupid, half-smile.

"Doesn't matter. I have nothing to say to you, Smith."

"You're still mad?"

Like this was some kind of revelation. "Yup!" She stormed off.

It occurred to Marcie how odd it was to find Smith outside the Chief's door, looking like a little boy who'd just been caught with his hand in the cookie jar. Number one, they weren't exactly on speaking terms at this point and hadn't been for a while, and two, could he be the one she'd seen? Why else was he there at that precise moment? The thing that bothered her the most was she *hadn't* told anyone she was going to speak to the Chief.

When the fire alarm clanged, Marcie shoved these disturbing thoughts about Smith to the back burner and got into her gear. It was a house fire and fairly close by. To be on the safe side, an ambulance accompanied them. Turned out this one was for the books, as well.

In her twenty-five years on this planet, Marcie had known several married couples. Most of those marriages had been unique adventures with their ups and downs and in some cases, sideways. No two were alike.

Take her parents, for starters. Their relationship was as lopsided as could be with her dad requiring fidelity from her mother while he played around. Every now and then her mother had complained, and it had earned her a shiner. Eventually she'd received enough badges of courage and accepted the status quo.

Then there was her sister's. Having begun on shaky ground, it had eventually collapsed under the weight of regret—Larry's. He merely waited until the right luxury train passed and bought a one-way ticket. Perhaps he figured he'd given enough time to the 'do the right thing' scenario. As far as she knew, Larry had never struck Eileen. He exercised his vocal chords instead. And that could be just as abusive.

And currently, the couple whose house was on fire had their own unparalleled story. By the time the hook-and-ladder arrived at the scene, Scott MacDonald was crawling out of the two-story structure, while his wife sat sobbing on a tattered, old lawn chair. No one was hurt; all the civilians were out of the house. Just the way firefighters liked it. They put out the fire that had ravaged half of the house and then heard what had occurred from the two police officers who'd caught the 911 call.

Maggie and Scott MacDonald had been married

A Heated Romance

eight years. She worked as a waitress and he was in construction. The officers were familiar with the MacDonalds, for they'd been there on a number of occasions to prevent them from killing one another. Mrs. MacDonald had an affinity for knives and Mr. MacDonald owned a nasty shotgun he loved to wave about.

The officers would read them both the riot act and then there'd be peace for a few short weeks before all hell broke loose again. This time was different, though.

The MacDonalds had fought earlier in the day. One of their neighbors had called it in. Although they were used to the noise, it often got out of hand. That was usually when one of the neighbors made the customary 911 call. The couple calmed down and the policemen left.

The original argument had been over another woman. According to Mrs. MacDonald, Mr. MacDonald had come home drunk the previous morning, reeking of booze and cheap perfume. The officers had successfully mediated a truce and left. Instead of maintaining the truce, however, the couple began to squabble again over Mr. MacDonald's lack of an income. His employment was seasonal and Mrs. MacDonald resented the fact that while she was out there busting her butt, he camped out in front of the TV knocking down beers. She felt he should get a temporary job to help pay the bills and his beer tab.

Unfortunately Mr. MacDonald, who was still very much hungover from the night before, was in no mood for his wife's nagging and told her to go to hell before he crawled back into bed to sleep it off. That seemed to infuriate Mrs. MacDonald, who was already fed up with his lazy and selfish attitude. She also hadn't quite forgiven him for cheating on her and was hell-bent on getting revenge. So she set their bed on fire with her husband sound asleep in it. If the acrid smoke hadn't made him choke and awakened him, he'd probably be dead.

Despite the fact that the policemen had had their fill

of the MacDonalds, they still found the entire scenario hilarious. With that in mind, perhaps it was time *they* put the fire out.

"They lived to fight," Officer Denby said taking off his hat to scratch his balding scalp.

"Yeah, they used it as foreplay," his partner, Officer Tisch, a baby-faced, shorter version of Denby added.

"We should make a movie. Call it *Fun and Games With Scott and Maggie*," Denby concluded, managing to crack everyone up.

Yup, it was all fun and games until someone ended up dead. Had anyone ever considered a marriage counselor—or divorce?

Chapter Twenty-one

After speaking with the Chief and him telling her to be careful, Marcie hadn't given too much thought to watching her back until a day or so later. She'd left the firehouse and was headed for home. It'd been quite a week and she was really tired and looking forward to a real good night's sleep. Perhaps a nice glass of wine and a book...

That was when she noticed the dark-colored pickup in her rearview mirror. For some reason, it looked familiar. Had she seen it before? Smith had a black pickup. Was it him? She tried to think if any of the other guys at the station had a black or dark blue pickup. She couldn't remember. But then, she really hadn't given it much thought before. Maybe subconsciously she'd noticed it following her at another time.

Now that she was aware of it behind her, she kept looking in her rearview mirror. It remained a couple of car-lengths behind, so she couldn't tell who was behind the wheel. Of course, being an avid reader of thrillers and mysteries, her mind began to weave the most intricate plot scenarios. It was a crazed psychopath who hated Jeeps. Or, the driver's mother was a redhead and he had this thing for her. The one thing she didn't want to think about, that it was somehow connected to her witnessing a fellow firefighter pick up a possible trip box, scared the living daylights out of her.

When the Chief told her to trust no one, he was warning her to be careful. She figured it was something he'd normally say in such a situation and not something he'd mention to upset or get her riled up. Yet, here she was letting her imagination get carried away, allowing herself to come apart at the seams by not thinking logically. She clutched the steering wheel so tightly her knuckles were as white as snow and her fingers ached. She had to calm down and become more rational. With great effort she loosened her grip and brought her breathing under control.

Once she'd calmed down, she shouted "Think, Marcie, think!" At the same time she kept an eye on the mirror and the pickup.

Then it came to her. She'd read a story where a young woman was being followed. She was smart and drove to a well-lighted gas station and the guy following her drove off. The last thing anybody should do was lead the person to their home or get stuck on a quiet, out-of-the-way road. So, she headed for a gas station. As she turned in, she watched the black pickup whiz by.

Then a new panic-laden question popped into her head. What if he was waiting a block or two away? If that were the case, she'd make a u-turn and come right back to the gas station and call the police. She felt much better after coming to that decision.

She got out, gave the guy in the booth twenty bucks and filled the Jeep. No change, so she slipped behind the steering wheel and locked the doors. Her hand shook as she turned the key in the ignition. Then she slowly drove off, looking all around as she proceeded toward home. The dark truck was nowhere in sight. She realized she'd been holding her breath and exhaled a long sigh.

Had she imagined the tail? Quite possibly. After all, she did possess an active imagination.

However, if it wasn't, what had she gotten herself into?

When she arrived home, she shut every shade after first checking to make sure all the windows were locked. Then she looked in every closet, checked under the bed and behind the couch. As scared as she was, she had to make sure she was alone. She even looked in the bathtub behind the shower curtain. After all, didn't all psychos hide there?

Discovering no unwanted guests, she returned to the kitchen. She began to regret talking to the Chief. No this wasn't because she'd told him. He wouldn't leak the information. This was because the guy *had* seen her. But there was a problem here. If she couldn't tell who he was, how could he know it was her? Had he seen her go in to talk with the Chief?

Suddenly, her stomach lurched and spiraled into a nose-dive as a snippet of memory teased at the edge of her thinking. Wasn't it Smith she'd run into as she left the Chief's office after confiding in him? An involuntary groan escaped her lips. Could it be possible that the man she'd slept with and loved—and probably still did—was now stalking her with the intention of harming her? It's said there's but a thin line between love and hate, but hey, she just gave herself new reasons not to trust any man.

Still, he was the last person she wanted it to be. Despite how she acted, and tried to lie to everyone, including herself, she was in love with him. Great. After he whacked her they could engrave 'She loved him 'til *her* end' on her tombstone. She laughed, but it didn't stop the tears from falling, emphasizing that this was far from a laughing matter. What was she going to do? She'd be a basket case in no time if she continued this way.

This is ridiculous. She grabbed a beer out of the fridge and sat at the kitchen table. After a few gulps, she realized her thinking had leapfrogged from a possible stalking to a definite murder. With that realization came the conclusion she was her own worst enemy, and she had to make a titanic effort to stop her foolish thinking and fix dinner. The telephone rang and she practically jumped out of the chair.

After slamming the phone receiver down on the telemarketer, she made a sandwich from leftovers. While eating, she turned on the small TV on the counter and watched some stupid sitcoms. Her mind focused on them for a while, but she needed to talk to someone. She had to unload before she exploded.

She keyed in Joanne's number, hoping she was free and they could get together. She really didn't want to be alone after all.

After the fourth ring, her friend answered.

"Hey, Jo, it's me."

"Hey, Marcie, how are things with the guys?"

She sighed. "Could be better. I was hoping we could get together tonight."

"No can do, girlfriend. I'm meeting this hot guy at the Digger."

For the moment Marcie couldn't place it and asked if it was a bar.

"Uh-huh. A small, intimate one across town."

The way she said it evoked naughty doings in Marcie's mind. "New guy?"

"Yeah. His name is Tony. And you know what they say about Latin lovers."

"Uh-huh. Give me a call when you're free."

"You sound down. Anything wrong?"

Marcie gave her the quick version of what had happened.

"Oh, boy. You really stepped into it this time, didn't you?"

She respected Joanne's advice, which was sound and usually went beyond *take two aspirin and call me in the morning.*

"I think you're doing it again."

"What?" Marcie asked, not certain what she was referring to.

"Obsessing on something and then drawing faulty conclusions."

"Okay, you've lost me."

"Are you certain the black pickup was definitely following you?"

"No."

"And how many dark colored pickups are there in this county alone?"

"Okay, I see your point."

"Stop reading all those scary thrillers. Put some romance in your life."

"Very funny," Marcie said.

"I just pulled into a spot by the place. Gotta go.

Promise to call you."

"Have a great time," she told her friend.

"I intend to," Joanne replied with a giggle.

Marcie thought about Joanne a moment. As kids when they were growing up, she'd often wished she could be her. To Marcie, Joanne was perfect in every way she wasn't. Joanne had matured more quickly and her body turned out to be quite the eye-opener. But it was her beautiful face, with those pouting full lips that men loved, that did it. Marcie would look in the mirror every morning hoping to find another face, preferably Joanne's or at least one with fuller lips staring back at her, but was always disappointed. Eventually, she comprehended that someone had to be her, as tough a job as it was, and took it on, even growing to like it.

Honestly, it was the freckles she hated the most. On her fair skin they stood out like polka dots, as if someone had sprinkled her with pepper. Thank God her hair was a deep auburn and not orange, which she associated with clown wigs. As much as she wanted to be delicate like Joanne, she was tall and ruggedly assembled. She was athletic and worked out with weights. Joanne's idea of working out was making love.

Despite all the differences, they remained the best of friends. And good friends were often hard to come by, let alone keep.

After talking to Joanne she felt somewhat better. A long, hot shower was in order. Just to be on the safe side, she brought a large carving knife into the bathroom.

The following day, Marcie straightened the apartment and ran some chores. She kept one eye on the road and the other behind her, paying attention to everyone she came into contact with that day. After seeing no suspicious pickups, she concluded the events of the day before may have been due to her overactive imagination.

The temperature had risen to the fifties, with practically no wind, under a bright sun. All things considered, the day had turned out quite pleasant. The chirping sounds of birds filled the air. One bird in particular often perched in a tree near her bedroom window. He wasn't a party animal, though. He didn't sing at night—only mornings.

She felt energetic and decided to wash her Jeep, which was covered with at least two inches of grime. It would never win beautiful car of the year, but it looked a helluva lot better than it did before she washed it. She nearly gashed her leg on the loose bumper. One of these days, when she got her hands on some extra cash, she'd have it fixed. But, hey, it got her where she needed to go and that was what mattered. Besides, that loose bumper gave it character and made it unique.

That night she had a sit down dinner, which meant she ate at the kitchen table and not standing at the sink. She'd gone all out and broiled a steak and baked a potato. It was edible. Perhaps her cooking skills were getting better. *Eat your heart out Betty Crocker.* She giggled at the stupid joke and cleaned up the kitchen.

She grabbed the garbage bag, twirled it closed and twisted a tie around it. Then she took it outside to the dumpster. As she walked back toward the apartment, she thought she saw a black pickup pass in front of the apartment building.

Racing inside, she slammed the door, standing with her back against it. Then she slowly sank to the floor. She buried her head in her hands, and sobbed her heart out.

So much for bravery.

Chapter Twenty-two

Marcie showed up at roll call a few moments before Assistant Chief Wiebolt. She decided to stay around others and not wander off by herself to read a book. Nor did she want to be alone with just one guy. In the company of two or more guys definitely seemed safer. Not knowing who her stalker was put her at a disadvantage, and she'd constantly have to watch her back. He, on the other hand, apparently knew she had ratted him out to the Chief. What he didn't know was she didn't know his identity.

Smith didn't even look her way. From guilt? In fact, hardly anyone spoke more than a few words to her. Did everyone know? Even though highly doubtful, her paranoia had kicked into gear.

As much as Marcie had hoped Smith wasn't her stalker, she couldn't think of anyone else who it might be. Unless the firefighter in the basement had seen her and figured out who she was, or perhaps somebody had seen her watching him, or even still, another guy saw her emerge from the Chief's office, the most likely suspect was Smith.

Her father had often told her not to believe in coincidence. The universe was way too quirky. Damn Smith! Why had he been standing outside the Chief's door?

It turned out to be a quiet day, and the squad ran through several practice drills. That helped take Marcie's mind off of things. The Chief insisted they perform at least one practice drill a month to keep their skills sharp. Periodically they went to the local community college to attend lectures on any new advances in fire protection and safety.

Marcie hardly spoke to a soul and was glad when the

shift ended. Even so, she didn't want to be alone and have to go home to an empty apartment. Joanne was going out so it left her with two choices: O'Leary's or her mother's.

She wasn't that desperate and headed toward the former.

Jerry Dodd sat at the bar. The constant, uneasy sensation someone was following her had her on edge. Possibly it was all in her head, but she didn't want to think she was losing it. It was a terrible thing, she decided, to watch little pieces of her mind break off and go running in totally different directions. Which part should she chase after?

She sat next to Dodd and signaled Tom for a beer. Tom was Ralph's son and the spitting image of his dad. If she didn't know better, she'd think Ralph had found some elixir from the Fountain of Youth or a special portrait like Dorian Gray.

Dodd looked so deep in thought with his head propped on a hand he didn't seem to realize she was there. She nudged him to get his attention.

"Hey, Dodd, you okay?"

He removed his hands and turned to face her. "Hey, O'Dwyer, what gives?" It came out flat, lacking his usual joviality.

"You seem down. Anything wrong? The kids and Cheryl okay?"

"Yeah, everyone's fine."

"So, why do you look like you've just been run over by a fire tanker?"

"Money. What else? I need to win Lotto."

"Don't we all?" she said. "No rich elderly relatives?"

"Nada."

"Seriously, if you need a few bucks..."

"Thanks, O'Dwyer, but I doubt if a few bucks will put a dent in the situation."

"This sounds serious."

"It is. I've got to come up with $55,000 a year to put my mom in a home. Her Alzheimer's has gotten so bad she needs constant supervision. It's too much for us to handle. I mean...with the babies and everything, poor Cheryl's constantly exhausted."

Marcie blew out air. "God, that's tough, Dodd. What will you do?"

She knew he was an only child and had no one who could share the burden. He'd been a good son and had taken in his mother to live with him and Cheryl after his father died. If he were putting her in a home, it was because it was damn necessary.

"I thought about asking the Chief if I could work some overtime."

"And?"

"I never got to ask him."

"Why not?"

"Somebody was in with him already and from what I could hear, it sounded like he had even worse financial problems than me."

"What do you mean?"

"Chief Mulvane was railing at him. From the way he went at the guy, he sounded like a father yelling at his son for being a bad boy."

"Could it have been Rory?"

He shrugged. "Dunno. I guess it could have been, but you know the Chief treats us all like family."

"So you really didn't see the guy."

"Nah. It could have been anybody. But man, whoever it was had to be in debt up to their chinstraps."

"How so?" Marcie asked, her curiosity now completely aroused.

"Gambling. Whoever it was owed over two-hundred grand."

She whistled. "Whoa! That's a great deal to be behind."

"Yeah, especially when loan sharks kill for less."

"Sounds like you'll be having company on your double shifts," she said.

"It would take much more than overtime to pay back a sum like that with all the interest."

Bringing the conversation back to Dodd, she reiterated, "Look, my offer still stands. If you need some cash, just ask."

He put a hand on her shoulder. "You're good people, O'Dwyer, but I'll get by." Then he gave her a forced half-smile. "Gotta go. I'm sure Cheryl needs me. She's got her hands full."

Not knowing what else to say, Marcie merely watched him pay Tom and walk out, looking like a guy who had the weight of the world on his shoulders.

After he left, she stared down at her beer thinking about what he'd just told her about the Chief chewing some guy out. A person that deep in a hole would need an awful lot of cash to pull himself out. And with deadlines looming, it would have to be fast. If it were Rory, she doubted he'd want to miss even one deadline. Self-preservation was his number one golden rule.

Unlike his brother, Jimmy, Rory would never run back into a burning building to rescue a civilian. He did his best to put out fires, but never went beyond that. It must have been tough to grow up in the shadow of a hero father and brother. The worst was probably getting beyond Jimmy and his citations. And the accolades continued long after his brother's death. Rory must have felt like a failure in his father's eyes.

But Marcie could hardly feel sorry for the guy. Blaming your shortcomings on others and not taking responsibility didn't cut it with her, especially after he'd been given some free passes along the way. He didn't have to work hard to join the fire department. His name magically opened doors.

It wasn't that she resented him. She just didn't like him. He wasn't a nice guy. It was difficult to like somebody whose only thought was of himself. Not to mention that kind of person didn't fit well into a family type atmosphere like a firehouse—like trying to fit a square peg into a round hole. Working twenty-four hour shifts provides ample opportunity to get to know one another. One has to learn to share their toys and play nicely.

Speaking of family, her mind shifted to Rory's wife, Angie. He'd met her when she jumped out of the cake at Sal DiMaggio's bachelor party held at a bar in Manhattan. Marcie hadn't been there, joining the house a few months later, but the stories she'd heard about it were vivid enough.

Marcie understood what the guys, especially Rory, saw in her. She was their ideal specimen of a woman—gorgeous, with a great body, which in male-speak meant she had big boobs. However, from what she'd been told by several other firemen, Angie liked to live well above their means. Marcie wondered if Rory gambled to pay for his wife's trinkets and fine house.

Enough! Marcie reined in her thoughts. Since she didn't know *who* the Chief had berated, this was all conjecture. But whoever it was could be in such dire financial straits they might be tempted to turn to arson for hire. That was when her overactive imagination spewed out a crazy thought.

What if Dodd was the guy? What if he'd made up the whole story to implicate Rory?

The guys at the house would sooner believe Rory capable of setting fires than a sweet guy like Dodd. She shook that crazy thought from her mind. Dodd was hardly the type. He'd been an altar boy, for God's sake. Yet, desperation drove people to commit heinous acts they'd never consider under different circumstances.

So who was following her? Was it somehow connected to arson, if indeed someone was intentionally torching places? Or was she being followed for other reasons? When had she first realized she was being stalked? It was after she'd spoken to Chief Mulvane about the trip box. Or maybe she just hadn't noticed until after that. Yet, if it hadn't been until then...could he have been yelling at the arsonist? Paying off a huge gambling debt would make a good motive. She wished she knew. Nancy Drew, she wasn't.

Then there was Smith. Had he a gambling problem? Did he need money? Obviously he liked nice things. As Tom poured her another beer, another idea crept into her thinking. What if Smith hadn't been eavesdropping on her at all, but wanted to speak to the Chief on his own behalf? Was he the man Dodd had overheard Chief

Mulvane admonishing? He might be stalking her for two reasons. Aside from her witnessing him picking up the trip box, he was pissed at her for not giving him a chance to explain about the woman he'd been embracing.

What if Smith were just mad at her for dumping him? What if he were stalking her for that reason alone? If his ego were that fragile, maybe. Or if he were some kind of a sociopath. Good Lord! Marcie had no idea what to think at this point. And her brain was getting tired from all the mental acrobatics.

The only thing she knew for certain was what she'd seen. Whether or not the fireman picking up the timing mechanism actually started the fire was the only uncertainty. It definitely appeared he was involved with torching the building. And if somehow he suspected she saw him, she was in big trouble. Maybe she shouldn't have told the Chief about it, after all. Loose lips sink ships. It could also get one killed. But...so could fires. No, she'd done the right thing.

Her biggest problem now was she didn't know who she could trust and had a terrible feeling the list now included the Chief.

Chapter Twenty-three

Marcie felt like a character in a suspense novel. Every time she left the apartment, she constantly looked over her shoulder to see if she were being followed. Whether or not her mind was playing tricks on her, she'd become so paranoid she feared she was losing her grip on sanity. Of one thing she was certain, though. She saw that black pickup much too often. Okay, maybe it was a different black pickup from time to time, but not *every* time. Just once she wished the guy would slip up and get close enough for her to see the license plate. Then she'd know for certain.

To say she was upset by all this would be the understatement of the year. So shaken, she even toyed with the idea of going back to her mother's. The thought of living under the same roof with Eileen and her two loony tunes was worse than being alone. Besides, knowing her mother hated she was a firefighter, the first thing she'd say was *I told you so*. Now wasn't the time Marcie wanted to hear that. Maybe she was falling apart from all the stress, but she wasn't certifiable. Not yet anyway. And that was what it would take to move her back into her mother's place.

Her mother held grudges. She'd always hated the fire department and everything associated with it. She'd never been cut out to be a fireman's wife and certainly not a firefighter's mother. Catherine Malone O'Dwyer felt she'd been born to a higher class and was forced to associate with those of inferior stock—namely, firefighters.

She'd loved Marcie's father in her own fashion, but she'd never forgiven him for becoming a fireman. Every time there was a barbecue or picnic, Marcie remembered the arguments. Her mother hated going and never seemed to enjoy herself at any of them.

"If I'd wanted to become a member of a tribe, I wouldn't pick this one," she'd said once during a heated argument.

The problem was her parents were from two planets—not Mars and Venus, but two unidentified ones from another galaxy. They lived to fight, or loved to fight—except for the times her dad clocked her one.

There was no way Marcie could talk to her mother about the terrible situation she'd gotten herself into any more than she could trust her advice. Only one person served as her confidante.

Marcie had waited nearly an entire week for Joanne to call after her date with Tony. When she finally called, Marcie was leaving the firehouse to go home, her nerves frayed.

"Hey, you were supposed to get back to me. That was nearly a week ago," Marcie snapped.

"I know. I know." Joanne's tone was apologetic. "I've been busy."

"With him?" Marcie replied testily.

"Yes and no. If you're free, I can meet you at the Metro."

"You know I'm free. I'll be there in fifteen."

"Marcie..."

"Yeah?"

"Leave the attitude in the car."

"Sorry. It's the way things are going lately."

"I know. But, I'm not the enemy."

Once outside, Marcie looked for any sign of the truck that had followed her. She'd gone through the parking lot day after day looking for black pickups. Ironically, Smith now drove a small blue Jeep to work. The dark pickup was like a ghost appearing out of nowhere.

Confident it was safe to get into her Jeep, she walked toward it quickly. The blood froze in her veins when she reached the car and saw white paper tucked under the windshield wiper on the driver's side. She glanced around to check if anyone was watching before she removed the folded piece of paper. Dodd was getting into his car several yards away, but didn't turn in her direction. Shakily, she swiftly unlocked the Jeep and slid inside. After relocking the doors, she turned on the interior light to read the note written with black magic marker.

Should have kept your big mouth closed. Now you'll be sorry.

She stared out at the growing darkness around her. Where was the creep? Crumpling the note in her hand, she sensed him watching and laughing. He had to be enjoying the fact he was scaring the hell out of her. She stuffed the note into her jacket pocket. Her hands shook as she put the key into the ignition. In some bizarre fashion, she found it consoling. At least now she knew she wasn't going crazy and imagining things. Great! She tried to get her erratic breathing back to normal. Hell, lately, she had no idea what normal was.

As she drove, Marcie checked the rearview mirror for the pickup. If it were around, she didn't see it. Then something occurred to her. It wasn't necessary for him to stalk her on a consistent basis any longer. Whether he was around or not, she was a nervous wreck. Perhaps that was his goal all along. He only made her aware of his presence in the beginning to scare her. How else would she know she was being stalked? Whether he was following her now or not, she'd still think he was. Stalking also served another purpose. While the stalker followed someone, he learned the places the person frequented. Then when he decided to escalate to murder...

"Stop it!" Marcie yelled at herself, trying to stop her errant thoughts, but it was too late. The little voice in her head had already concluded that if he'd stopped stalking her, he was ready to take the step to the next level.

She pulled into the parking lot and parked. Joanne's red Xtera was nowhere in sight. Normally, she'd wait for her outside, but tonight she preferred crowds and lots of people. Parking as close as she could to the building, she wiped the sweat from her face and got out of the car. She nearly did a 360-degree swivel with her head, like Linda Blair in the Exorcist, before rushing to the door.

The Metro Diner was a typical eating place, open 24/7, and served the usual diner fare, which was a little of everything. Personally, she wasn't crazy about the food. She doubted Joanne was either. They merely used it as a convenient place to meet at off hours.

Inside, it wasn't busy and she was able to get a booth facing the door, allowing her to feel a little safer. She ordered coffee, and when it came she wished it were stronger. With a sigh, she leaned back and relaxed as best she could, waiting for Joanne. She realized all this precaution was for naught, since she had no idea who was stalking her. But if one of the guys from the squad happened to show up, she would find that more than a mere coincidence.

Joanne entered and Marcie waved her over. She looked like a model stepping off a page from Vogue Magazine even though she wore sweats. As she slid onto the opposite bench, she let out a yelp.

"They need to fix these worn seats," she said angrily after getting jabbed by the frayed vinyl.

The place did need a major overhaul, from the cracked seats to the scarred tabletops that had seen more action than an ice skating rink. Marcie consoled herself knowing the food was fresh. The aroma wafting from somebody's meal nearby had stimulated her appetite.

"Okay, give me an update," Joanne said.

Before Marcie could say a word, the waitress shuffled over and handed them two menus. She looked just as tired as the menus in their frayed yellowing plastic jackets. They glanced at them and ordered BLTs and coffee. After she left, Marcie updated Joanne on everything that had happened since they'd last spoken, including the note she'd just found on her windshield.

"Where's the note?"

Marcie retrieved it from her pocket and handed it to

her. The color drained from Joanne's face as she read it. She was about to say something when the waitress returned with their sandwiches and refilled their cups. Marcie looked at the BLT, but her appetite had disappeared along with the waitress.

"This is *not* a joke, Marcie. You've got to go to the police."

"And tell them what?"

"That you're being stalked. The note proves it."

"That won't help," Marcie subconsciously shredded her napkin.

Joanne looked at her incredulously as if she were speaking some foreign language. "And why not?"

"Because there's nothing they can do until he tries to harm me."

"Oh, so after you're hurt they come and try to put you back together again like Humpty Dumpty?" Joanne replied angrily.

Marcie looked down into her coffee cup as if she'd find answers hidden among the grounds.

"Marcie, you just can't wait for something bad to happen."

"So what do you suggest I do? Run away, leave town, take an extended vacation?"

"Stay with me."

"I doubt your flavor of the month would appreciate having me underfoot."

"First of all, you're my dearest friend and you come first. *Mr. Flavor of the Month* or whatever you call him will just have to understand. And I doubt you'll be underfoot—unless you join us," she said with that little x-rated suggestive smile of hers.

"I love you, Jo, but a ménage à trois is not my thing. Thanks for the offer."

"What about crashing at your mother's?"

"That's called crash and burn. I'm not suicidal, yet."

"Look at you. You're a nervous wreck. How much longer can you go on this way? You've got to do something," Joanne pleaded.

"I don't think things will remain like this much

longer." Marcie put the crumpled note back into her jacket pocket.

"There's *got* to be something you can do."

"Until the guy tries to hurt me, no crime has been committed. Unfortunately, I doubt if writing threatening notes is any more a crime than unsubstantiated stalking."

"You should go to the police anyway!"

"Shhh! People are looking at us," Marcie warned.

"I'm just frightened for you," Joanne said, lowering her voice.

"You know something? I think maybe this note is telling me not to go any further with this. He just wants to scare me so I don't sign any formal statements."

"And you're not going to, right?"

"I have to. People's lives depend on it. What if this guy doesn't stop setting fires?"

"Marcie, listen to yourself. You're about to jump from the frying pan into the fire. How can you avoid getting burned?" Exasperated, Joanne slumped back in her seat. "You have a death wish, girl." With jaw set and eyes narrowed, she glared at Marcie a long moment. "You didn't call me here to ask for my advice, did you? Why am I here?"

"I needed to talk to someone I trust."

"So I can worry my head off whether you're safe or not?" Joanne spit out.

"No. I do respect your advice, Jo, but I just can't walk away from this and put my head in the sand."

"But you *can* alert the police. That way, they'll know what's been going on...in case this jerk *does* do something."

"Maybe you're right—"

"I *am* right!"

Before they parted and went their separate ways, Joanne had Marcie promise she'd tell the police about the stalking. Since it was late and she was tired, Marcie went home to sleep on it. *That is if lying in bed, tossing and turning all night, is considered sleep.*

A Heated Romance

The following day Marcie barricaded herself in the apartment. She figured if she didn't go anywhere, she was safe. Especially after the terrible nightmare she'd had. Somehow between the tossing and turning, she'd caught a few terrifying winks.

It had a stellar cast. Her dad and grandpa had starring roles. So did Smith and the entire firehouse crew, both shifts, including the Chief and Assistant Chief. Eileen played a cameo. Much of the details remained sketchy, but what she remembered was horrible enough. Most of the nightmare took place in a courtroom where she was on trial for her life. Everyone served as witnesses for the prosecution and bad-mouthed her. The only witness for the defense was Joanne, and Marcie's attorney was soon forced to label her a hostile witness. Just before the judge was going to pass sentence on her, she woke up.

At this point, things didn't look good. Not knowing what else to do, she was ready to go to the police. Things had spiraled out of hand and she needed whatever legal advice and help she could get. She took a shower, washing off the perspiration of fear from the nightmare as she mentally gathered the information she needed to tell the police. She wanted to sound rational rather than like some off-the-wall lunatic.

After toweling dry, she slipped into jeans and a sweater. She was hungry and downed a cup of instant coffee along with a heaping bowl of cereal. Fortified, she pulled on her jacket, grabbed her purse and keys, and went out to the Jeep. No notes; no black pickup. Taking that as a good omen, she got inside and locked all four doors before heading out to the police station. Only she never made it.

Chapter Twenty-four

Halfway to the police station, one of the Jeep's tires suddenly went flat. Luckily it wasn't on the highway and she wasn't going fast when it happened. She was able to control the car and wrestle it to a stop on the side of the road.

She looked in the back for the spare and nearly began to cry when she saw it was just as flat. Having no choice, she called for service. The good part was they were coming. The bad part was it would take them about an hour. A very unhappy camper, she got back into the Jeep and relocked the doors.

Sitting and waiting for the cavalry to come, Marcie had nothing to do but think. Why was her spare tire flat? The last time she'd checked, it had been hard as a rock. Pretty coincidental for it to be flat when she got a flat. And that made her nervous. As she waited, she felt like a sitting duck, and half expected a black pickup to appear out of nowhere. She felt as though she'd been transported into a Stephen King movie.

She leaned back in the seat, hoping no one would stop before the mechanic got there. Tired from the terrible night she'd had, she dozed off. The knocking on her window startled her. All she saw at first was the black pickup in her mirror. Her throat constricted as panic overwhelmed her. She turned slowly to look at the face staring at her through the window.

He knocked again. Angrily, he said, "Lady, roll down the window."

Not certain if he were friend or foe, she slowly lowered the window a crack.

"You the lady who called for help?" he asked gruffly.

"Are you from Bailey's?" That was the name of the service she'd called.

He pointed to the insignia on his jacket. "Is this okay or do you wanna see a check stub?" he asked sarcastically.

She rolled the window up, opened the door. "Look, you never know who's going to stop to help," she said.

He gave her a nod and went to look at the tire. It wasn't long before he told her, "The tire can't be fixed—broken valve. I'll have to put on a new one."

"Okay. I haven't much choice since my spare is just as useless."

After he was done, he told her to drive to the shop soon and get the tire balanced. She paid and thanked him.

"No problem. You be careful now."

Marcie watched him drive off. Glancing at her watch, it was now time to head over to her mother's. She'd gotten roped into coming for dinner when her mother called to tell her the news about her sister. Eileen and the girls had moved out. In the same breath she'd mentioned her sister was seeing a new guy, hinting he was a possible husband number two and Marcie still hadn't even had a number one. It sounded like she was in for some major fun and games. Though she'd rather be going to the police station, it would have to wait.

Marcie went to her mother's house early in order to spend time with Grandpa. Since her sister and the duo from Hell had moved out, his life had gotten back on track. He was less stressed and seemed a great deal happier. While her mother prepared dinner, they sat in the den and she told him about some of the strange fires the squad had been faced with lately.

He chuckled and told her people never really changed. "Some remain as dumb as a post and there just ain't no teaching them about the dangers of fire. Fire needs to be respected."

She had to agree with him about that. Their talk was rudely interrupted when the front door flew open.

Eileen pranced in, gracing them with her eccentric

entourage, her two girls and the guy she was now living with, Edward. Marcie was *definitely* not prepared for the likes of Edward.

He was a mountain of a man—better yet, the side of the mountain since he seemed nearly as wide as he was tall. Well over six feet and close to three hundred pounds, or more in her estimation. All she kept thinking when she first saw him was that it would take an awful lot of mashed potatoes to fill him.

His corn-yellow hair was tied back in a ponytail, rivaling her own in length. On his tree stump of a neck, a colorful tattoo of a dragon peeked out from under his hair giving her pause to wonder what else might lie on the canvas of his body. His voice complemented his body—loud and deep.

When he laughed, which was often, it resembled the rumblings of distant thunder. Even though he seemed jovial, his gray eyes were steely and cold as bullets. Marcie sensed she wouldn't want to get on the bad side of him.

Edward had two gold incisors only a vampire would admire and a diamond embedded in his top right front tooth. This guy would be mugged not just for his jewelry, but his teeth—that is, if the would be mugger had a death wish.

When he first walked in wearing his leather jacket, a chill ran right through Marcie. The insignia on the back, Righteous Saints, said it all. Eileen had hooked up with someone who ran with a motorcycle gang. Had she jumped from the frying pan into the fire? Marcie worried the girls would be burned from the resulting sparks. The two loonies could become psychos.

Of course the biggest question was, what the hell was her sister doing with a guy like Edward? They were like night and day, total opposites.

Sarah blurted out to her grandmother that Edward had taken her and her sister for rides on his big motorcycle. The color drained so quickly from her mother's face she looked as if she were going into cardiac arrest.

"Isn't that awfully dangerous?" Catherine O'Dwyer asked, directing her question at Edward.

However it wasn't Edward who replied, but Eileen. "Not really, Mother. I now ride my own bike."

Her mother's eyes widened to the size of saucers in surprise and she was speechless. Marcie, on the other hand, got with the program and asked Eileen, "Do you have a cute matching leather jacket like Edward's?"

Her sister glared at her before turning back to their mother. "FYI, most accidents between motorists and bikers are caused by the stupidity of the motorists."

Well, Marcie was so glad Eileen cleared that point up for them and reassured their mother, who looked like she was ready to scream. Personally, Marcie was totally surprised her sister had the nerve to even ride a bike. Could there be a side to Eileen she'd never seen?

"I'll just bet those biker mamas are real sweet," Grandpa said out of the blue.

Marcie thought his comment funny, but stifled her laughter as Edward said, "Damn straight, old man." He patted Eileen's knee.

Watching, Marcie winced, clenching her teeth. Those love taps *had* to hurt. The man had hands the size of snowshoes.

Grandpa turned to her. "Maybe you should get a bike, Marcie?"

"Maybe I will. Sounds like fun."

"Fun my—" Her mother caught herself. "It's all fun and games until someone gets hurt. Enough of this—"

"Now, now, Catherine," Gramps chided, "you were always something of a killjoy."

"If you're really interested, Marcie, I can hook you up with a real beauty," Edward said.

That was when her mother finally erupted. Marcie was close enough to her to see her eyes had darkened into two storm clouds, as her words rained down on them in torrents. "No *more* stupid talk about motorcycles. Everyone into the dining room, *now*. Dinner is ready."

Before Marcie's father died, it had been difficult for

her mother to speak her mind. Now there were no physical or mental restraints on her and she did so. And often. As they all marched into the other room and took their places around the table, the subject of motorcycles was put to rest. The dinner went along smoothly. Shoveling enough mashed potatoes to sculpt an entire mountain range, Edward hardly had time to speak. And for once, Catherine O'Dwyer didn't have leftovers.

Leaving her mother's, Marcie looked around to see if any black pickups lurked about ready to pounce on her. She hadn't seen one in two days. This left her ambivalent. As glad as she was *not* to have the creep following her, she hoped he was busy doing something else and not getting ready to take the stalking to the next level.

On the drive back to her apartment, Marcie thought about her sister. She smiled as she imagined her astride a motorcycle. Their father had to be laughing from his grave.

Chapter Twenty-five

Marcie walked out to the Jeep the next morning and found a note under one of the windshield wipers. Fear fluttered like ugly moths in the pit of her stomach. As much as she desired to ignore it, she couldn't. She imagined it was a reminder to let her know that although he was out of sight, he was still around. Her hands trembled as she reached for the slip of paper. The tremor worsened as she slowly unfolded it and read:

"My sister's in town. Thought you might want to meet her. Come to Lazy Lou's tonight at 8:00.

"Smith."

She exhaled the breath she'd been holding and sucked in air greedily as she reread the note. What was Smith up to? His sister was dead. Then it hit her. The note...maybe it wasn't from Smith at all? He never left notes for her. The only time she'd found a note, it had been from the stalker. Was this from him or was Smith the stalker after all? Maybe this was only a ploy to get her someplace where he could...she stopped and swallowed hard, not wanting to go where her thoughts lead her.

Then again, maybe the note really was from Smith. How else could he communicate with her? Was it possible one of his sisters hadn't been in that fatal fire and lived? She could ask Smith if he'd left the note. It was easy as that. However, if it weren't, would he think she was missing him and wanted him back? Then she realized something important. Who else knew she and Smith used to go to Lazy Lou's?

Lazy Lou's, a small restaurant on the other side of town, served the hottest chicken wings and best ribs around. Hot didn't come close to describing the wings. They torched your mouth and as they made their way down your digestive tract they incinerated everything in their path, giving reflux new meaning.

She drove to the supermarket thinking about this. Halfway there, she thought she caught a glimpse of a black pickup behind her, but it turned off at the next intersection. This was crazy. She wished the guy would stop this game he was playing. Not knowing who he was, coupled with the fact he could come at her anytime, had frayed her nerves to the point of breaking. She was afraid of a meltdown and knew she should go to the police. The problem was there was little they could do about it and dragging the police into this might anger the guy into really doing something stupid.

She knew, when she first told the Chief, it wouldn't be a picnic. And if it were getting to her now, how was she going to get through the formal board of inquiry when she'd have to testify before a board of commissioners? She knew the Chief was awaiting the results of the fire inspector's report. Then, to make matters worse, somewhere at the back of her mind a small voice kept telling her she may never get the chance to testify at all.

Marcie wasn't exactly certain when she made the decision to meet Smith. Though there was always the possibility he could be the stalker, Joanne's words kept haunting her. She hadn't played fair with him. Had never given him the opportunity to explain himself. Of course, she was curious about his sister, too. And lastly, though she hated to admit it, even to herself, she still had feelings for the big oaf.

As she applied some makeup, she looked into the mirror and silently asked herself if this was really what she wanted to do. Was it worth risking her life to go to Lazy Lou's? What were the chances the note was actually from Smith? Then the strangest thought popped into her head. If her sissy of a sister could find the courage to ride a motorcycle, why couldn't she find the courage to ride over to the restaurant? A tiny little voice tried to tell her the two weren't quite the same, but she did her usual best to ignore it.

Just as she left the apartment and closed the door, Mrs. Brass appeared out of nowhere. She was clad in a bright yellow and purple print muumuu. "Hello, Marcie. How's that hunk of yours?"

Surely she knew they'd broken up. After all, Smith hadn't been around for quite some time and something like that would have never escaped her prying eyes. Obviously, she was trying to irritate her.

"Funny you should ask. I'm going to meet him tonight and I'm already late." She looked at her watch, lying about the time.

"Well, I won't keep you then."

The look on the old lady's face told Marcie she hadn't believed her. She couldn't have cared less. What that crazy woman thought was the least of her problems. She murmured goodnight and headed for the Jeep. No notes. Who knew if that were a good sign or not?

She got in and started the engine. As she pulled away, she silently prayed it was Smith she was going to meet.

It was a beautiful evening. Not a cloud could be found in the star-studded sky and the crescent moon looked laid back as if it were watching the twinkling stars at play. A perfect evening for lovers to stroll and whisper tender words of love to one another, but Marcie hardly noticed.

Every few moments, she checked her rearview mirror for the pickup. Traffic was light on the road she'd taken and he'd stand out like a sore thumb. Because of several hairpin turns, not many people took this way at night. But it was the most direct and fastest route to the restaurant.

As she drove, her thoughts strayed to Smith. She'd missed him a lot, remembering how his green eyes, filled with desire, could turn her insides to mush. Instinctively, Marcie touched her lips as if she'd been kissed. Tears filled her eyes.

Straight ahead the road narrowed into a small one-lane bridge that covered a ravine. She slowed as she neared. More than one drunk had driven through the barriers and crashed below. It was well-traveled during the daytime, linking the roads up to 95, but at night it could be treacherous, especially in bad weather. Wanting to get to Lazy Lou's more quickly, she hadn't given any thought to the road.

Suddenly a pair of headlights appeared in the distance behind her. She was going the speed limit—about 30 mph. She'd just reached the narrowed road and had nowhere to go but straight across. She looked into the mirror again. The lights approached rapidly, so the driver was obviously exceeding the speed limit, which made her nervous. Only a crazy fool would operate a vehicle so recklessly on this road. If he didn't slow down, he was going to ram her. That was when the lightbulb snapped on inside her head. Rear-ending her was *exactly* what he *intended* to do. And she didn't have to be a genius to figure out who the driver was.

Her mouth went dry as she clutched the wheel so tightly her knuckles ached. She was a sitting duck. Even if she pressed the pedal to the metal, she'd never make it across the ravine before he overtook her. The best she could do was brace herself for the impact. Silently her mind counted the seconds down...

The vehicle slammed into her right rear fender with such force her Jeep lifted off the road and sailed toward the guardrail. Suddenly it was film at 11:00 as a kaleidoscopic montage of her life flashed before her eyes. The Jeep crashed through the rail and would have gone over, dropping into the black unknown below, had her bent fender not caught on the remaining guardrail.

The creaking of the car as it slowly swayed in the air sent shivers of ice through her veins. She was all too aware that at any given moment the rail could break loose and the Jeep would tumble into the yawning black mouth of the ravine below.

As her car clung to the railing by only a twisted scrap of metal, Marcie thanked God she hadn't had it repaired. Poverty had its advantages. For whatever reason she'd been spared, she didn't intend to blow it. The sands of time in her life's hourglass were running out. The weight of the Jeep was too heavy for the railing to bear much longer. However, her stalker had even less patience. She heard him shift his gears into reverse and watched him back up. He was going to finish her off! She had to get out.

Easier said than done. One false move and she was in the ravine anyway.

And if she somehow managed to leap from the Jeep to safety, wouldn't the guy see her? If she sat there and did nothing, she was as good as dead. So what did she have to lose?

Marcie didn't want to die on some isolated highway. Quickly she took in her surroundings. There were bushes and scrub-like plants growing along the ridge on both sides of the rail. If she could somehow bail out of the Jeep safely and hide among the bushes, in the darkness he might not see her.

In the still night's air she heard him shift gears once more. He would be coming at her in a flash. She had no time to think about it any longer. Her hand shaking, she grabbed the door handle. It didn't move. Was the door stuck? Dear Lord, she was going over after all. Then she remembered, all the doors were locked. Quickly, she flipped the lock and opened the door. She tossed out her purse and leapt from the car...

Chapter Twenty-six

Arms outstretched like a leaping cat, she hit the side of the ridge with such a thud she nearly bounced off. Quickly grabbing onto exposed roots, she hastily clawed her way up and burrowed into the bushes just as the pickup slammed into the Jeep.

The noise was deafening. The force of the impact tore the bumper from the Jeep, causing it to sail across the ravine until it lost its invisible wings and spiraled down to the bottom like a lead sinker. Seconds later, she heard an ear-piercing explosion. From where she hid she couldn't see below, but the Jeep must have caught fire because the stench of burning rubber, gasoline and undercoating wafted up and filled the air. Her breath caught in her throat as she heard a car door creak open, followed by the unmistakable crunch of gravel as her assailant stepped down from the truck and walked toward her.

From the brush Marcie had crawled behind, all she could see was the tall silhouette of a man dressed in dark clothes and a baseball cap. She held her breath as he walked past her to the edge of the broken rail and stared down at the wreckage of the Jeep. She wished he'd leave already.

She'd pulled herself in so tightly her legs were beginning to cramp—which at the moment seemed to be the least of her problems.

Suddenly he turned in her direction. Had he seen her? Or had her labored breathing given her away? Realizing there wasn't time to bargain with God, Marcie snapped her eyes shut and began to recite the Lord's Prayer in her head as a token of good faith.

Gravel crunched. Marcie's heart nearly stopped mid-beat. She clenched her teeth and prepared herself. But the crunching sound continued past her, growing fainter and fainter. She opened her eyes. Her would be assailant had walked away! Then a door slammed, but she didn't move a muscle until she heard the whine of the engine as he drove away.

Marcie slowly emerged from the bushes and cleaned herself off as best she could. The cool night air stung the scratches on her face and hands from the nettles and quickly dried her perspiration. Shivering from the cold, she nearly came apart at the seams when the realization of how close she'd come to death actually hit her. Wrapping her arms around herself, she rocked back and forth.

From the deepest recess of her mind a new galvanizing thought emerged. What if he decided to return? She had to get the hell out of here. Her purse—she remembered having thrown it. She crawled around in the dark, hands groping her way through the bushes like a blind person in a desperate attempt to find it.

With bloody hands, she recovered it from the bush it had fallen into. She emptied the contents on the ground and retrieved her cell phone and keyed in 911. Her voice, high-pitched and strained, sounded like some stranger's. The dispatcher told her to sit tight and a squad car would be there in ten minutes. As if she had any place to go.

Ten minutes felt like a century. Marcie walked to the edge of the ravine and peered down into the darkness. Tears slipped silently from her eyes partly from relief and partly for her poor Jeep that now lay at the bottom of the drop. She truly had loved that car. Now, she'd have to notify the insurance company of its untimely demise.

She glanced at her watch. It was too dark to see the time. Was Smith at Lazy Lou's waiting for her to show? *Or had it been Smith behind the wheel?* That would explain how the stalker knew where she'd be. She reasoned whoever had left that note on her windshield was most probably the guy who tried to kill her tonight. And as much as it hurt to admit it, all the facts and fingers pointed to Smith.

Approaching headlights caught her attention and she straightened up from the railing she'd been leaning on. Was this the police? Or had the stalker decided to come back and make doubly certain she'd gone over the side with the Jeep?

Deciding to play it safe, she hid once more and waited for the car to come close enough for her to tell if it was friend or foe. A squad car slowly appeared and she jumped from the bushes so the officer would see her.

The officer pulled the car off the road as far as he could. Leaving the engine running and the headlights on, he got out.

"Ma'am, are you the one who made the call?"

She looked at the tall, lanky policeman, who appeared to have just entered puberty, wondering if he was for real. Did he happen to see anyone else here in the middle of nowhere? She had to be a sight.

Marcie nodded.

"Are you all right?" he asked.

An understatement. "I guess so."

Shining his flashlight on her, he said, "Those cuts look pretty nasty. Do you want me to take you to the hospital?"

"No. All I want is for you to get that guy."

"What guy?"

"The guy who's been stalking me!" she shrieked. "Didn't the dispatcher tell you? Someone tried to kill me tonight!"

She knew she sounded hysterical, but she didn't care. She couldn't take any more of this.

"The call I caught only said there had been an accident on the 258 by the Narrows Bridge."

"I told that idiot—"

"Maybe he couldn't understand you—"

"Maybe he should learn English!"

He chewed his bottom lip. "That makes this a different ball game." He got back into his vehicle and called in.

The officer, flashlight still in hand, emerged again. "Show me the spot."

Marcie brought him to the place where her Jeep had gone over. He shined the light at the gaping hole in the railing and looked back at her.

"That's some drop. You're lucky to be here talking to me." He shook his head and repeated, "Damn lucky!"

She nodded and wrapped her arms around herself.

"Cold?"

"A little," she replied.

"Get into the car. I'll turn on the heat."

She got into the squad car with him and waited for the forensics team to arrive. The heater kicked in quickly, but Marcie doubted any amount of heat would be able to warm the chill which had taken root in the depths of her being. Even though she knew she'd have to repeat everything to a detective at the station, she told Officer Shaw the entire story. She didn't mind. She was glad to be alive.

The forensics team showed up in an SUV about fifteen minutes later. The officers brought lights and took snapshots of evidence they found. While the others went to work, a woman came over to the squad car, introduced herself as Ann Dunlop from the Crime Lab, and began to ask Marcie questions. She was a no-nonsense type, compact-looking woman somewhere in her forties, and having reached whatever rank she now possessed, aimed to keep it. Especially, if she'd worked her way up the ladder the hard way.

"Tough night, huh?"

"Worse than a fire. At least you can fight a fire," Marcie said.

Officer Dunlop looked at the surroundings and then gave her a knowing look. "Okay, so he came up from behind and rammed you. Take me through what happened next."

Marcie repeated the story, trying to remember every detail of her ordeal.

Hundreds of pictures were taken of the area with special attention to the tire treads and footprints. The railing was dusted for fingerprints.

"O'Dwyer, I know it's tough, but hang in there. We'll get this guy," Officer Dunlop said.

Marcie pursed her cracked, dry lips. They felt like sandpaper. "I hope so...because my life sort of depends on it."

Later, at the police station, Marcie suddenly felt as spent as a used cartridge. She'd just finished telling Detective Arnold, a barrel of a man who looked as if he'd been poured into his desk chair, about the suspicious fire and why she felt the man she'd observed rooting through the rubble in the basement was the one who tried to kill her. Arnold tapped the tip of his pen against his fleshy lips, nodding to himself, his dark eyes narrowed in thought. Sitting there in his rumpled suit and loosened tie, peering at her above half-glasses perched precariously on his bulbous nose that looked more like a road map, he appeared to have been there for days and had taken root.

"You really got yourself involved in some prime, grade-A manure, little lady," he said.

She nodded.

"The minute you show your face at the firehouse, the guy's gonna know you're alive."

"I know that."

"Perhaps, you should consider a little vacation, while we sort this out." he suggested.

"I can't hide forever."

"No, but you don't have to put yourself in harm's way, either," Detective Arnold snapped.

"I have to go back to work."

"Why? You have some kind of a death wish?"

"No. It's nothing like that," Marcie protested.

"Enlighten me, Ms. O'Dwyer. Tell me why you want to make my job more difficult."

"Look, Detective, this isn't about you. I worked hard to get respect. I can't just run away now."

He shook his large, meaty head in a manner Marcie perceived as he thought she was acting stupid. Yet, instead of lecturing her to drive home his thoughts, he let out a huge sigh before shaking his head again. She half expected the heavy mass to swivel off its short, stump-like neck and roll onto the desk.

"You're a spunky one, for sure. But, I guess you have to be in order to do a man's job."

From the corner of her eye Marcie saw a uniformed policewoman walk by and was about to say something to that effect when he held up a beefy hand. "It takes a tough woman to be a cop, as well. I guess I'd expect no less from Liz over there." He jerked his finger in the policewoman's direction.

Marcie did a double take. She never expected the likes of him to say something so profoundly supportive of women. Perhaps she'd misjudged him.

"What say I have someone keep an eye on you going to and from the station?" he suggested.

"*That* would be super," Marcie said.

He grinned. "I thought you might go for that. I never took you for a fool."

Officer Shaw took her home and opened the door. He turned on the lights and handed back her keys. "Stay right here until I check the place out."

Marcie complied and waited for him to return. It took only a few minutes to check out her entire apartment.

"Everything looks clear," he said.

"Can I make you a cup of coffee, Officer Shaw?"

At first he looked like he might turn her down, but after a beat said, "I guess I could use a cup, thanks."

He followed her into the kitchen and sat at the table. She took the coffee out of the refrigerator and filled the coffeemaker. The clock on the wall read 12:45, but it felt much later.

She joined him at the table while the coffee dripped into the carafe.

"This is nice of you," Officer Shaw said.

"It's the least I can do. You've been my chauffeur all night."

"Just doing my job, ma'am."

"Call me Marcie. Ma'am sounds like my mom."

He grinned. "Okay, Marcie."

"How long have you been a cop?"

"I'm finishing up my second year."

"You like it?"

"For the most part, yeah, I do. What about you? You're the only female firefighter I know."

She got up to get the coffee, filled two mugs, and carefully carried them to the table. Not knowing how he took his, she went back and grabbed milk and sugar.

"Three years. Up until now I've loved it, yet the last few weeks have been rough."

"If tonight is an example, I can just imagine. Hey, don't take this the wrong way, 'cause I admire you for doing such a tough job, but what compelled you to become one?"

"Both my grandfather and dad were firemen. I guess I wanted to continue the tradition."

"Must have been tough breaking in."

"Yeah, it was and sometimes I think it'll never end. Men are very proprietary."

He laughed, his eyes twinkling with a knowledge that belied his age. "Good choice of words."

Marcie realized her first impression of him had been all wrong. He was smarter than she'd originally thought and liked him.

"So why'd you become a cop?"

"I wanted to put the bad guys away. I watched a man get shot in a drive-by when I was a kid. Gave me nightmares for a long time."

His dark brown eyes had grown serious. Marcie studied his youthful-looking face. Most people were affected by things that occurred during their childhoods. They seldom think about them until hit by some kind of a crisis. That was usually when they pull out the microscope and reexamine their lives in an attempt to find the reason why.

"So you decided to do something about it."

"You think I'm crazy?"

"No. I admire you for trying to make things better. How many people only give it lip service?"

"I took the job with my eyes wide open, knowing it would be an uphill struggle."

"That sums it all up in a nutshell," Marcie said. "We gotta keep trying. If we give up, the bad guys win."

"I guess that goes for the both of us," he said.

She refilled his cup.

"That's why, as scared as I am, I've got to go back to work."

He put down his cup and looked her squarely in the eye. "But you know what's going to happen. It's almost suicidal."

Marcie half-smiled and said with false bravado, "I'll just have to be careful, won't I?"

It was getting late. Officer Shaw finished his second cup of coffee and used the bathroom before she walked him to the front door. He turned to face her. "Thanks for the coffee. You be careful out there now."

"I will. Thanks again for bringing me home."

After she closed and locked the door, she turned on every light in the apartment. She didn't intend to let anyone sneak up on her.

Chapter Twenty-seven

With the destruction of her Jeep, Marcie drove a rental until the few measly bucks from the insurance were sent to her. She strongly doubted it would even cover a down payment on another Jeep.

A squad car followed a short distance behind and she felt safe driving to the firehouse. A guy would have to be insane to try something. She wasn't certain how long she'd have a police escort, but for now it helped settle her frazzled nerves. When she told Joanne about her narrow escape with death, Jo blasted her for not having gone to the police sooner. Marcie realized that whether or not she was right was conjecture at this point. What's done is done. Besides, she was still here... for now, anyways.

She walked toward the room where the roll call was taken every morning. The sound of footsteps approaching fast behind her caused Marcie to turn her head. It was Mulvane, Rory, not the Chief. For a brief instant, their eyes met and held. His were unsmiling and cold, giving the impression he wasn't too happy to see her. But, hey, there was nothing unusual about that.

Rory was a typical male chauvinist who hadn't liked the idea of working with a woman from the moment they'd met. They'd bumped heads numerous times in the past.

He'd made a really nasty comment once. "If God had wanted you to be a man, O'Dwyer, He'd have given you real balls." Ironically being married to Angela, he no longer had any himself.

As she sat waiting for roll call, she looked over and saw Smith glaring at her. She recognized the controlled anger, his green eyes as hard as two emeralds fixed on her. Was he angry at her for not showing up at Lazy

Lou's to meet him last night or because she was still alive? Her thoughts were interrupted as Assistant Chief Wiebolt walked to the podium in the front of the room.

As the AC droned on, Marcie thought about all the other men sitting around her. Her assailant could be any one of them. Chasing the green was a very strong motive. Who among them didn't desire to possess nice things or want to pay their bills? Including herself, thinking about having to buy a new car.

Sitting there, she felt like a lamb amongst a pack of wolves. And one wolf would eventually emerge from the pack and try to kill her again. It was worse than waiting on death row. At least there you knew the exact hour you were going to die.

Since the day she watched the firefighter pull the trip box out of the burned rubble, she'd thought about little else. The consequences resulting from that action had dominated her waking as well as sleeping hours. She'd decided not to be an easy target. If one of these guys wanted to yank her plug, he was going to be in for a fight.

Marcie needed to call the insurance company, but had left all the information in the glove compartment of the rental. On her way back inside, a small cat came out of the bushes and brushed against her legs, meowing and purring its little head off. She bent and picked up the adorable ball of striped orange fur.

"Hello, fella. Hungry?"

She got a long purr in response. "I'll take that as a yes."

Marcie kept a quart of skim soy milk in the fridge for her coffee. It usually lasted the week since nobody else in the company liked it. Grabbing a bowl, she poured some milk and took it outside. The poor little thing was ravenous and lapped it up quickly, so she added more to the bowl. It finished that and walked away. She started to turn and take the milk back to the fridge, when out of the corner of her eye she saw the cat suddenly come to a stop and keel over. By the time she rushed over, the cat was dead. The implication wasn't lost on her. Somebody had poisoned her milk. Had she drank it, she might have been lying there on the cold, hard ground instead of the cat.

One question entered her mind. Had she only one strike left?

McGuiness, Mulvane, Smith and Marcie were dispatched to a home a few miles from the interstate where a five-year-old boy had fallen into a well. The rest of the squad went to put out a house fire. Riding over to the place, her own personal fear of possibly rubbing shoulders with her assailant had been replaced by another.

Abandoned wells scared her. She'd watched a childhood friend fall into one. There were a number of old unused wells in the area that had been covered and for the most part, forgotten. They remained a potential hazard for people and animals. Children, especially during play, were susceptible to falling into a well that had an unsecured cover or was in disrepair.

One of the most publicized accidents was that of Jessica McClure, the toddler who'd fallen into an abandoned well and was trapped for almost sixty hours. The sad part was, that accident, as well as so many others, could have been prevented by taking the precaution of properly sealing the well.

This accident proved no different. Had the unused shaft been adequately sealed, it wouldn't have happened. The cops had arrived on the scene first and gave the firefighters an update. They had to see the well before deciding how best to rescue the child. At this point nobody even knew if the child was hurt.

A frantic, middle-aged woman led them behind the house to where the well was located.

"I'd forgotten it was even there. Please help Peter," she cried.

"Was this the cover?" Smith pointed to a thin sheet of broken fiberglass.

The woman nodded, her chin quivering.

Over time, grass had grown over the well, hiding it from view. The opening was approximately 2 feet by 2 feet. They were faced with several problems. The most difficult was how to lift the little boy out. They couldn't just throw a rope down and tell the kid to grab onto it. One of them had to go down and retrieve him.

Since Marcie was the smallest, she'd have to be lowered into the well. The thought of being dangled by a rope by someone looking to kill her gave her pause. However, on the bright side, he wasn't alone. He wouldn't try anything stupid in front of the other two men, would he? She pushed that thought aside remembering the little boy down there who could be badly hurt. How could she refuse?

They tied the rope into a harness and lowered her slowly into the dark, gloomy hole. She aimed the flashlight into the blackness as she called out, "Peter!" When she got no reply, she feared the worst. Then she saw him, lying there in a fetal position.

"I see him," she spoke into her walkie-talkie. "I'm almost there."

Finally, Marcie's feet hit bottom and she rushed to the little boy. His eyes were closed and his thumb was in his mouth. He was very still—too still. Please God, let him be all right.

She ripped off her glove and touched his neck. It was cool, but she felt a pulse. The boy was alive!

Quietly she said, "Peter, I'm here to help you."

The boy's eyelids fluttered open. His eyes were wide with fear. Marcie gently touched his face.

"Are you hurt?"

"My arm hurts."

"Okay, kiddo, everything's gonna be all right," she tried to reassure him.

"Guys, he's alive, but hurt. Definitely a broken arm. I have to carry him up. I'll pull on the rope when we're ready." She spoke again to the little boy. "Peter, I'm going to pick you up now. Okay?" The child nodded. "Then I'll hold you and together we're going to be pulled out of here. Okay?"

His head moved again and she gently scooped him up and hung him over her shoulder. She saw him wince in pain, and he moaned as she got him into place and tugged on the rope. He whimpered as they were slowly lifted up to safety. When her head broke the surface, the grandmother let out a cry of relief.

A medic whisked the child from her arms and he was airlifted to a hospital. They later found out he'd suffered only a broken arm and some bruises. He was indeed, a lucky little boy.

The public needed to be informed about the dangers of abandoned wells. They needed to seal them adequately. Today they were lucky. It was tomorrow that worried Marcie. What if some child wasn't as lucky?

Chapter Twenty-eight

The Chief called Marcie into his office when she returned. She wondered if it was for more than to pat her on the back for doing a good job.

She knocked on the Chief's door.

"Enter!"

She poked her head inside. "You wanted to see me, sir?"

"Come inside, O'Dwyer, and shut the door. You did real good today."

"Thank you, sir. Is there something else?"

"Yeah, there is."

Marcie swallowed hard.

"A Detective Arnold filled me in about the little *adventure* you had last night. Why didn't you take his advice and go sun yourself in Florida?"

"With all due respect, sir, that would be running away. And I'm not a quitter."

"This isn't a game, Marcie."

"Believe me, sir, I know that."

"There's nothing I can do to help you change your mind?"

"No."

He gave out a sigh. "Just as well. You'll be giving your formal statement on Thursday."

Well, if things had been a little hairy up until now, Marcie could just imagine how they'd be after the hearing—that is, of course, if she lived long enough to be there. Just thinking about it gave her the willies.

"I'll be there, sir," she said, knowing it was fifty-percent bravado and the rest pure prayer.

She didn't tell him about the milk incident. In fact, no one else knew, except the killer. She rose from the seat and turned to leave.

"Oh, O'Dwyer, I don't have to tell you to be careful, do I?"

"Not anymore," she quipped. "It sort of comes with the territory, so to speak."

Marcie knew she had to get out of there before she fell apart. All the kidding around could only keep her together just so far.

He nodded and she skedaddled. She walked out of the Chief's office to find three pairs of eyes waiting for her. They belonged to Dodd, Mulvane and McGuiness.

"What's up, guys?"

Dodd, the spokesman of the group, said, "We think you deserve a pint on us tonight at O'Leary's."

"That's nice, but I'm a little out of sorts."

"If it's female troubles, we can put it off." Mulvane's voice was doused with syrupy sarcasm.

Marcie always hated when a guy tried to show how understanding he was about certain female *conditions* when he actually wasn't. Usually, he was silently cursing you and his bad timing. From Mulvane's tone, she'd gotten the distinct feeling this was one of those times. Looking Mulvane squarely in the eye, she clarified she was only very tired. After her drop in the well, it should have been easily understandable.

"Can I take a rain check?" she asked, walking away without waiting for an answer.

She wandered into the kitchen and poured herself a cup of coffee. They always kept a fresh pot on. She used the dry creamer that was kept on hand. For the moment, milk was off limits. The guys had been coming over to congratulate her on the rescue. If one more guy clapped her on the back, she'd be sore for a week.

Sitting with her coffee, Marcie took a few moments to reflect on life and her place in the universe. She felt she had free will and could basically decide how to live her life. But so did everyone else. Sometimes their decisions collided, causing conflict. Add to all those possibilities the fact that everyone's strings were held by a Grand Puppet Master sitting high above and it presented one giant dramatic crapshoot called life.

Thinking along those lines, she wondered if He had the next few moves worked out on His heavenly chessboard.

The fire bell sounded at 2:30 in the morning. It was a six-story walkup in a part of town that had seen more than its share of economic decline. Years back, there'd been a few weeks of unrest when civilians torched their own apartment buildings in disgust. The landlords hadn't kept up the maintenance, but continued to grab their rent. Frequently the heating and plumbing in the units were substandard at best and often on the fritz. As a result, the City had cracked down on delinquent landlords to avoid future occurrences, but there was still much to be done.

Multi-floored buildings were difficult fires to put out. The firefighters had to face a great number of unknown factors. If structural integrity was questionable, they had to be doubly careful of cave-ins. Another worrisome aspect was that usually the building occupancy standards exceeded their maximum limits.

The media was attracted to this kind of blaze like a moth to flame. It was simple economics. Disasters sold papers. Because of the coverage and potential political fallout, the Chief accompanied the squad to this fire and called the shots. He knew the mayor and possibly the DA would also show their faces. If it developed into a political football, he wanted to be in control and take it all the way to the goal line.

When Marcie and her squad arrived, the fire had overrun most of the first floor, causing sheer bedlam. A man who lived in a basement apartment had been awakened by smoke. He placed the 911 call. After he got his wife and three kids out to safety, he proceeded to knock on the doors of the other apartments in the basement and got those people out. He tried to alert the upper floors, but ran into trouble when he discovered the stairs, the only way up, were already ablaze.

Upper story occupants would have to jump from the windows into nets. One woman on the fourth floor was so frightened she jumped to her death without waiting for help. She'd been one of the few tenants still able to open her window. Over the years, most of the windows in these apartments had been painted shut, while others were covered by iron bars for protection. This meant they'd either have to use an acetylene torch on the bars or somehow get the civilians to the roof and take them down from there.

The Chief called for backup and two more companies responded. He'd stationed firemen around the perimeter of the building with nets and sent others inside to get people out of their apartments. It would be the call of the firefighters to decide what to do with the civilians once they found them. Even as the Chief barked orders, hoses had been hooked up to numerous fire hydrants and the building was being doused with water. It was going to be a long, cold morning.

Most of Marcie's squad went on the search and rescue mission. They climbed up to the second floor and smashed a window. Precious minutes were lost as they used the acetylene torch to remove the bars, but it had to be done. Marcie found people screaming in the halls. These were taken to the closest accessible window and were assisted to jump into a net. Then she, Dodd, Smith, Mulvane, McGuiness and the Assistant Chief went from apartment to apartment looking for civilians. Some people were so frightened they hid under beds.

Some time back, Dodd and Marcie were asked to speak to a group of elementary school kids. They'd reserved time at the end of the presentation for the kids to ask questions. One little girl stood and asked Marcie, "What do you think about when you run into a burning house?" Marcie told her she thought about the fire and what she had to do to put it out. All she focused on was that and everything that might be related to it, like saving a trapped person. Nothing else mattered. She'd tried to convey the idea that whatever personal problems you had took a back burner. All you saw and thought about was that fire. She hadn't been certain whether or not the child understood what she meant.

Now, this was exactly what Marcie was attempting

to do. She'd put her own personal fears about somebody wanting to remove her on the back burner. Like a robot, she performed her job trying to save as many people as possible.

They'd made it to the fourth floor. Dark acrid smoke filled the hall writhing about the ceiling like serpents. Marcie reached a door and pounded on it. No answer. She doubted the people were out of the apartment. Wanting to err on the side of precaution, she broke down the door and went inside to search for civilians. She heard someone come in after her.

She slowly turned and watched in horror as a fellow fireman charged at her with an axe.

Chapter Twenty-nine

For a split second, Marcie stood immobilized by shock watching him approach. But just as he reached her, axe poised to strike, another fireman appeared and tackled him from behind. The two men came down hard and the axe wedged into the flooring. They struggled, crashing into furniture and walls. Suddenly, the crying of children was heard from another room. This halted the fight momentarily, allowing one of the men to escape into the hall. Marcie ran in search of the children, while the other guy chased after the fleeing fireman.

She found two little girls huddled together under a bed.

"Come on out." She reached for them.

They were too frightened to move. She didn't have time to coax them out, so she lifted the bed off of them. Then she scooped them up and tried to open the windows in the room. They were stuck. She decided to carry the girls out and headed for the steps to the roof. She nearly collided in the hall with the other two firemen who were still fighting.

Then all hell broke loose as the ceiling collapsed, plummeting down on all of them.

When Marcie opened her eyes all she saw was white. The brightness caused her eyes to water and she squeezed them shut again, wondering if she were in heaven. Not completely certain she'd made the qualifying cut, she reopened her eyes as the white moved away. It had been the uniform of a nurse adjusting the IV bag hanging on the pole next to the hospital bed she lay in.

When the nurse noticed Marcie was conscious, she

gave her a hospital-approved smile. "Welcome back," she said as if Marcie had taken a vacation.

Marcie opened her mouth to speak. She wanted to ask the nurse if she'd had a nice time, but her throat felt as if she'd swallowed a wad of cotton balls and she couldn't speak.

"Would you like some water?"

Marcie nodded. The nurse poured water into a cup and added a flexible straw. It felt good and Marcie drank greedily, nearly choking.

"Slowly," the nurse cautioned. "I'll let the doctor know you're awake. He'll catch you up on things."

Just looking around, she was able to do some assessment on her own. Her left arm was in a cast and when she tried to move her head, the room spun like an amusement ride. She closed her eyes and tried to take deep breaths. The fact she could breathe easily with no pain meant she had no broken ribs.

Then she remembered the fire. Apprehension gripped her like a vise as she recalled holding the two little girls. Were they safe? She had to find out. And she hadn't been alone in the hall. The two firemen...they'd been fighting. What had happened to them? Better still, how long had she been here?

Her mother appeared at the door like an apparition. For Mom to be here, her accident had to have been serious. Hospitals terrified Catherine O'Dwyer. "Marcie, are you awake? The nurse told me you were conscious."

She came into the room and brought a chair close to the bed. "You scared me half out of my mind," she admonished. Vintage Mom—it was always about her, wasn't it?

"Mom, you know if I'm going to intentionally scare you, I'm not going to do a half-assed job."

"Always the smart mouth. How do you feel?"

"Like I belong here."

"Can't you ever be serious?" her mother said.

Marcie could see the dark circles of worry that hung like bags under her mother's eyes. She'd been worried enough and didn't need any more of her sarcasm. This was *déjà vu* for her mother, Marcie realized, thinking about her father. Funny how you tend to forget about those things.

"Sorry, Mom. Thanks for coming."

"That's what mothers do, Marcie."

The doctor, followed by the same nurse as before, walked into the room. Marcie's mother got up and moved the chair out of the way. He greeted her by name. They'd already met.

"Glad to see you've decided to finally rejoin us," the doctor said cheerfully. His tag read Adam Chandler. At least her eyes were working.

"I guess this is the part where I ask you what's wrong with me, right?"

He smiled. "Well, for starters, you're going to live to fight another fire."

Marcie heard her mother groan in the background. She rolled her eyes and the doctor picked up where he'd left off.

"You fractured your arm in a couple of places. We had to use pins to keep it in place."

"So I'm now bionic and will cause the alarms to go off in airports?"

Everyone laughed, except for Mother of course. Marcie saw her bury her head in her hands.

"You also have a large knot on the side of your head the size of an orange. Nothing to worry about. No brain swelling or bleeding. Actually, you're a very lucky young woman."

"I'm glad. What about the two children I was carrying? Do you know if they're okay?"

"They're fine. You protected them from the falling debris by covering them with your body."

"That's good, Doc. I was worried."

"Two other firefighters were brought in with you. One is in a coma, while the other should be released today."

"Do you know who they are?"

"The luckier one is the Chief's son...Rory Mulvane I believe. The other guy's Ray Smith."

Before she realized it, she'd said, "Poor Smith. Is *he* going to be all right?"

"Time will tell."

The nurse moved closer to wipe the tears that had slipped from Marcie's eyes. She hadn't realized she'd started crying.

"I'll check in on you later," Dr. Chandler said.

She thanked him as he walked away, then closed her eyes.

The nurse told Marcie to ring for her if she needed anything. She, too, left the room.

Catherine O'Dwyer walked over to the bed and called Marcie's name softly.

Her eyes fluttered open. "I know how hard it was for you to come, Mom. Thanks."

"I'm going to let you rest. I'll be back tomorrow."

"Mom, you don't have to. I mean, there's no need to come every day."

"It's easier now that I know you're going to be okay. Feel good, Marcie." Her mother leaned over and kissed Marcie's forehead. She smelled of wildflowers. Come to think of it, she'd always worn that perfume. For the moment, it made Marcie feel good. She closed her eyes and must have dozed off.

When she reopened them, her mother was gone.

Chapter Thirty

Dodd, DiMaggio and Ed Clark came to see her. Tethered to a hospital bed, Marcie realized time had a way of slipping away. From the shadows on the wall she guessed it was late afternoon. They'd brought her a pile of magazines and books.

"How long do you think I'm going to be here, guys? Oh, I get it now. You want me to stay here indefinitely. I thought you missed me."

They knew she was goofing with them and Dodd replied, "Yeah, we miss that convoluted sarcastic wit of yours. Don't we guys?"

DiMaggio made a motion as if he were going to throw up. Everyone laughed. After that the conversation turned serious.

"How are you feeling, O'Dwyer? For real," Clark asked.

"I'm not sure. They keep pumping meds into me."

"Heard you've gone bionic," DiMaggio added.

"Just a couple of pins. Boy, those nurses have loose lips."

"Just takes a few hunks like us," he replied.

Marcie laughed. She needed a good laugh. Her mind was still more like mush than anything else, since she first opened her eyes and discovered she was in the hospital. But it was still a whole lot better than the alternative.

She wanted to ask them about Smith and Mulvane. She also wondered if the fact she'd been stalked and nearly killed had become common knowledge around the house yet. Even though she hadn't told anyone, she knew it was hard to keep things under wraps for very long. There was no way she could ask without opening the proverbial can of worms, though in this case the can would probably contain venomous snakes. Then Dodd brought up Smith.

"You heard about Smith, right?" Dodd casually asked.

"The doctor told me he's in a coma. Has there been any change?"

"You sound awfully concerned for someone who tried to kill you," DiMaggio spoke up.

"What...? Who...who told you this?" Suddenly she felt as if she'd been mowed down by a fire truck. Then the image of a fireman coming at her with an axe replayed in her mind. Had that been Smith?

"Mulvane told the Chief from his hospital bed," Clark said.

"He's in the hospital, too?" she asked, trying to hold onto everything they were telling her, not trusting her drugged mind.

"No, he was lucky. Had a few bruises. Smith was on top of him and got the brunt of the falling debris," Clark added.

"Wait a sec. Go back to the part about Smith. Mulvane told the Chief that Smith attacked me?"

"Yeah. That's what he said. Don't you remember?" Clark asked.

"Does she sound like she's functioning on all her cylinders, let alone remember what happened?" Dodd asked.

"Well, whether she remembers or not, that's what's going around the house," DiMaggio said. "And only three people know the truth, you, Mulvane and Smith. And Smith is down for the count and he ain't talkin'."

Either the painkillers had begun to wear off or the possibility Smith was actually her assailant caused the dull throb in her head to vibrate like a gong struck by a heavy mallet. Not being content with just targeting one area, the pain shot down her left side. It felt as if her entire body were on fire. Perhaps she moaned involuntarily or her face registered pain. Whatever, the guys took the hint.

"I think we've stayed too long, O'Dwyer," Dodd said.

"We'll come see you again."

Marcie nodded and somehow muttered, "Thanks," before she hit the call button for the nurse.

In her drug-laden mind, she, Smith and Mulvane rode a carousel. Round and round they went, trying to keep their balance without falling off. None of this made any sense. Then out of nowhere, the Chief appeared and clobbered her over the head with an axe.

Whoever thought drugs were cool had obviously taken too many.

Marcie wasn't certain whether she sensed someone in her room or just happened to wake up. When she did, a voice said, "Good to see you awake, O'Dwyer."

It was the Chief. She looked to see if he had an axe with him. He didn't.

"How are you feeling?"

"As good as one can feel with a broken arm after having a ceiling fall on their head," she said. "However, the doctor has assured me I'm going to live."

An amused look formed across the Chief's face. Even the usual deep crease between his bushy brows momentarily grew smooth. At least her glib answer didn't anger him. It just slipped out—with the drugs and all. Usually, she was more formal—and a great deal more careful.

"That's good to hear, O'Dwyer, because you can also breathe easier now. We've got the guy."

"The arsonist?" she asked.

"Who also just happens to be the guy who tried to push you into the ravine," he added.

"Who is it, sir?"

"Ray Smith. I thought you knew already."

Marcie shook her head, unable to find the words to describe what she felt.

"You know, O'Dwyer..."

"What, sir?" she asked, finally able to speak.

"I find the entire situation unbelievable," he said.

You're not the only one, she wanted to say, but didn't. "Why's that?" She was still reeling over the fact he'd just declared Smith an arsonist.

"I thought you two were an item."

"Short fling. We took the dislike, fight, dislike route. You obviously hadn't noticed we'd moved on to the latter phase. But, sir..."

"What's on your mind, O'Dwyer? You should be beaming from ear-to-ear."

"It's this...I don't think Smith is an arsonist and—"

"Do you recall anything before the ceiling caved in?"

"Yes, but I don't know who came at me—or who came to my rescue."

Marcie thought she detected a glimmer of relief pass over his expression after she told him that. Keeping things in perspective, she hadn't forgotten, despite everything, Rory Mulvane was still his son and his flesh and blood.

"Then with Rory's testimony, we can put this entire affair to bed and get on with our lives." He punctuated the statement with a smile.

Marcie realized it would be futile to debate with the man. He'd already made up his mind. She decided to let the subject drop for now.

He stood to leave. "You get well soon, O'Dwyer."

She managed a smile and nodded.

He returned her gesture and strode from the room. Marcie was glad to see him go. She needed to think. A ton of unanswered questions clamored around in her drug-impaired brain. One thing she was damn certain of. If Smith woke up and she was able to ask him what happened, she might get a totally new perspective of the incident. And it would be his word against Mulvane's. Somehow, she'd be inclined to believe Smith, for if track record accounts for anything, when did Mulvane ever risk his neck for anyone? She recalled again the poker game where her father and some other firefighters had discussed Rory and Jimmy Mulvane.

She'd bet a year's salary Rory *did not* rush in after Smith to save her. Okay, to be honest, unless Smith came out of his coma and confessed, she'd never believe he tried to kill her. Even if he wanted to, would he have chosen to do it then? Smith was a true fireman, through and through. He'd save the civilians first. And then take care of her.

Marcie suddenly recalled something that occurred while she and Smith were out on a date early in their relationship. They were having dinner at Lazy Lou's when a commotion at a table a short distance away caught his eye. He vaulted out of his chair and rushed over. A young boy around seven was choking. In a time when frivolous lawsuits were on the rise causing most doctors to shy away from helping strangers, Smith dove right in with both feet, never considering the repercussions.

He grabbed the kid and performed the Heimlich maneuver on him. Marcie had followed him over to lend her help if necessary. However, hers was superfluous. Smith had dislodged the chunk of steak from the child's windpipe. It flew across the table and landed with a plop onto the plate of the child's panic stricken mother. Marcie nervously looked around for any ambulance chasing lawyers lurking in the area hoping for cracked ribs. The parents were more than grateful and decided to take their pale, but lucky to be alive, child home. The dinner had been in celebration of his sixth birthday. Marcie was certain it would be one he'd always remember.

Even if she didn't still have some feelings left for the guy, Marcie didn't think Smith could change in character any more than Mulvane could. She doubted her breaking up with him would drive him to murder. Stalking was one thing, murder was something else entirely.

Marcie was aware she wasn't a great thinker. Throw in the painkillers, and her thought processes might be a little fuzzy, but at that moment she realized something crucial. As long as Smith remained in a coma, there was no one to refute Mulvane's version of what had taken place at that fire. She certainly couldn't. That meant Mulvane wouldn't want Smith to recover. Taking this idea one step further, if Mulvane was capable of murder, why would one more added to his list matter? What would stop him from killing Smith, to prevent him from talking?

Slow down, girl, she counseled herself. This was all supposition. What if one guy were the arsonist and the other guy the stalker? Couldn't that be possible? If you want to go there, her inner voice cautioned, anything is possible at this point in your befuddled mind.

One thing bothered her the most, though. If Smith were innocent and had gone after Mulvane to save her, then if he died, his noble actions would be the direct cause of his death. Would she be able to live with such guilt?

Marcie knew the answer despite her drug-sodden mind. She had to learn the truth. But first she had to get out of this damned hospital bed.

The wheels of the dinner cart clattered on the tile floor outside her room, waking her. When the last tendrils of sleep had fled from her eyes, she noticed her intravenous drip had been removed. On what planet had she been when they did this? Despite her bewilderment, she realized the implication of being served food and took it as a good sign she was closer to getting released.

She raised the bed and drew the table closer to her. She opened the cover and stared at what they'd given her for dinner. It appeared to be some kind of mystery meat stew on a bed of wide noodles. Whether or not it looked appetizing, she had to eat. Getting out of here was her main goal. As she continued to inspect the food on the tray, Dr. Chandler strolled in as if he were taking a constitutional. He had a smile on his round, boyish looking face reminding her of a cuddly cherub. She was tempted to ask him if he ever moonlighted on Valentine's Day.

"I'm glad to see you awake and alert, Marcie," he said as he whipped out his penlight and peered into her eyes, one at a time.

"That makes two of us. When can I make my great

escape?"

"I see no reason why you can't go home tomorrow."

Her mind did mental cartwheels of joy, since her body couldn't. "Good call, Doc."

"Speaking of call, make one to your mother. Tell her early afternoon."

The man had a sense of humor. That was a big plus in her book.

He turned to leave. "And don't forget to eat up."

Yup, he was a funny man, all right.

The following morning, Marcie got out of bed after some trial and tribulation. She finally succeeded in making it to the bathroom and back without taking a header. A faint throb still thrummed in her head along with some dizziness, but she could deal with it. However, the cast made her feel terribly unbalanced. She sometimes felt as if she were going to keel over. Her mother was bringing her clothes, and they'd have to fit whatever top she brought around her arm. She had a sling to wear to help her manage, but she didn't relish the idea of having to wear a cast for six or more weeks.

Her mother had brought a bathrobe the day before. Marcie draped it around her as best as she could and decided to go in search of Smith. She slowly raised herself out of bed, using the chair for leverage. Resting against it, she stood taking deep breaths as she tried to regain her strength. She had to step slowly in order to keep her balance. She felt as though she were walking with a book perched on her head. The damn cast had to be gotten used to.

Taking baby steps Marcie made her way to the door and poked her head out of the room. She knew Smith was somewhere on this floor, but had no idea where. She began to read the names from the cards on the doors of the rooms she passed, hoping to find him before her strength gave out. On the fourth door she read Smith's name and walked inside. Her eyes nearly popped out of her head when she saw the chair next to Smith's bed was occupied.

Chapter Thirty-one

The same pretty, dark-haired woman Marcie had seen kissing Smith the night of his birthday sat by him, holding his hand. Her first instinct was to turn around and go straight back to her room. The second one, which came to mind, was to slug her. Of course, in her present condition, Marcie had to rethink that one. With a new tear in her heart, she turned to leave and nearly lost her balance. She braced herself against the door to avoid falling.

"Don't go." The woman said, evidently having noticed her. Marcie wasn't surprised. She'd made enough noise. However, she didn't need more hurt and had no desire to talk to this woman.

"Please, come inside," the woman said in a soft pleasant voice. It wasn't the voice of someone merely looking to gloat.

Marcie felt at a disadvantage. It almost seemed as if the woman knew who Marcie was and had been waiting for her. Or was Marcie reading into this? Whatever, her curiosity drew her to the stranger like a magnet? The woman's dark eyes were moist and filled with sadness. She obviously loved Smith very much.

"Please don't go, *Marcie*," she pleaded. Calling her by name rooted Marcie to the spot.

"How do you know who I am?"

"You're exactly as Ray described you to me. Beautiful, red hair and eyes as blue as the sky."

"Smith told you that?" Marcie stammered, more surprised than anything else.

"On more than one occasion."

Why would Smith talk about an old girlfriend to a new one? Is she that much in love with him and secure with his love that she can bear to hear him praise an old girlfriend? Marcie wouldn't have tolerated her guy spewing the wonderful charms of an ex lover. No self-respecting woman could.

Totally amazed and at a loss for words, she merely nodded and asked how Smith was doing. His head was bandaged and the betadine solution had stained his forehead orange. It was the only color on his waxen complexion.

"Each day that he remains in a coma, his prognosis worsens."

Marcie felt a sharp pain in her chest. It only confirmed what she already knew about comas. Though she tried so very hard not to ask the one question which was ripping her to shreds inside, it came tumbling out.

"How long have you and Smith been seeing each other?"

The woman laughed and shook her head.

"You find that funny?"

"You've got it all wrong. Smith told me you were headstrong and stubborn, but—"

"But what?" Marcie interrupted, fuming now. If the woman kept this up, Marcie was going to clobber her with her cast.

"But, I never thought you'd carry things this far."

"Lady, what the hell are you talking about?"

"My name is Carol Rogers. My maiden name is Smith."

"How can that be? Your mother killed you in the fire."

"You can obviously see it wasn't me."

"So who died instead of you?" Marcie asked, without hiding the accusation in her voice.

"My cousin."

"Why should I believe you?" Marcie asked as she stood there looking at her through narrowed eyes. Just because she said her maiden name was Smith didn't necessarily prove to Marcie it was.

The woman read the disbelief in Marcie's eyes and removed her purse from the nightstand and opened it. She pulled a small, worn photograph from her wallet and handed it to her. Marcie had seen a similar one in Smith's place of him and his brother and sisters. Even so, she could have gotten it from Smith. When doubt still lingered on Marcie's face, Carol Rogers sharpened her tone.

"Why would I lie? What motive could I possibly have to pretend to be Ray's sister?"

Putting it that way, if possession is nine-tenths of the law, Carol already had Smith. No need to pretend anything to anyone. News stories are often wrong. Marcie, of all people, knew that. When she received a medal of valor from the mayor, the name under the photo had been written as Marcy O'Leary. The newspaper had to print an apology in the following issue.

"My brother and I waited two hours for you to show the other night. You could have had the decency to let him know you weren't coming."

"Believe it or not, I was on my way when someone tried to push me off the bridge on Narrows Road into the ravine below. Luckily, only my Jeep hit bottom."

Carol sighed heavily. "I wish he'd known before this happened," she said, tenderly touching his face.

Marcie understood what she meant and felt the same way. As she stood there, she was so overcome by guilt, she nearly lost her balance. Carol jumped from the chair to steady her.

"Here, Marcie, why don't you sit down?" She helped Marcie into another chair.

"I feel so awful. I should have believed him." Hot tears slipped down Marcie's cheeks. She looked at Smith lying there so still, like some wax figure from the Madame Tussaud's museum.

"My brother loves you very much. You were the one girl who got under his skin."

That statement hit Marcie funny, making her giggle. "Oh, boy, did I get under his skin," she replied, thinking of all the irritation she must have caused him before remembering it was a two-way street.

Then with a half-smile, Carol added, "But he did say

he was never bored when you were around. You made each new day special."

As Marcie looked at Smith, she thought of Snow White lying in her glass coffin. All it took to bring her back to life was a kiss from Prince Charming. Marcie doubted he'd want a kiss from a prince. She reached for his hand and kissed it. After hearing his sister talk, she knew there was no way Smith tried to hurt her. Now she was positive Rory Mulvane had lied. And if worried before for Smith's safety, she was now frantic.

"Carol there's something you should know."

"What's wrong?"

"Are you aware the Fire Chief's son has concocted a story blaming Smith for arson and trying to kill me?"

She looked at Marcie as if she had two heads instead of one. "That's preposterous!"

"Just as I thought."

"But how could any of it be true?" she protested. "He loved his job—and you..."

"Only three people know that—me, Smith and Mulvane. Smith can't talk and I had no idea who tried to kill me—until now. Since the guy has tried to kill me twice and now that I know Smith was with you at Lazy Lou's during the attempt at the bridge, that leaves Mulvane. But Mulvane doesn't know I figured this out."

Carol's face drained quickly of color as she followed what Marcie was saying. "That would mean...if this Mulvane thinks my brother's a risk, he might try to kill him, right?"

Marcie nodded. "Not if *I* can help it."

"What can *you* do?" she asked.

"I'm going to talk to Detective Arnold. Maybe he can keep tabs on Mulvane or place a guard outside this door."

"You think it'll help?" Carol asked, hope sounding in her voice.

"I won't know until I talk to the guy. But, one thing I *do* know."

"What's that?"

"Doing nothing is worse."

Marcie stood and leaned over. Balancing herself by her good arm, she kissed Smith's lips. She'd forgotten how good they tasted. As she pulled away, she thought she saw his eyelids flutter. Probably wishful thinking and nothing else.

"Would you mind staying with Ray for a few minutes? I'd like to go down and grab a sandwich or something."

"Go ahead, I'll wait for you to return." Marcie was glad to have a few moments alone with Smith.

When Carol was gone, Marcie leaned closer to Smith and covered his flaccid hand with hers once again. A half-smile covered her face as she recalled how this very hand had touched her, on many occasions, making her quiver with delight.

"I owe you an apology, Smith. I jumped to my usual harebrained conclusions. You were right; I can be pigheaded at times. But believe me; I've never stopped loving you, though, of course, I'd never tell you that. Come back to me and love me again. I promise—no I swear—I'll never let you go. I know about Mulvane. Rest assured I'll find some way to deal with him. If he harms one hair on your head, I'll kill him myself. Just wake up. Please, baby. I need you! I never knew how much until now. I love you, Smith. Don't leave me now. Please!"

She laid her head on his chest and let the tears flow as she prayed for him. A thought occurred to her as she listened to the shallow rhythm of his heartbeat. Her father would have really liked him.

"I'm back," Carol said, walking over to the bed.

"What time is it?" Marcie quickly wiped her eyes with her good hand as she lifted her head.

"Eleven-twenty."

"Look, I've got to go back to my room. My mother's coming to take me home. I'll let you know what the detective says."

"What should I do in the meantime?" Carol's face was full of worry.

"Sit tight. Mulvane's next day off is in two days. That's when things could turn nasty—especially if Smith wakes up."

Carol turned to look at her brother and sighed. She gazed back at Marcie. "I'm glad we finally got to meet, Marcie O'Dwyer."

Still subdued, Marcie nodded. "Me, too."

Chapter Thirty-three

By the time Marcie got back to her room, her mother had already been there, dropped off a bag of clothing, and left. She found her at the nurses' station making a general nuisance of herself, complaining about her daughter being lost. Marcie went over and grabbed Catherine O'Dwyer's arm, stopping her diatribe in mid-sentence. The two nurses sitting behind the desk looked more than relieved to see her.

"And where the devil have you been?" her mother scolded.

"I stopped in to see Smith."

Upon hearing Smith's name, her mother's face softened. "How is he?"

"Pretty much the same."

"Such a shame...a nice handsome boy like him."

The way she said it, Marcie wondered if she'd care about his health and well-being if he wore glasses and had an overbite. Whatever, it wasn't in the least important.

"Look, Mom, I've got to get out of here."

"You sound as if you've been locked up for years. Think about poor Smith."

"I am. That's why I've got to leave." Marcie nudged her in the direction of her room.

"Marcie, I can live another hundred years and still won't understand you."

"I'll explain when we get there."

"Where?"

"My room, Mom."

While her mother helped her dress, Marcie told her about Mulvane and the danger Smith was in. Her mother's eyes immediately widened like saucers, her face as white as a tablecloth for them to rest on.

"Is any of this part of your job description?" she asked. "You know how much I hate what you do and now you have all this to contend with. Is it worth it?"

Marcie looked at her mother. "Mom, I love Smith and I'll never be able to live or forgive myself if anything happens to him. Damn it! It's *my* fault he's in there lying like a vegetable in the first place."

She collapsed onto the bed. The outburst had momentarily sapped her strength. Catherine sat down next to her and put her arm around her shoulder. She kissed Marcie's head. "Okay. What do you want to do?"

"Take me to the police."

Of course her mother exacted her price for her aid. Marcie agreed to stay with her mother until she was self-sufficient again. Since Catherine was willing to help her, it was a small price to pay. Besides, she needed someone to help her dress.

The orderly came with the wheelchair and together they descended in the elevator to the main lobby where the orderly waited with Marcie until her mother drove the car up under the portico. Catherine O'Dwyer parked at the curb and the orderly, a young man with biceps the size of basketballs, helped Marcie out of the chair and into the car. When she thanked him, he gave her a huge smile filled with large white teeth, saluted and hurried inside.

"Are you certain you want to go straight to the police station?" her mother asked.

"Time is a factor, Mom."

She nodded and started the engine. Marcie felt safe enough to tell her the entire story. Catherine's face grew pale again, but she didn't take her eyes off the road.

"Why didn't you tell me any of this before?"

"Why upset you needlessly?"

"I'm your mother, Marcie."

"What could you have done? Besides, I know how much you hate my job."

"With good reason!"

"Still, I love my job and I'm able to make a difference."

"Not if you're hurt, or God-forbid killed," she sniped, the barb hitting its mark.

"I know. Believe me, I know. This will all be over soon."

Her mother sighed.

Detective Arnold took one look at Marcie. "*This* is how you take care?"

Ignoring his remark, she introduced him to her mother.

"Pleased to meet you, Mrs. O'Dwyer. Do you know what your daughter does for a living?" His idea of a joke.

"Don't remind me."

"What can I do for you, Ms. O'Dwyer?"

"Has Chief Mulvane spoken to you?"

"He seems to feel we got the guy behind everything."

"He wants to believe that, but he of all people should know better."

"What do you mean?" Arnold shifted his massive body weight forward.

"Rory Mulvane is the Chief's son. I think he has a gambling problem which led him to accept money in exchange for arson."

"Do you have proof of this?"

"Nothing tangible. Just things I've heard. But, if track record counts for anything, Rory Mulvane wouldn't save his own mother if his life depended on it. He didn't rush in to save me at the fire. He was the one who tried to kill me. It was Smith who tried to save me."

"Are you certain?" he asked, his eyes cold and hard as pebbles. "You said you couldn't recognize the guy."

"I'd bet my life on it."

"You may very well be doing just that." His eyes narrowed as he looked at Marcie.

"And Smith's. As long as he's breathing, he can come out of the coma and tell his side of what happened. I doubt if Mulvane will risk that."

Detective Arnold quickly realized what was at stake. "We can put a man on the door under the pretense of keeping Smith from escaping and perhaps catch Mulvane if he tries anything."

"At least Smith will be safe. Thank you."

He nodded. Marcie began to rise out of her chair. Her mother had to steady it from toppling over.

"Nice meeting you, Mrs. O'Dwyer."

"Same here," she replied.

"Oh...and Mrs. O' Dwyer...try to keep an eye on her."

"I intend to, Detective."

Chapter Thirty-four

Marcie called Carol at Smith's place later that night to tell her about the police guard. However, she was more concerned about how Smith was doing. If it were at all possible, Marcie wouldn't have left his side.

"No, the police hadn't arrived while I was there," Carol said.

"I was hoping the detective would have sent a guy over immediately."

"Look, I don't want to get your hopes up—"

"What happened? Did he wake up?" Marcie's heart banged against her chest.

"No, but Ray's eyelids fluttered. At first I thought I'd imagined it. But, he did it again. And—"

"What? Please tell me!"

"His fingers twitched as I held his hand."

"Oh, that's marvelous!" Marcie cried into the phone. "He could be coming out of it."

"Yes. Will you be by tomorrow?"

"Even if I have to walk," Marcie replied. "Good night, Carol."

Carol wished her a good night as well.

Marcie's heart had lightened with the new knowledge Smith might be coming out of the coma. Now she knew she hadn't imagined the fluttering of his eyelids earlier. However, there was a slight damper on the good news. He was going to be in a lot more danger when he regained consciousness.

The following morning Catherine had errands to run so she dropped Marcie off at the hospital, intending to come back for her in the afternoon. That worked for

Marcie and she was greeted by a policeman outside Smith's door. Detective Arnold had kept his promise.

Carol had already arrived by the time Marcie walked into Smith's room. She smiled brightly when she saw it was Marcie.

"You're here early," Marcie said.

"What else do I have to do? My husband, Steve, says everything's okay back home and the kids hardly know I'm gone."

"Like you might believe that."

"No. Steve can handle them. If not, I'd have gone home by now."

"That's good. Smith needs you."

"And you," she added. "I think hearing your voice helped."

They both turned at the sound of the bed linens ruffling. Smith was moving his legs. The two women gasped collectively. Marcie felt tears of joy welling up in her eyes.

"Come on, baby! That's it. You've slept enough," she said breathless with excitement.

Smith's eyes slowly fluttered open. He turned in their direction and smiled. Marcie's heart nearly exploded with delight. Without a doubt, Carol shared her happiness.

"My two favorite girls," he said in a hoarse voice.

"Then you forgive me?" Marcie rushed to offer him some water with a flexible straw.

"Help me sit up," he replied, not answering her question.

Marcie helped lift him with her good arm, as Carol tucked pillows behind to make him more comfortable.

Carol smiled at her brother and said, "Thanks for the memories, kid."

He tried to laugh, but instead began to cough. Marcie grabbed the glass again and held the straw to his lips and he sucked in more water. When the coughing subsided, he lay back against the propped pillows. Marcie was so glad her prayers had been answered and Smith was awake, she didn't care if he ever forgave her.

If that were the price she had to pay for his recovery, she'd learn to deal with it.

"You don't have to talk now," Marcie said.

"Want to."

"Maybe you should rest."

"Enough rest. Where's Mulvane?" he asked, causing the temperature of the room to plunge.

"I don't know. You have a guard stationed outside your room."

"Mulvane tried to kill you. Why?"

Marcie realized Smith had no idea of the events that had transpired leading up to the attempt on her life at the fire. She told him about having seen Mulvane remove the trip box and going to the Chief with the info. He sighed. She was certain pieces of the puzzle clicked into place for him as she spoke.

"I have to get out of here."

"Not until the doctor says you can leave," Carol said with an older sister's authority.

As if on cue, Dr. Chandler and a nurse walked in. Like the MasterCard commercials on TV, the looks on their faces were priceless. However, the doctor, with his keen sense of humor, had a quick comeback.

"So, you've had enough rest, Mr. Smith, and decided to get back on the roller coaster, huh?" The doctor used his penlight to peer into each of Smith's eyes and checked the glands in his neck.

Marcie expected Smith to say something sarcastic in reply, but he only smirked.

"Before I release you, I want to run several tests to make sure you're okay. Hopefully, you won't need rehabilitation."

A playful thought ran through Marcie's mind. She'd like to give Smith her own brand of rehab. On a more serious note, she realized he hadn't tried to walk yet. Having been in a coma for a few days, his muscles had to have weakened.

"If everything goes well, I'll have you out of here in a day or so."

"Thank you, Dr. Chandler," Smith said, reading his name tag.

"You're very welcome, Mr. Smith. I'll have you know you were my quietest patient."

A collective groan answered his levity.

"Okay, Allison, I guess that was our cue to leave and continue our rounds," the doctor replied.

Marcie didn't care how long it took Smith to recover. He'd come back to her. She intended to honor her apology and make up for all the lost time. And she pledged to never lose him again—if he'd take her back, of course.

Carol decided to go for a walk to stretch her legs and Marcie was thrilled to finally be alone with Smith. She had the distinct impression Carol was providing time for them to clear the air. Right after she left, Smith closed his eyes and looked as if he were going to sleep again. Tired, he catnapped frequently. It was understandable. He'd been through a great deal of trauma. Obviously, Marcie had a harder head than he did. She certainly proved to be more stubborn, anyway. She figured she'd let him sleep and started to move away from the bed.

He reached out and touched her arm. "No. Don't go, O'Dwyer. Not yet."

She turned and looked directly into his green jewels. Instantly her eyes filled with tears.

"I'm truly sorry, Smith. I should have believed you."

"I wasn't Jack."

She nodded. "I know that—now."

"He must have hurt you terribly. I'd never do what he did."

"Because you don't like men?"

He tried to laugh, but ended up choking. His face turned blue, alarming her. She fumbled with the water carafe pouring more water on the table than in the glass. She held the glass for him with her bad arm and positioned his head better with the other so he could drink. Being one armed was definitely making her life more difficult.

After he'd settled back down again, he asked, "Tell me, O'Dwyer, did you come here to kill me?"

Marcie knew he said it in jest, but she gave a serious reply as tears suddenly filled her eyes. "No, Smith, if I could turn the hands of time back to the way we were, I'd do it in a heartbeat."

"We can't do that."

She felt her heart crash and burn when he said that. He didn't love her anymore. How could she blame him? It was her own stupid fault.

"But we can go on and make it better."

At first she wasn't certain she'd heard him correctly. But he smiled at her and touched her arm.

"I had a dream, O'Dwyer. You were with me and told me how much you loved me. I knew it was a dream, because you told me how stupid and pigheaded you are."

The 'dream' depicted her heart-to-heart with him yesterday. Could he have been semiconscious? She decided to let it remain a dream.

"Okay, what else did I tell you in this dream?"

"You told me if I came back to you, you'd never let me go again. Is that true?"

Marcie gave him a crooked little smile. "It works for me."

"Good, I'm just checking."

Fresh tears filled her eyes. "I love you, Smith. It took nearly losing you to make me realize how much."

"I'll keep you reminded."

"I'm sure you will." She bent and kissed his lips.

"Sorry to interrupt," Carol said as she walked in holding a cup of coffee for Marcie. "Lunch is on its way for you, Ray."

Marcie knew they had more serious issues to discuss before her mother came to get her and asked, "What about Mulvane?"

"Didn't you mention that the detective was going to leave the guard outside my brother's room?" Carol asked Marcie.

"He mentioned he'd try to keep him there as long as he could spare the manpower. I hope he wasn't just humoring me. I'll rip him another—"

"Now that's the woman we all know and love," Smith interjected. "As for Mulvane, let him come. I'll give him a warm reception."

Carol looked at her brother and then Marcie as if they were both crazy. "All this stupid, macho banter. Neither one of you is able to fend off this guy. We need an armed policeman."

Marcie realized she was right. Smith needed time to strengthen his muscles that hadn't been used in days. And she was just as useless. Everyone looked toward the door. People were approaching, their voices echoing off the walls of the corridor. Smith had visitors.

Chapter Thirty-five

Well, if they wanted to keep Smith's recovery a secret, that idea had gone up in smoke. DiMaggio and Maguire, along with Mulvane at their side, sauntered in. Marcie detected a fleeting look on Mulvane's face which didn't equate as happiness for Smith. He probably surmised Smith had told her what had happened by now. More than ever, they needed official protection for Smith.

A nurse with a policeman in tow entered the room. "So we're having a party, are we? How you all managed to get up here is beyond me, but hospital policy is still two people max. I don't care who leaves, but when I return, that's all I better see in here."

"You heard the nurse," the officer piped up. "Let's clear out the room."

"We'll be going," Mulvane spoke up for all the firefighters. "We just wanted to check on him. Make certain he was okay." He smiled and saluted Smith.

"Thanks for stopping by, guys," Smith said.

"We miss you around the house," DiMaggio replied.

"Yeah, things aren't the same without you both," added Maguire.

Marcie noticed how the cop looked at Mulvane. He obviously knew who he was having been briefed by Detective Arnold. He remained after the firemen left.

"Are we glad to see you," Marcie said, breathing a deep sigh of relief. "I thought maybe Detective Arnold had forgotten."

"My name's John Newell. I'll be guarding the room tonight."

"The detective briefed you?"

He nodded. "In my experience, if this guy intends to make a move, it'll be tonight."

"It makes sense. Now that I'm conscious, he has to assume I'll be out of here soon," Smith said.

"Why not wait until you're alone, like Marcie was?" Carol asked.

Marcie added her two-and-a-half cents to the mix. "Either way is possible. He may try tonight and if he fails or changes his mind, go to plan B."

"If he does make his move, I'll be here," the young officer assured them.

"Marcie, are you ready to leave?" her mother said from behind.

No one had heard her come in. Her face brightened when she saw Smith sitting up and very much awake.

"It's so very good to see you feeling better, Ray," she said.

"Why, thank you, Mrs. O'Dwyer," he said politely.

They had their own mutual admiration society. Marcie introduced Carol and the policeman to her mother. Then she kissed Smith and Carol goodbye. She was a nice person and in the short time she'd known his sister, they had bonded. Though she felt a great deal better knowing Officer Newell was there, Marcie couldn't shake the apprehension that had settled deep within her.

The oversized cast had made it difficult to find a comfortable position, but Marcie eventually fell into an exhausted sleep. She dreamed she stood in a field of lilies surrounded by a dozen churches on a Sunday morning. Suddenly, all the church bells began to peal. Marcie covered her ears.

The noise continued. Finally, she poked her head out from under the pillow and realized her cell phone was chirping. The clock on the nightstand glared 2:45 in bold green numbers. Who on earth would be calling at this ungodly hour?

"'Lo?" she managed to say.

"Ms. O'Dwyer, Detective Arnold—"

"Don't you ever sleep? You a robot or something?"

"I wish. Look, I just got word from Newell that

Mulvane made an attempt on Ray Smith's life—"

"Is Smith okay?"

"Yes, but Mulvane might be headed your way."

"What happened?" The last remnants of fog cleared from her head. She was now fully awake and trembling. Too bad the cause wasn't from the chill in the room. A bathrobe could cure that.

"Mulvane distracted the officer on guard by setting up a smoke bomb in an empty storage closet down the hall. The officer went down to see where the smoke was coming from. Upon opening the door and not seeing any flames, he realized he'd been duped. He rushed back to Smith's room to find the two men struggling. Mulvane nearly put Newell through the wall trying to get out of there."

"Mulvane got away."

"Yeah. There's an APB out on him."

"You think he may come after me?"

"There's a chance, though if he's got any brains, he'll get lost. I had a car placed out front of your mother's place."

She shifted her weight and nearly rolled off the bed in order to look out the window. Sure enough, a patrol car was parked across the street. She couldn't say she'd ever seen a more beautiful sight.

Marcie thanked the detective and tried to go back to sleep, which proved impossible. Her mind was too wired to shut down. Apprehension kept her from relaxing. And she was sick at heart for endangering her mother and grandfather.

Chapter Thirty-six

Mulvane must have high-tailed it out of town as fast as he could. Angie swore to the police she had no idea where her husband was. For the following few weeks the police kept an eye on her activities in case Mulvane tried to contact her. But, wherever he was hiding out, he appeared to be staying put. Never knowing if and when he'd show up was like hoping a warranty didn't run out before something broke down.

In the meantime, the hospital released Smith and he began physical therapy to tone his unused muscles. Carol returned home to her family and Marcie hated to see her leave. She seemed more of an older sister than Eileen ever was.

Since both Marcie and Smith were on medical leave, they had lots of time to get *reacquainted*. Thanks to her cast, Marcie was more than certain they'd added a new position or two to the Kama Sutra.

One beautiful spring morning Smith picked Marcie up at her mother's and they stopped at the deli for sandwiches and sodas. They wanted to take advantage of the nice weather and picnic at the park.

As they drove toward the park, Smith looked over at her. "Are you nervous?"

"Why do you ask?"

"You don't even realize what you're doing, do you?"

"What do you mean?"

"You constantly look in the mirror to see if we're being followed and won't get into the car until you make sure no one is in it."

"I'm sorry. I probably won't be able to stop until Mulvane's behind bars."

"He's probably long gone by now. I know I would be

if I had an APB out on me."

"I don't know. I've read and seen enough legal thrillers to know if the key witnesses disappear, there's no case."

"Aren't you forgetting about the arson and the death of the night watchman, O'Dwyer?"

"Yeah, but that can be bargained down to practically no jail time."

"There's also another huge hole in your theory," he said.

"What's that?" Marcie thought she'd covered all the bases.

"You and me...we're not going anyplace."

"Third strike, you're out?"

He shook his head. "If he gets within three feet of you, he's a dead man."

She didn't have to see his eyes to know he meant it. The tone of his voice said it all. Marcie only hoped that when they married and vowed 'til death do us part, it didn't include any help on Mulvane's part.

They picked out a nice peaceful spot near the lake and spread their blanket out. Several other people had the same idea and sat reading books or listening to music with their MP3s. Joggers coursed along the winding pavement and mothers out walking pushed their strollers on the path. Everyone taking advantage of the mild weather.

Despite the tranquil setting, Marcie felt ill at ease, almost jumpy. Something wasn't right. She didn't have a special sixth sense or anything, but just knew. It was like a prickly feeling one sometimes got and couldn't put a name to it. In her case, though, she had a name, but didn't want to speak it.

But it didn't make sense that Mulvane would be out there somewhere spying on them. If she mentioned this to Smith, he'd laugh and possibly think she was crazy. Was her imagination playing tricks on her again? When they snuggled and Smith told her how much he loved her, all was better in her world.

Smith took Marcie to the doctor to have her cast removed. Her arm was as good as new and the doctor advised her to keep it that way. "Slowly tone up the muscles," he said, making sure there was light behind her eyes. She had no idea why he didn't trust her. She always followed orders—well, she tried to, anyway. It was good to have a matching pair of arms again. The first thing she did was hug Smith.

"Hey, watch it, lady," he said. "You don't want to snap it or break one of *my* bones."

"Your bones?" She laughed. "I feel...so...so free again!"

"How do you want to celebrate?" he asked.

She felt sure she had that *come on, boy* look on her face. He quickly got the message and they drove back to his place. The first thing she did was jump into the shower. It was the first normal shower she'd taken in weeks. It felt so good, she actually sang as she stood under the cascading water.

The glass door slid open, interrupting her song and Smith stepped inside behind her. He kissed her neck as he slipped his hands around her. She was certain he had her cleanliness in mind when he thoughtfully soaped her breasts and all the not so easily reachable parts. Honestly, there's nothing more erotic than being made love to in the shower. If there weren't any danger of shriveling up like a prune, she'd have remained under the warm water forever. They got out and toweled dry. The good part was they could continue where they left off, in bed. And that was exactly what they did.

Cuddling together in Smith's round love nest, enjoying the afterglow of their romantic antics, he kissed the top of her head. "I've been doing some thinking about my life lately."

"This sounds serious." Marcie snuggled closer, taking in his unique scent that she loved.

"It's time I settled down and had some kids. Wanna help?"

She looked up into his eyes to see if he were fooling around and saw that small stitch in his forehead. The man was dead serious.

"Is this some new type of marriage proposal, Smith?"

He shrugged. "So what do you say?"

Marcie was overwhelmed, unable to speak for a heartbeat or two.

"Don't tell me you have to think about it?" A hint of anger bled through in his voice. "It's a simple yes or no."

She reached up and grabbed his face between her hands and kissed him with every ounce of love and passion she felt.

When she released him, he said, "Well, what's your answer?"

If he hadn't broken out in laughter, she would have clobbered him.

"You, idiot," she said. "I almost battered you with my *new* arm."

When the laughter quieted down and they were almost serious again, Smith kissed her. Then out of nowhere, he asked, "Are you going to marry me or not?"

"You're a persistent little devil, aren't you?"

He gave her a quirky little smile—the one she loved so much.

She tilted her head, watching him closely. "I love you. Doesn't that say it all?"

"Nope. It's a yes or no question."

"Yes!!!!"

"Now why was that so hard?" He rolled over and covered her body with his.

Chapter Thirty-seven

Things settled down in West Burg. With Mulvane gone, there'd been no new suspicious fires. The Chief was forced to reassess the hard fact that his son had lied to him. Marcie was fairly certain this wasn't the first time Rory had let his father down.

Ironically, the police weren't the only ones looking for the Chief's son. The shouting match Dodd had overheard so many months before had been between Rory and his father. Word had spread via the firehouse grapevine that Rory Mulvane hadn't paid back a loan shark in full and enforcers were scouting for his scalp. It was a toss-up who would track him down first—the police or the racketeers.

Logically speaking, if Mulvane had any sense, he'd never show his face back here again. That was exactly what the police and Smith believed. Marcie wanted to agree, but couldn't. She had a gut feeling Mulvane wasn't the kind of guy who'd merely disappear into the woodwork.

On the home front, now that she and Smith were officially engaged, her mother kept pressing them for a date. The topic had come up from time to time between Smith and Marcie, but since she was practically living at his place already, there was no rush. The situation drove her mother bonkers. Since Eileen and her biker boyfriend had shacked up together, Catherine O'Dwyer was hoping to salvage one of her errant daughters and keep her from hurdling down that rocky path toward damnation. At every family meal she'd creatively find a way to bring up the subject.

"I called your apartment yesterday to ask you to bring a loaf of bread tonight, Marcie."

"Why wouldn't you have called my cell phone,

Mom?"

She waved her hand in a circle. "I couldn't remember the number. You know how it is when you get old."

"You're not old. Grandpa is old."

"Who's old?" Grandpa clattered his fork against his plate. "Watch who you're calling old, young lady," he snapped, giving her his two-cents worth.

"It wouldn't matter what number I used had you been there."

Several minutes later she understood where her mother was going with this line of thought. "This is about me staying at Smith's place, isn't it?"

"Is this where the fireworks go off? Should I leave?" Smith half-stood from his chair.

Not wanting him to get up, Marcie put her hand on his shoulder. "Okay, Mom, tell us what's *really* on your mind."

"You know I'm not going to live forever—"

"Mom..."

"Oh, all right. When are you two going to get married in the eyes of God?"

"We're working on it." Marcie sighed.

"Well, work faster before He loses patience."

Smith raised an eyebrow when he heard that and Marcie saw him gulp down a chuckle.

"Mom, as soon as we know, you'll know. I promise."

"Marriage is for suckers," Grandpa said out of nowhere.

"Is this coming from the man who was married to the same woman for forty-eight years?" her mother asked.

"Living in sin is much more exciting." Grandpa winked at her and Smith.

"That's just the filth you watch speaking." Her mother gave him a nasty glare.

"Since you brought it up, Mom, I want you to know I don't want a fancy wedding."

"Now, why aren't I surprised?" she said.

Even as a child, it had never been easy for Mother to

get her to wear a dress. She practically had to be hog-tied on Sundays to get her to wear one for church.

"Smith and I really just want to get married in front of a Justice of the Peace."

No sooner had Marcie said this when her mother's face reddened and the tiny blue vein on the side of her head grew in proportion, threatening to explode. "You're not getting married in church by a priest?" She made it sound as if Marcie were speaking blasphemy. For Catherine, she imagined, she was.

Smith cleared his throat. "If it means that much to you, Mrs. O'Dwyer, I'm sure we can manage a *small* church ceremony."

Marcie nodded her agreement. She'd never thought her mother would go ballistic over the damn thing. Unfortunately, now Marcie would have to get a white dress. So much for best laid plans. Actually, when Smith and she first discussed getting married, she suggested eloping to Las Vegas and getting married by an Elvis impersonator in one of those wedding chapels along the strip. He laughed, thinking she was kidding, but she wasn't.

Now that her mother had won that battle, she sought one more victory. "Why don't you two pick a date?"

Marcie was about to say why, what's the hurry, when she caught the steel in Catherine's dark eyes. Turning to Smith, she suggested, "What about the following spring?"

His green eyes twinkled. "Nah, let's do it sooner, say in September."

"Why September?" Marcie asked.

"No special reason. It's the halfway point between now and spring."

Marcie turned to her mother. "Are you okay with that?"

Her mother knew well enough to leave things alone and nodded.

"Good. Then it's settled," Marcie said.

Smith covered Marcie's hand with his and grinned.

A year ago, she wouldn't have dreamed they'd be talking about marriage. She'd bet that right about now her mother adored Smith, who was fast becoming her favorite almost son-in-law.

The following months felt as if Marcie's life had been hitched to a runaway star. Though they'd opted for a small wedding, even small things have a way of getting blown out of proportion and snowballing. Marcie had no idea about all the planning that went into a wedding—and quickly learned being small made no difference.

Ironically, she found an ally to shoulder much of the work. Her mother had blossomed and seemed to thrive on the flurry of activity. Now in her own element, she quickly took charge. Every so often, Marcie had to remind her not to go for the gusto, since she and Smith were paying for the shindig and their combined bank accounts were pitiful at best. Besides, she already had to pay over three-hundred dollars a month for a new Jeep thanks to Mulvane.

Despite some of the unnecessary additions made by Catherine that needed to be excised, she did a splendid job and Marcie was fortunate to have her help. Unfortunately, Smith didn't always agree with her assessment. And they nearly came to blows over a few things.

Marcie agreed to wear a white dress for the ceremony. In her mind, it meant a white dress and not necessarily a gown. Catherine interpreted it differently.

"When are you and I going to go shopping for a wedding dress, Marcie?" Her mother was calling to let Marcie know Father Andrew would be performing the ceremony on September 9th.

"No hurry, Mom. I can pick up any old white dress—"

"This is your *wedding*, Marcie."

"I didn't forget. Grandpa's the senile one, remember?"

"Don't be sarcastic. You know what I mean."

"I don't want to shell out big bucks for a gown I'll

never wear again."

"What about the pictures? What will you show your children?"

"I can have pictures taken no matter what I wear."

"It won't be the same. And you'll regret it later."

Whining wasn't going to be far behind. "No, I won't." Marcie stood her ground.

Realizing she was losing the argument, her mother shifted gears at this point and came at Marcie from another angle.

"Joanne is going to join us and make this a girls' day at the mall."

"You spoke to Joanne about this already?" Marcie was amazed at the woman's audacity.

"It's a big moment for all of us."

Marcie knew how much this meant to Catherine. And she *was* doing a great deal of the planning and work for her...

"Okay, Mom. I'll get a gown—only not a frilly one. Is that understood?"

"Yes," came the answer.

Marcie could picture her mother doing a one-arm pull down on the other end, and trying hard not to gloat over her win.

Yet another expense Marcie had to run past Smith. He'd already agreed to a small reception following the ceremony. She figured the best time to tell him would be after they'd made love and his defenses were down. She discovered she'd chosen the wrong time, though probably no time would have proven better.

"You're going where with Joanne and your mother?" He'd hiked one eyebrow toward the ceiling.

"For a wedding gown," she replied meekly.

"I thought we discussed this already."

"We did, but Mom brought up some poignant things—"

"Has she forgotten who's getting married here and who's going to foot the bill?"

"No. She's been good and trying to work within our guidelines. I owe her a great deal for the help she's giving us."

"Yeah. And don't forget how much less our wedding would cost without her wonderful help."

"It's a once in a lifetime thing."

"It better be," he replied, "for at the rate she's going, we'll be paying it off for the rest of our lives."

"I want to marry you in a pretty dress," she said, throwing her arms around his neck and kissing him.

"Does that mean I have to wear a monkey suit?"

Now it was her turn to raise a brow. "Are you referring to a tux?"

"Yeah."

She shook her head.

His facial expression suddenly changed to a smirk. She could just imagine what was on his mind.

"You know something, O'Dwyer, I'd like to see you in one of those dresses."

Marcie had a funny feeling this was going to be a costly victory for her in more ways than one.

Despite all the potholes, bumps and detours along the planning route, the wedding turned out lovely. Forty guests showed up to help them celebrate. For Marcie, the day was a glorious blur of kaleidoscopic moments. When Smith and she stood before the priest and exchanged vows, her heart actually stood still. This was the one moment of her life she wished she could bottle and save forever. No matter what the future held, she'd always love him. If something happened, she wanted to remember this exact moment until she took her last dying breath.

They danced the night away, so close their hearts beat as one. When they whispered their undying love into one another's ears, Marcie felt a step closer to heaven. Her mother had been right. She would remember this day forever.

Chapter Thirty-eight

Marcie and Smith didn't need a warm, sunny tropical isle to express their love for each other. A rented cabin by a lovely lake in the Poconos served their purposes. And they couldn't scoff at the off-season pricing. It had everything they needed—a bed. 'Being married' was a weird feeling for Marcie and when she and Smith registered as Mr. and Mrs. Smith, they got a *yeah, really* look from the desk clerk. She guessed he must get a lot of people using their name.

While on the subject of names, Marcie hadn't given much thought to what Smith would call her after they married. She soon discovered some habits were hard to break. He continued calling her O'Dwyer. She toyed with the idea of hyphenating her name to make things easier, but she doubted her macho man would go for that any more than he'd call her Marcie. So she figured she'd always be O'Dwyer to him. And if he survived her and had to give the stone engraver her full name, she was sure it would be O'Dwyer Smith because he'd never remember her given name was Marcie.

By the third day of loving nearly 24/7, they came up for air and decided to explore the place. Picturesque and secluded, all twelve cabins were bordered by woods on one side and mountains on the other. One building housed the main office and dining room and was situated between the sixth and seventh cabins, so no guests had to walk too far to eat. Of course, they could drive to another restaurant or resort for entertainment. But if a person wanted quiet, you simply remained in your cabin, which came with all the amenities: hot and cold running water in a spacious bathroom, cable TV, internet hookups, a small kitchenette complete with a refrigerator, oven and microwave, and last, but far from least, a king-size round bed. She thought it was the bed and the fact they were secluded that had sold Smith on the place. He felt as if he were home.

On the fourth day, they visited the dining room for dinner and met a few of the other couples staying at the resort. One couple was working on their second marriage for them both. They were regular Barbie and Ken dolls, blonde, blue-eyed matching look-alikes from Florida who could pass for brother and sister. She was called Suzie and he was Brad. How perfect was that? Marcie pegged them both in their late thirties.

Jan and Robert Delaney were from Massachusetts. They were younger, in their twenties, and didn't look like matching bookends. He was as dark and tall as she was short and fair. This was their first shot at marriage.

The third couple, Rena and Joel Bloom, looked like refugees from a science convention—nerdy, with matching black-frame glasses. Socially, their skills appeared retarded. Either that or they were probably afraid the rest of us wouldn't comprehend. They, too, were in their twenties and came from downstate New York. Some place on Long Island. Rena Bloom seemed shy and studied her hands a great deal. She reminded Marcie of a girl she once knew in school, named Rachel. She'd been a wizard in math and science, but stuttered whenever she had to speak in front of the class. And, of course, all the kids laughed, making her more nervous. Marcie used to think that Mr. Phelan, the physics teacher, was a closet sadist because he always called on her. Now looking back, she realized he didn't have much choice. She'd been the only one who knew the answers.

Everyone finished eating and talked as a group for a while until certain urges began to splinter the group. When Smith rubbed her back, Marcie knew exactly what his urge was about.

They kissed their way back to the cabin. Stopping every few feet to refuel, it took them twice as long to get there. What all this kissing did, in essence, was to send doses of desire through Marcie, stoking her passion like adding gasoline to a fire. By the time they closed the cabin door behind them, she was aflame. They practically ripped the clothes off one another.

As Smith's body covered hers, they quickly found the tempo which bound their bodies together and the world disappeared around them.

Afterward, as they embarked on further lovemaking, Marcie spoke. "Smith, you know what's wrong with this place?"

Smith raised his head from where he'd been feasting on her body. "What'd ya say?"

"There's no room service."

"So?"

"So, I'm hungry," she said.

"I'm not."

With *I wonder why* written across her face, he got the message.

"Okay, then, I could go to the office and see if they have something for you to snack on."

She granted him a tremendous smile of gratitude.

"I figured you'd like that." Rolling over, he got out of bed.

Her eyes danced in delight as she watched him pick up his jeans from the floor and slip them on, neatly tucking his manhood in before he zipped. She couldn't help sighing as he bent down giving her a bird's eye view of his perfect buns nestled in the seat of his jeans as he searched for his tee shirt.

"Come back soon," she called to him.

"You're that hungry? By any chance, are you...?"

"No, babe. Hungry for you."

He grinned and closed the door behind him.

She got out of bed to catch a quick shower while he was gone. In the shower she thought about Smith's question. To tell the truth, after spending too many hours with her nieces, she didn't want to rush right out and get knocked up. Smith and she had spoken about kids, but it was considered a future project. When he brought up the subject tonight, she nearly wished she was. Weird. Guess that was what love can do, she mused.

A few minutes later, she heard the bathroom door open. "Smith, join me. The water is delicious."

"'Fraid not." A strange male voice turned her blood to ice as the shower curtain was roughly pushed aside.

She gasped. "Smith's coming right back," she managed to squeeze out while trying to cover her nakedness.

"That's what I'm counting on." Mulvane threw a towel at her. She soon discovered it wasn't a nicety on his part. He didn't want her to drip water through the cabin. And this was no social call. The gun he held said a thousand unspoken words.

She shivered as she tried to towel herself dry. Mulvane hadn't taken his eyes off of her. She tried to think, but fear was getting the better of her. In all the books she'd read, when the hero found himself in a tight position he tried to get the villain to talk. But Mulvane didn't seem to be in a very talkative mood.

"Hurry up!" he commanded.

"Why are you doing this? You could have stayed away. In time, who'd remember—"

"Shut up and get the hell out of there!" He threw her terry robe at her.

Marcie feared Smith would walk in and get shot. Somehow, she had to warn him.

"Now get out here before I plug you right where you stand."

She slipped into the robe. She didn't like the way he was eyeing her. In a way she might be lucky Smith was coming right back. Mulvane nudged her toward the bed with his gun, while she chatted insanely, asking him stupid questions like why'd he do it in the first place and didn't he know how much he'd hurt his father and wife. Each time she asked another question, he jabbed her in the back harder.

"Take your robe off and get on the bed."

"Hey, you sure you'll have time for this?"

He answered her with a glare. "Do what I say."

"What for? Aren't you going to kill me anyway?"

"Okay, funny girl. You don't cooperate, I'll hurt Smith more and make you watch. Or maybe, I'll maim him just enough to make him a vegetable. How does that sound?"

Like more guilt. She let her robe drop and quickly slipped under the covers. He opened a small bag and took out a roll of duct tape. She used to call her father the duct tape king. He used it to fix practically everything. How funny to think of something so stupid at a time like this, she thought. He finished wrapping her hands and cautioned her as he pulled the sheet to her chin. "Try to warn him and he'll suffer."

Less than five minutes later, Smith opened the door. Mulvane had positioned himself behind it. She tried to prevent Smith from coming inside by yelling, "Don't bother coming back without the aspirin."

Mulvane glared at her. Smith must have stopped to think about what she'd screamed out, but instead of going back to get aspirin, he came inside holding a bunch of candy bars and soda cans, looking confused. "What's wrong with you?"

He never finished the question. Marcie's heart skipped and went offline as she saw Mulvane clobber him on the back of his head with the gun butt. Smith crumpled to the floor. Mulvane then wrapped Smith's hands with duct tape and dragged him to the bed. He put him next to her and taped both of their mouths.

Studying his accomplishment, he smiled. "You both have been a thorn in my side. Now it's payback time."

He looked at his watch. "Tick-tock, tick-tock. Have to get a move on it. By the time help comes, you both should be ash. Tsk-tsk. Didn't anyone ever tell you smoking in bed is a killer?" He broke into evil laughter.

She struggled against the tape wound tightly around her hands as she watched him prepare to set them ablaze. Smith had come to. His eyes opened wide when he focused on Mulvane. He looked at her apologetically. She knew he felt guilty that he was helpless. It was she who should bear the guilt for so many reasons. She snuggled closer to him. Tears welled in her eyes. At least, they'd go together. She wanted to tell him how much she loved him. And that she was so very sorry...

"Enjoy eternity together." Mulvane drenched them in gasoline.

Marcie looked at Smith before closing her eyes. His face was the last thing she wanted to see before she died—not Mulvane's. Silently, she asked Smith to forgive her as she heard Mulvane move away from the bed. He must have lit a cigarette, because she smelled smoke. She began to pray.

Chapter Thirty-nine

A wood-splintering noise accompanied by shouting interrupted her prayer as armed men in bulletproof vests and helmets filled the cabin and overpowered Mulvane, dragging him outside.

Detective Arnold and another man approached the bed.

"What kind of aftershave do you use, Smith?" Arnold crinkled his nose as he ripped the tape from his mouth and then Marcie's.

"You're just about the last person I expected to see," Marcie told Arnold.

"Better than your Maker, eh?"

"I'll drink to that," Smith said.

The other man was the sheriff of the township they were in. Conklin, she believed he said his name was. Since she was still dealing with the fact she was alive and not ash in an urn, her brain could have been used in an omelet. Besides, the gasoline smell had given her a headache the size of Texas and she needed some aspirin for real. She'd had enough excitement that day to last a lifetime.

Marcie and Smith met the next morning with Detective Arnold at Conklin's office, which was nothing more than a postage stamp size room with a view of the parking lot. The details of the events leading up to their miraculous rescue were shared.

Detective Arnold did much of the talking. "How's your head, Smith?" he asked first off.

"I'll live," he said. However, Marcie knew how badly it still hurt even with the painkillers.

"Just for the record," Arnold began, "Mulvane never left town."

"I knew it!" Marcie practically shouted.

"Instead, he holed up at the home of a relative. Eleanor Mulvane pumped the Chief for information and passed it on to her son. No matter what Rory had done, he was still her child."

"So Mulvane knew where we'd come on our honeymoon from the get-go," Marcie said.

"Most likely," Arnold replied. "However, I realized this might be the case when his license plate was tagged at an E-ZPass along the Thruway. To be on the safe side, I had Sheriff Conklin post a man at the lodge."

"When the officer didn't call in with his report, I knew something was wrong," Conklin took over. "I got on the horn to Detective Arnold immediately."

"In New York?" she said, incredulously wondering how he'd gotten here so fast.

"No. I was already here at a motel down the road," Arnold replied. "Did you think I'd hang you both out to dry? Besides, I wanted Mulvane."

"When we arrived, we found the officer's car empty and began to search for him," Conklin continued. "Mulvane had killed him and covered the body with leaves and brush."

Marcie was horrified and guilt ridden.

Detective Arnold picked up on it. "It's not your fault."

"If you guys had shown up a few minutes later, we'd both be toast," Smith said.

"You worked with this guy and never knew he was this bent?" Conklin asked.

Smith and Marcie said no in unison. Who knew if Mulvane was always a bad seed or whether circumstances twisted him. No matter what, he had a great deal to answer for. And Smith and she weren't the only ones who could now rest easier.

With all the commotion caused by becoming the target of a *psycho pyromaniac*, as one reporter had tagged Mulvane, Smith and Marcie knew they couldn't remain at the lodge. The media were like flies on a dead carcass. One would think after what the newlyweds had been through they'd be sympathetic and give them space. Not when money was the bottom line. Crime sells newspapers, just like disaster.

Slamming and locking the door to the cabin, Smith said, "I feel like a piece of cheese surrounded by a hundred rats."

"Great minds think alike, but here's the $64,000 question: What are we going to do?"

"For starters, babe, we're getting out of here."

"Where will we go?"

Smith's face broke into that yummy crooked grin she loved. "I have a plan."

"Tell me what you're thinking." Marcie's voice sounded like a beg.

"Las Vegas. With all the hotels, there's got to be an available room."

Forty minutes later they were booked on a plane out of Pennsylvania bound for Nevada. And of all places, they were going to stay at New York, New York. Marcie was psyched and Smith seemed to be, too. Neither had ever been there.

The very best part of the plan was that absolutely no one knew they were going. That meant no reporters. They'd be alone.

Las Vegas was a blast. Like two kids in a candy shop, they were awed by the millions of lights on the strip at night. Smith played some poker and won $250. Marcie lost about $15 in the slots. The highlight was seeing Celine Dion's show. Costly, but well worth it. They'd fallen in love with Las Vegas and agreed they'd come back some day. As the cliché went: all good things must come to an end. So did what was left of their honeymoon.

Smith and Marcie returned to work. The Chief looked as if he'd aged twenty years. What could they say to him? He had to realize they hadn't put his son behind bars. Rory Mulvane had put himself there through his own actions.

That night at work she went behind the partition where she normally slept. It was the first night in a long time she and Smith weren't together. She was busy pounding her pillow into a more perfect shape when she heard Smith call out to her.

"Want me to come tuck you in and read you a bedtime story, O'Dwyer?" he cooed from the other side. She could hear the snickers and muffled laughter from the other guys.

She remembered the first time he'd asked her that. Boy, they had come a long way.

"You know I'd love you to, but tonight Goofy's getting my business."

She heard a murmur of huhs? and whats? but Smith had broken into gales of laughter. She could just picture the other guys looking at him as if he were crazy, not being privy to their inside joke.

"I love you, Smith," Marcie whispered.

Lonely, she consoled herself. After all, it was only one night. They had a lifetime of nights to look forward to and be together.

A lifetime to love and cherish one another.

And no matter what heat life sent them along the way, their love would withstand it.

Author Information

A member of RWA, LIRW and LIW, Candace has been a freelance writer for over ten years, having been fortunate to have nearly 200 short stories and novels in print. Her work has appeared in Strictly Romance, Woman's World, CHICKEN SOUP FOR THE KID'S SOUL, A Hint of Seduction, the publications of Sterling/Macfadden, Dorchester Media, Highland Press Publishing, Ocean's Mist Press, DiskUs in April 2008, Whiskey Creek Press and Tiger Publications, 2010. She lives in New York with her husband, Robert.

Stop by her website www.candacegold.com or write her at truconfwrtr@optonline.net.

A Heated Romance

Candace Gold

Also Available from Highland Press

Deborah MacGillivray
Cat O'Nine Tales
Leanne Burroughs
Highland Wishes
Ashley Kath-Bilsky
The Sense of Honor
Isabel Mere
Almost Taken
R.R. Smythe
Into the Woods
(A Young Adult Fantasy)
Leanne Burroughs
Her Highland Rogue
Jacquie Rogers
Faery Special Romances
Katherine Deauxville
The Crystal Heart
Rebecca Andrews
The Millennium Phrase Book
Chris Holmes
Blood on the Tartan
Jean Harrington
The Barefoot Queen
Anne Kimberly
Dark Well of Decision
Isabel Mere
Almost Guilty
Young/Ivey/Chai
Brides of the West
Cynthia Owens
In Sunshine or In Shadow
Jannine Corti Petska
Rebel Heart
Phyllis Campbell
Pretend I'm Yours
Holiday Romance Anthology

A Heated Romance

Christmas Wishes
Holiday Romance Anthology
Holiday in the Heart
Romance Anthology
No Law Against Love
Romance Anthology
Blue Moon Magic
Romance Anthology
Blue Moon Enchantment
Romance Anthology
Recipe for Love
Holiday Romance Anthology
Love Under the Mistletoe
Holiday Romance Anthology
Romance Upon A Midnight Clear

Upcoming

John Nieman & Karen Laurence
The Amazing Rabbitini
(Children's Illustrated)
Brynn Chapman
Bride of Blackbeard
Diane Davis White
Moon of Falling Leaves
Romance Anthology
No Law Against Love 2
Katherine Deauxville
Southern Fried Trouble
Eric Fullilove
The Zero Day Event
Jacquie Rogers
Down Home Ever Lovin' Mule Blues
Romance Anthology
The Way to a Man's Heart
Romance Anthology
Love on a Harley
*MacGillivray/Burroughs/Bowen/
Ahlers/Houseman*
Dance en L'Aire

Lance Martin
The Little Hermit
(Children's Illustrated)
Sorter/MacGillivray/Burroughs
Faith, Hope and Redemption
Jo Webnar
Saving Tampa
Sandra Cox
The Sundial
Freddie Currie
Changing Wind
Molly Zenk
Chasing Byron
Anne Holman
The Master of Strathgian
Romance Anthology
Second Time Around
Linda Bilodeau
The Wine Seekers
Cleora Comer
Just DeEtta
Don Brookes
With Silence and Tears
Romance Anthology
Love and Glory
Jeanmarie Hamilton
Seduction
Katherine Shaw
Love Thy Neighbor
Jean Harrington
In the Lion's Mouth
Inspirational Romance Anthology
The Miracle of Love
Katherine Deauxville
The Amethyst Crown
Katherine Deauxville
Enraptured
Katherine Deauxville
Eyes of Love

A Heated Romance

Check our website frequently for future Highland Press releases.

www.highlandpress.org

Cover by Deborah MacGillivray

Candace Gold

A Heated Romance